The Girl With A Curl

Margarite St. John

[handwritten inscription] John Brown

[handwritten signature] Margaret Yoder

The Girl With A Curl

www.margaritestjohn.com

This book was previously published as an e-Book through Kindle.

Cover photograph by Bonnie Manning, marthabook@gmail.com

Cover design by Sara Norwood, www.norwoodarts.com.

Other Books by Margarite St. John

FICTION:
Face Off
Monuments to Murder
Murder for Old Times' Sake

NON-FICTION:
Finding Mrs. Hyde:
Writing Your First Popular Novel

Our Loyal Readers Say About:

Face Off

"I really enjoyed *Face Off*. It is far better than James Patterson, Patricia Cornwell & Stuart Woods I also read over the past few months. I have recommended it to friends!"
- Jamie

"*Face Off* is easy and enjoyable reading. . . . The pace compelled me to read just one more chapter. . . . A good mystery with an explosive beginning and end."
- A fan, Marco Island

"*Face Off* is well-written and fast-paced. It's kind of a twisted romance as well as a murder mystery. The characters are thoroughly fleshed out, which is different from a lot of mystery novels. . . . I like the way the books ends. Surprising and very exciting."
- Anne-Marie

"The author has given us interesting characters involved in a compelling story line. An easy comfortable writing style keeps you involved and draws you on, chapter to chapter. I'm left wishing for more!"
- pageturner

"Couldn't put the book down! Extremely well-written with a suspenseful plot and interesting characters. Each chapter ended with a hook, so I couldn't wait to start the next one! All of the requirements of a great suspense novel were woven into the book with great thought. A definite must-read! I can't wait to read more from this author!"
- Heather

Monuments to Murder

"It took me only two days to read this book. It was funny, disturbing, educational, enlightening, and ended with a good twist. I'm hooked on this author."
- Anne-Marie

"This is the second book from this author that I have read and I absolutely loved it!! Suspenseful, interesting characters with whom it was easy to identify, and a plot that was both intriguing and yet easy to follow. I literally could not put down my Kindle for 2 days until I finished it! I would say that this author has exactly what it takes to please the suspense novel fan and keep them coming back for more! Can't wait to read her next novel."
- Heather

Murder for Old Times' Sake

"The characters are very interesting, the story compelling, and the who–done–it suspense kept me reading to the funny and fitting end. The author fleshes out the good guys, bad guys, and the somewhere in-betweens, as people the reader can sympathize with and understand their motivations and mindsets. I am looking forward to the fourth book."
- Anne-Marie

"Third book from this author that I have read and just a wonderful suspense novel all the way around! Very interesting characters combine with an exiting plot to keep the reader coming back for more. Details are woven in carefully giving the reader the sense that they "are there" as things are happening. Just loved it!"
- Heather

The Girl With A Curl

"I eagerly awaited Margarite St. John's fourth mystery novel and was not disappointed. It is a story that deals with two peoples' decision to correct as humanly as possible a past transgression that went unknown for years. But their good intentions unleash a chain of events that affects not only themselves, but those around them. I really enjoyed the perspectives of each character, good, bad, and indifferent, as they dealt with these changes. The ending was a complete surprise and makes the reader ponder just how hard it is to decide what to do in the face of evil. "
- Anne-Marie

Finding Mrs. Hyde: Writing Your First Popular Novel

"I am a fan of Margarite St. John. She's written three mystery novels in the past year and I have enjoyed every one of the stories (see my reviews). This short guide for women writers is funny and on the mark. The book takes you on a short and sweet step by step process through the stages of writing a good mystery story. Read this before you write."
- Anne-Marie

Table of Contents

Part Three

Part One

There was a little girl who had a little curl
Right in the middle of her forehead

First lines of an old nursery rhyme

"Before I formed you in the womb I knew you . . . ."

The Lord speaking, Jeremiah 1:5

1

Scuttlebutt's
Saturday, May 22, 2010

Miss Honeypot was tired and it hurt to shake her money-makers, but a gaggle of twenty-something newcomers, probably a bachelor party, was yelling at her to move that honeypot. Their manic enthusiasm kept her going. On Saturday nights, Scuttlebutt's was always crowded near midnight, and tips were good, especially from bachelor parties. From her viewpoint on the stage, the smoke cloud hovering over the room sometimes struck an ethereal note, obscuring life's hard edges, but not tonight. Everything was all too real. She'd sprayed every part of herself in patchouli oil, but still the odoriferous smog of beer and masculine funk made her feel faint.

Perhaps the faintness came from something else though. The puffy tenderness in her breasts suggested she was pregnant again. Normally she kept her gaze fixed just above the heads of the sweaty, raucous strangers below her, occasionally deigning to catch the eye of a big-tipping regular, but she decided to chance a quick glance downward at her body to see if she glowed the way pregnant women were said to glow. That was a sign, wasn't it? She did glow, but maybe it was only the effect of the rosy spots directed at the stage. Still, the other signs weren't good. Her lacy thigh-high stockings were cutting into her flesh so hard her legs were going numb, and the waistband on her old fringed thong kept rolling over. She must be gaining weight. She hoped it was just water weight or that time of the month, but in her heart she knew it wasn't. All her life, her luck had been bad.

When Bobby Valentino began imitating a police siren in *Mrs. Officer*, the crowd-pleasing, bass-heavy song favored by Scuttlebutt's younger customers, Miss Honeypot slithered back to the pole to the cries of "honeypot, honeypot" and began her final gyrations. As she slid up and down and twirled around, she tried to calculate when she must have gotten pregnant and by whom, but the calculation evaded her. She couldn't remember most of the men's names, and even then she could never be sure the names she heard were real anyway. How long could she hide her condition from Percy "Scut" Scutter, the owner's son who was somewhere in the crowd, keeping an eye on things and urging the men, with jovial backslaps, to have another drink? Scut had an eye for secrets, both those of the women he employed and the men he fleeced. If he took a good look at her, he'd know and she'd be out the door. But she needed the money. Perhaps a different costume would help for awhile.

Once her act had finished, she left the stage, the rictus of a smile on her horsey face, and began mingling with the crowd, smiling for drinks, offering lap dances, and finally sitting for a half hour with Mick, the fat, balding truck driver who always wanted to talk to her. It was the only amusing part of the night. Mick pretended they had a life together, a life of yachting and making love by moonlight and buying out fancy shops in Vegas after a winning hour at the craps table. So far as she knew, he never did anything more exciting than drinking watered highballs and dreaming with her. But she happily went along with his fantasy in exchange for the chance to rest her feet and to let him slip a hundred into the waistband of her too-tight thong.

When she finally reached the badly lit concrete room Scut called a dressing room, she found Little Red getting ready to go on but wanting to talk a few minutes first. "Girl, you look tired," she said, smiling at Miss Honeypot's reflection in the mirror.

"I am." Miss Honeypot began removing her false eyelashes and taking out the rhinestone combs from her bird's nest hairdo. Glancing at her friend, she once again wished her hair was as straight as Little Red's, but she just didn't have the strength to iron it out every day. "You know of any bar tending jobs? I'm thinking of doing something else."

Little Red glanced at her friend's swollen breasts and belly. "You pregnant again?"

"Maybe." She sighed. "Probably."

Little Red shook her head, her silky red hair brushing her shoulders like a bead curtain. "In case you haven't noticed, Jen, practically every day another bar or restaurant goes out of business in Fort Wayne, so, no, I haven't heard of any bar tending jobs. How far gone are you?"

"God knows. I don't."

"You gonna keep it?"

"Yeah."

"Why?"

"I like babies."

"So do I, but I'm not having any until I'm done with my degree."

"What's it in again?"

"Accounting."

"That's what I should have done, Sally, but, of course, I was never good with numbers, and anyway it's too late now. Oh, God, I gotta pee. Now." Miss Honeypot kicked off her four-inch mules, rushed to the dark hallway, and ran to the bathroom, but the door wouldn't open. She pulled and jerked and swore, but whoever was in there must have set the hook.

"Who's in there?" She considered bending down to peer under the door but was afraid the pressure on her bladder might be too much. "This is not fair," she cried, pounding her fist on the warped wood in frustration.

She rushed back to the dressing room. "The door's locked and the light's on. Who's in there?"

"Tawny, I think. She's filling in for Lois." Little Red was bending over to shake her breasts into a stiff new bra. "She's been in there since a few minutes after I got here. Sneak into Scut's private bathroom down the hall. That's what I did."

3

"He'll kill me if he finds out, but I've gotta go now. A minute longer and it'll be too late. If you see him, tell him our bathroom door won't open."

Little Red left for the stage. After using Scut's private bathroom Miss Honeypot returned to the dressing room, where she began her transformation into plain Jen Ricky, mother of twin girls aged four, by donning her street clothes -- gray jersey shorts with a stretch waistband, a white dago-t, and a pair of broken-at-the-heel sneakers, once white, now gray. She let down her hair and pulled it into a loose ponytail with a busted-out scrunchy, then picked up her oversized fake alligator tote (a gift-with-purchase from Estée Lauder) to check that her billfold was in place.

She had just pulled open the metal door to the parking lot when she heard Scut stomping through the hallway, loudly swearing that women were nothing but a pain in the ass, literally. Despite her fatigue, she turned around to have a word with Tawny.

She watched Scut slip a credit card into the opening between the door of the girls' bathroom and the jamb to push the hook up, then jerk the door open to show just how mad he was at being forced to do something this simple and stupid.

Jen stood behind him, prepared to scold Tawny for locking the door and commandeering the only toilet, but her indignation instantly changed to shock. Tawny, her chestnut curls framing her raddled face, was lying on the floor, green vomit frothing out of her mouth. Strangely, the smell was sweet.

2

Wild Child
Sunday, May 23, 2010

Jacintha Delamarter, tangled in a cheap cotton throw, was dozing on the stained pull-out couch, which she never bothered to pull out, when she heard the lock turning on the front door of the mobile home. She'd just been brought back to half-consciousness by a bad dream she couldn't recall, so even if she'd been so inclined, she wouldn't have made it to the door in time to welcome the owner home.

Instead, Jacintha pretended to be deeply asleep. She needed the baby-sitting money, but she scorned Jen Ricky, who always wanted to talk a little while after getting home. Jacintha had no interest in her employer's litany of complaints about the bad hand life had dealt her, her questions about the noisy twins' behavior, or her boring stories about life at Scuttlebutt's. Jacintha just wanted the money and then the chance to run home -- though home was just another dreary doublewide, even messier and dustier than this one, a few doors away. She also scorned her mother, but at least Antoinette wouldn't be there tonight. Jacintha would have the place to herself.

She felt Jen's hand on her shoulder. "Jacintha. I'm home."

Jacintha didn't move. She felt her shoulder being shaken more urgently.

"Are you awake?"

"No."

"You are. I can tell. Would you sit up for me?"

For a long minute, Jacintha refused to move, making her point. Finally, she untangled herself from the cotton throw and slowly pushed herself into a sitting position as if it were a great burden to do it, felt around for her glasses with the thick lenses, and put them on. She gave Jen -- Horsey-Face, as she was known behind her back -- her surliest look. "What time is it, for Christ's sake?"

"Jacintha! That's no way to talk at your age."

"So what?"

"So . . . ." Jen trailed off, thinking the poor girl was so homely at least good manners would give her some chance in life, but she didn't want to say so. "So I have to talk to you about something serious."

"Like what?" Jacintha asked, pretending to struggle to her feet.

Jen moved to the refrigerator, removed a bottle of Mike's Hard Lemonade, snapped off the cap, and took a long swallow. The girls' drinks at Scuttlebutt's contained no liquor, though the men paid big bucks for "champagne cocktails," so once she was home she had a drink to calm herself down. Without turning around, she called over her shoulder, "I think you better sit down again. It's about your mother."

Jacintha, with a pouty look on her face, simply held out her hand. "Just give me the money and I'll get out of here. I don't want to hear about her."

Jen found her tote, extracted her billfold, and pulled out a twenty. "Sit down and you can have this."

"I'm not a dog. I don't sit on command when you offer me a treat."

Jen almost laughed as she took a chair near the pull-out sofa. *Actually, you foolish girl, you are a dog. Little chits with the kind of teeth and ears you have are called dogs behind their back. The only thing you've got going for you is your mother's beautiful, curly chestnut hair.* "Sit down anyway. You'll need to." She took another swallow of lemonade and waited to speak until Jacintha sat back on the sofa. "Your mother's very sick. We found her in the bathroom at Scuttlebutt's, frothing at the mouth."

"Really."

Jen was dismayed but not surprised by the girl's lack of interest. "Really."

"What's that mean?"

"Frothing? I don't know. It looked like she'd been throwing up. Green stuff. It smelled sweet."

"What green stuff? You think she's, like, pregnant?"

"Not that I know of." Jen wanted to have a cozy little chat about her own fear that she was pregnant again, but this wasn't the time. "They took her to St. Joe's. If I can get my mother to stay here with the twins for a few hours, I'll take you there myself."

"Why should I go there? What could I do this time of night?" She made her voice tremble. "I'm tired. Girls my age need sleep and I never get enough."

"I'm tired too, and I never get enough either, but that's what friends and daughters do for each other. You can hold her hand, let her know somebody cares. You can say a prayer for her."

"Ick. If she's frothing at the mouth, I don't want to touch her."

"For heaven's sake, Jacintha, have a heart. She's your mother. She's been raising you all by herself since you were born."

"Which she doesn't have to do. She could make my father pay so we could live somewhere other than this dump."

Jen was stung. "Cedar Grove Parke is not a dump, and if Antoinette knew who your father was, I'm sure she'd go to court."

"I know who he is."

Girl, if you only knew, sometimes a woman doesn't know. Jen's mood quickly shifted from a sense of guilt about not knowing who her babies' fathers were to scorn for the angry girl. "You think you know more than your mother about that? Is that what you think?"

Jacintha's face was stubborn. "I know what I know."

Jen lit a cigarette and considered what to do next. Before she could speak, Jacintha grabbed the pack, shook out a cigarette, and lit it.

"You smoke? Does Antoinette know?"

"Yes." The girl's face was defiant.

Jen looked at her curiously. She wouldn't put it past Antoinette to allow such behavior. "Well, there's nothing we can do about your father right now, so I'm calling my mother to come over here so I can take you to the hospital."

"Let me borrow your car. Or take me to Ma's. I know where St. Joe is. I'll drive there myself."

"You're only fifteen, Jacintha."

"I'm sixteen soon."

"How soon?"

"The end of this month."

"So you don't have a license yet."

"But I can drive. I've driven Ma to Scuttlebutt's more than once. I have a second set of keys to the car, so if you take me over to Scuttlebutt's, you won't have to go to the hospital with me."

"You're kidding."

"About what?"

"Driving."

"I'm not."

"Well, I'm not letting you drive my car, that's for damn sure, and I think the cops towed your mother's car away."

"I wanna go home first."

"You shouldn't be alone at a time like this."

Jacintha walked to the door. "I've got something to do." She squinted her eyes. "Brush my teeth, change my shirt. Give me, like, half an hour. Okay?"

"Okay."

The only person who saw the girl throwing a black garbage bag in the dumpster a little after four in the morning was a clerk coming home after a late shift at Walgreens, but when her headlights illuminated the girl's face, she thought nothing of it. Antoinette Delamarter, the worst housekeeper she'd ever known, kept strange hours and exercised no control over her wild-child teenage daughter -- an ugly duckling if there ever was one.

★ ★ ★ ★ ★

But Antoinette "Tawny" Delamarter would never keep strange hours again, and whatever little control she might once have had over her ugly duckling was lost forever. She was dead before the ambulance reached St. Joseph Hospital.

3

The Pool Man
Monday, May 24, 2010

Monday morning Phyllis Whitlow was interviewing applicants sent to her by the employment agency for the position of maid -- a ridiculous term, she thought, for a full-time cleaning woman. The house Lexie and Steve had built was so huge she could no longer manage the housekeeping duties of cleaning, laundry, scheduling repairs, dog-walking, shopping, miscellaneous errands, and cooking, so having been given a choice, she chose to be the housekeeper and cook. Though Whitlow was her maiden name, which she'd returned to after her husband's death twenty years earlier, she recently adopted the honorific of "Mrs.," as she'd discovered from *Gosford Park* that English cooks and housekeepers always did.

She had help with the outside work from Todd Fingerhutt, the pool man, though he was much more than that. He did all the handyman work and landscaping. He mowed the vast lawn, trimmed bushes, cleaned the garages and kept the Wrights' various vehicles gleaming, washed the windows, atrium, and skylights, changed the ceiling and coach light bulbs, cleaned the courtyards and terraces every morning, and generally found something to do all day long.

She had interviewed at least a dozen women, none of whom she thought would be a suitable maid or someone she could stand to have under foot all day. The most qualified woman showed up wearing short shorts and a patronizing look on her face, sure that, given her experience in a nursing home, she was the only woman in Allen County who knew the proper way to clean a bathroom. She grated so hard on every last nerve that Phyllis dismissed her without a tour of the house.

Phyllis was authorized to offer the finalist a rent-free apartment above the five-car garage, and though she'd been made the same offer, she decided to keep her house in Huntertown so she'd have privacy when her six-month-old twin grandsons, Phillip Whitlow Bott and Lucius Flowers Bott, came to visit. Phil and Luke were the best things that ever happened to her other than her own son, Drago. The babies were just like Drago when he was a baby -- bright-eyed, colicky, handsome, willful, sleepy during the day and wide awake all night. They were driving Lucy and Drago crazy and they had only just begun to crawl.

The last applicant of the morning was a woman she guessed to be about forty. Sadie wore a black lace scarf on the bun at the back of her head, a long denim skirt, and white-white sneakers. Intelligent, soft-spoken, and modest, she revealed that as a Mennonite she did not work on Sundays. Not ever. Period. She would happily stay in the garage apartment during the week, but on Saturday afternoon, she would leave for the Ohio farm where she grew up and return early Monday morning. Upon learning that she could entertain her boyfriend but not give him a key, she said there would be no male visitors; she was firm about that. Yes, she had a car; that was her Ford Focus on the street.

She assured Phyllis that she was used to hard work, knew all there was to know about cleaning and laundry, and never got sick. She'd be happy to walk Henry any time it was necessary because she loved dogs; in fact he could stay in her apartment if that was convenient or go to the farm with her if the owners were going to be away for the weekend. She would wear a uniform but only if it included a long skirt (no trousers) and was otherwise modest. Babies? She liked them, and if any made their appearance, she'd consider the occasional baby-sitting duty. She did not drink coffee; tea only. She had never learned to cook and was glad to hear her meals would be provided. She'd never smoked in her life, though if anybody else in the house smoked, that was fine. Live and let live.

"I see you haven't listed any references."

"This would be my first job away from home. My father just died, and my brother and his wife are taking over the farm, so I've got to earn some money. But you could talk to my pastor or my mother."

Phyllis got up to make Sadie another cup of tea. This woman was too good to be true. So it was time for a little personal information. "Do you read much, Sadie?"

"No, other than the local papers. I'm too tired after I'm done working. But I read a passage from the Bible every day."

"What's your favorite television program?"

"I have more than one. I guess my favorites are *The Young and the Restless* and *The Days of Our Lives*, but I like a lot of the game shows too, especially *The Price Is Right* and *Wheel of Fortune*. At night I watch re-runs of my favorite soaps just before I go to sleep. How about you?"

"The soaps mostly. *General Hospital's* pretty good, don't you think? And I like *Jeopardy.*"

They discussed their favorite characters for awhile. "So, Sadie, you'd take a lunch break with me to watch *The Young and the Restless?*"

Sadie allowed herself a small smile. "If that's allowed."

"Of course, it's allowed. Mizz Royce is the easiest woman you'll ever work for."

"Mizz Royce?"

"Mrs. Alexandra Wright, for some purposes, but she didn't take her husband's name. He's Sterling Steven Wright, the construction guy building this development. Wright Construction? I'm sure you've heard of that. Anyway, Mizz Royce is a good wife but way too famous to change her name."

"Famous? For what?"

"Business. She owns Summit City Metals and Scrapyard -- inherited from her father. My son works there. She owns lots of other businesses too, companies you've never heard of -- wind turbines, ethanol producers, that kind of thing. When she was still in her twenties, she got rich starting various scrap collection companies, which she sold a few years ago. Now she's getting ready to publish a book in New York, and with her luck, it'll become a best-seller." Phyllis watched Sadie's face, curious to see whether she'd be impressed by the grandeur of her potential employers. She wasn't.

Sadie sipped her tea. "So doesn't that make her hard to work for? Is she spoiled?"

"Spoiled?" Phyllis looked away a second. "Compared to what? She's used to things being done well. She expects a lot, assumes things will be done right, and she does get mad sometimes, but unless you watch her face, you wouldn't know it. No yelling or anything. Something about her, the way she looks at you . . . Mizz Royce is the kind of woman you want to make happy even though she doesn't demand it. Some people just have that quality. Failing her would be like failing your mother."

Sadie, Phillis discovered, was truly rock-hard when it came to being impressed. After a tour of the mansion and grounds, she asked the woman what she thought.

Sadie looked around. "It's a big place, practically a hotel."

"Very grand, don't you think?"

Sadie cocked her head noncommittally. "You could say that."

"You think you could handle it?"

Sadie looked at her as if she were crazy. "Of course. It just takes organization and steady work, day after day. Never let anything get ahead of you. I'm good at that."

They were standing in the courtyard when the door from the pool area opened. "Oh, let me introduce you to the pool man." She watched Todd approach, carrying a skimming net in his right hand, a coil of hose draped over the other shoulder, and a container of pool chemicals swinging from his left hand. He was a stocky, heavy-boned guy in his late thirties, very friendly, never at a loss for words. "Sadie, this is Todd."

His face crinkled. "Glad to meet you. Can't shake hands, though. I've been cleaning the pool. So, you're the new maid?"

Sadie didn't return his smile. "Don't know."

"What's that scarfy thing on your head? Looks real nice, very ladylike, like you just came from church. You Amish or something?"

"Mennonite."

Todd set down the container and shrugged off the hose but held onto the pool net. "Oh, I know all about the Mennonites. My cousin was born Mennonite. I went to his wedding, years ago, had a blast. Food was good and lots of it, but those clothes -- not much to look at, right? Very plain." He caught Phyllis' look. "Oh, except you look real nice, don't mean anything by it. I've never seen cleaner sneakers. My mouth gets ahead of me sometimes. So, years ago your people came over from Sweden, didn't they?"

"Switzerland."

He slapped himself with the pool net. "Oh, yeah, always get those two places mixed up. Both start with 'S,' I guess that's the trouble. But at least the Mennonites aren't allergic to cars like the Amish -- well, that's just nuts, if you ask me, driving in a horse and buggy ten miles an hour down a country road at night. Don't know why there aren't more dead Amish along the highway. You drive, I hope."

"I do."

"Well, that's good. People are born Mennonite, you know. Nobody ever converts, so they've gotta keep having babies if they want a church. Not like the Baptists -- which is what I am. Something strange about a religion where no one ever joins except by being born to the right parents. That's not a bad thing, of course. I'm just sayin'."

Looking confused, Sadie merely nodded.

"My cousin says Mennonites are Anti-Baptists -- the opposite of what I am. The religion started in the Middle Ages, he said, back in Sweden -- I mean Switzerland. Gotta get that straight. Switzerland."

"Anabaptist," Sadie said, pronouncing it elaborately. "That's what your cousin meant."

"Anna what?"

"Anabaptist." She spelled out the word. "We aren't *anti*

14

Baptists. Infant baptism doesn't count so adults that accept the faith have to be baptized again. That's what it means."

"Why not call yourselves Rebaptists then? I'm no language expert, of course. I'm just sayin'."

Frowning in confusion, Sadie shrugged.

"Well, that's a new one, that is," Todd said, undaunted by her silence. "I'll have to look that up on Wikipedia. Learn something everyday, I do. I've gotta computer you know, on its last legs, I'm afraid, but you gotta keep up. Just listen to people, that's my motto. Listen and learn. I like that. Anabaptist. I'll remember that word. You know, if you say the same new word ten times in a day, it's with you forever."

"I'll bet you have no trouble saying something ten times a day."

He laughed loudly. "You got me there, miss, yes you do. That's fresh, that is. I like that. I like a woman who says what's on her mind, no beating around the bush. No sir. That's our lovely Mrs. Whitlow to a tee. Straight as an arrow."

Phyllis cut him off or they'd never get back in the house. "We have some things to discuss, Todd, so we're going back in for a few minutes."

As always, Todd was concerned about Mrs. Whitlow and wasn't ready to be dismissed. He was moved by her pale, narrow face, her sharp chin, her china blue eyes that looked like they'd seen too many tragedies. His little talks with Mrs. Whitlow were the highlight of his day. Though she was the most competent woman he'd ever met, Phyl -- as he called her in private -- seemed unsure of herself. That always puzzled him. What did she have to be unsure about? The set of her shoulders, the stiffness of her rounded back, suggested she was especially tense today. Todd patted her back, testing his observation. Yes, she was stiff as a board. He wished she'd let him massage her shoulders. "Anything you need me to do, Phyl?" he asked in a whisper. "I'm going to shut down the fountain and give it a good scrubbing, then I'm going to repot that ornamental boxwood Henry tore up, but after that, you want your car washed? Some new dish you want me to taste, anything like that?"

"Not right now, Todd, but I'll let you know when lunch is ready."

"So is Sadie here the one?" he asked, leaning in so he couldn't be overheard while shooting a reassuring smile over Phyl's shoulder to the woman with the scarfy thing on her head.

Phyllis frowned. Her new responsibilities weighed on her, and though she appreciated Todd's concern, she didn't want to be distracted from the vetting process, which she had to get exactly right. "You'll be the first to know if she is."

4

At Home
Monday, May 24, 2010

Monday evening Steve was grilling filet mignon on his magnificent built-in, gas-plumbed, stainless steel Viking grill in the Tuscan-themed outdoor kitchen. At first he'd been so intimidated by the sheer size and gleaming sleekness of the grill that he was reluctant to fire it up or get it dirty. He longed for his old battered Weber, fed by a propane tank, with a bent hood that no longer closed properly, but he was gradually getting used to this new contraption. Lexie wisely watched him in silence. Steve never read instructions manuals and did not like wifely help in the outdoor kitchen. Grilling was a man's domain.

"The furniture for the media room is coming tomorrow," she said. "You don't have to do anything, just letting you know."

He turned around, looked at his watch, took a beer out of the under-counter refrigerator, and sat down at the engineered-quartz countertop in Liguria green. "Is Liguria really green?" he'd asked when months ago she consulted him about the color. "And if it is, why did the manufacturer choose the name Liguria? Why not Vermont? Because anything Italian costs more than anything American?" Lexie had made a face. She was so harried by all the choices she had to make that she wasn't in the mood for jokes about countertop colors. She had no idea that building a custom house involved so much work on her part.

Their Bermuda wedding in September of the previous year now seemed eight years ago, not eight months. At Carroll, they'd been high-school sweethearts but had broken up before college, married other people, then divorced. When they accidentally met again fifteen years later, the old spark was reignited but it had taken awhile to burst into flame. Steve's girlfriend had been murdered, followed by the murder of Lexie's ex-husband's girlfriend and her half-brother. Then both of them had almost been killed by an old family friend. The failing economy had imperiled Steve's construction business, and Lexie had lost about ten percent of her assets to her financial advisor's corruption. So when they got married, they hoped they were setting sail on placid waters.

It wasn't to be. They didn't face a perfect storm when they returned to Fort Wayne, but they faced a storm nevertheless. They had a rambunctious puppy to train and a huge house to design and build. Lexie had a book to write, plus a family business needing a big injection of discipline, capital, and intelligence. And Steve had committed himself to a risky venture, building Elysian Fields, an up-scale development, in a faltering economy. Because the development had gotten off to a bad start, he changed the name from Elysian Fields to Gretna Green and gave the streets Scottish place names. He hoped the name change was a good omen.

Like all honeymooning couples, they also faced the little stumbling stones strewn across the moors of married life. Ed Singer's toast in Bermuda rang in their heads. "A second marriage is the triumph of hope over experience." And then there was Jean Arnold's joke, which she didn't think Lexie overheard: "Love is a disease and marriage is the cure." Still, getting married was the best thing they ever did.

That was months ago. The little tiff over outdoor countertops was long past, though others were just waiting over the horizon. Now Steve leaned toward his wife to give her a kiss, then took a sip of his beer. "Finally. How long has it been since you ordered that furniture?"

Lexie smiled encouragingly. The time it was taking to furnish their new house was a sore point. Steve could not understand why they just didn't go to Klopfenstein or Ethan Allen and buy whatever was in the showroom that day. He was impatient with rooms that were only half-furnished and very uncomfortable. "It's only been seven months." She spread out catalog pages to show him how beautiful it all was. "Jessica knew about this manufacturer in Italy."

He merely glanced at the pictures. "For the Italians, I suppose seven months is fast. I think they build furniture about the same way they do everything else. A few hours of work followed by a siesta, a parade, a strike, indictment of the prime minister, and installation of a new government." He leaned to the side to look behind her. "Henry's rearranging the lavender bed again."

She looked around. "Oh, Henry, get out of there!" She rushed over to try to pick him up but that was no longer possible. The German Shepherd was almost a year old and weighed over seventy pounds. When he was intent on something, usually destruction, he was practically immovable. She tugged on his collar. "I thought the shelter said he was the unwanted runt of the litter. How big do you think he's going to get?"

"About the size of a small pickup, I'm afraid, but without first gear or brakes. And no return policy."

She laughed as she brushed off Henry's paws. "I can't wait till he's out of the puppy stage. Todd says at fifteen months he'll be a new dog. He'll stop chewing shoes and digging up flower beds."

"Todd says!" Steve said, his expressive brown eyes at last sparkling with humor. "That man is an expert on everything. I'm just sayin'."

"Phyllis said he told one of the women she was interviewing that he knows all about the Mennonites because he has a cousin who's one. He said they're anti-Baptists."

"Everybody knows that," he said. "Time to turn the filets."

"Did you hear that one of our high-school classmates was found dead Saturday at Scuttlebutt's?"

"No," he said, turning to look at her. "Who?"

"Antoinette Delamarter. The class skank. How many times was she sent home to put on something that covered her midriff and her thighs? Remember that time she came to school wearing a red bandanna as a halter top?"

Steve turned back to the grill. "How'd she die?"

"The newspaper said poisoning is suspected."

"You're kidding. People in Fort Wayne get shot or stabbed if it's murder, electrocuted by downed power lines or crushed in a car crash if it's an accident. But they don't get poisoned."

"You want to know the least surprising part? She was an exotic dancer using the name 'Tawny.'"

"That was always her nickname, wasn't it?"

"To tell you the truth, Steve, I don't remember. We didn't exactly run in the same circles. The paper says she's survived only by her half-sister and a fifteen-year-old daughter."

"No husband?"

"None mentioned."

Steve tapped the filets with his finger. According to Todd, that's the way master chefs in good steakhouses did it. He hated to admit Todd was right. "The meat's done. Medium rare. You want me to give the hamburgers to Henry now or wait?"

"Wait till we sit down. Otherwise, he won't leave us alone."

"That puppy training -- so glad we did it. Otherwise, he'd be begging for food and digging up flower beds." He set the platter on the table. "Oh, wait. He is -- ."

Lexie cut him off. "I know, I know. Maybe I've got to take him to class instead of leaving it to Phyllis."

"Well, don't start tomorrow. We have a golf date, remember, in the afternoon."

"Oh, Steve, my darling, you don't really want me along, do you? I'm still an embarrassment."

"Nothing embarrassing about being the worst in the foursome. Makes everybody else feel good. Hal Linkerman's new wife is going to join us and she may be in the same class as you, so it'll work out."

"Linkerman. I've heard that name before."

"He's the guy who took his family whitewater rafting in Colorado, killing his wife and two kids, plus a neighbor's kid who was on the trip. He survived. Now he's remarried."

"And still whitewater rafting?"

"He is."

"What's he do? For a living, I mean."

"Plastic extrusion, I believe. He has half a dozen plants in Indiana and Ohio."

"By the way, congratulations on this filet. It's perfect."

"Let's give credit where credit's due -- Todd's expertise on testing meat without a thermometer. Anyway, Linkerman is thinking of buying a double lot here and building a bigger house than this one. His new wife refuses to move into the house he owns in the Canyons because that's where the first wife lived, so they're bunking in an apartment he owns downtown and, according to him, she's getting restless."

"What's his new wife's name?"

"Martine. She's French."

"If she's married to a rich industrialist, I don't suppose she works."

"Oh, she does. She's descended from the French aristocracy and spends her time raising money for various international charities. The Linkermans have a foundation called The Link -- Linking the World."

Lexie made a gagging gesture. "Giving fish away instead of teaching people to fish. I can't stand it."

"Well, do your best. I need the Linkermans."

"Good thing you finished the golf course before anything else. It's the greatest selling point you have."

"That and this house. The model house is great, but this is the one that sells prospective buyers. They like to know the developer is confident enough to live in his own subdivision. So if it's all right with you, we'll make this the nineteenth hole, give them a drink and a tour."

"I'll warn Phyllis."

"Speaking of Phyllis, has she found anyone she thinks would be good enough to clean this place?"

"I'm meeting the woman she's recommending tomorrow.

Sadie Blosser, fortyish, lives on a farm near Van Wert, loves dogs, never lived away from home before. Todd told me before he left this afternoon that she wears a 'scarfy' thing on her head, a long skirt, and the whitest sneakers he ever saw. Very ladylike, he said."

"Well, then, that's that. If Todd approves, what more do we have to know?" Pushing his empty plate to the side, he imitated Todd's voice. "I'm just sayin'."

It took Lexie a few minutes to stop laughing. "Should we plan something for this weekend? Jessica and Ed are coming. She wants to be sure the media room furniture is what she ordered and it's arranged the way she planned."

"Why does she get to decide how it's arranged?"

"Because she's the designer. And because she's Jessica Singer."

"I'm drawing a blank. All I can think of for entertainment is a round of golf and a movie, try out the furniture Jessica selected. We could take them out to dinner, I suppose, but since there's no smoking in Fort Wayne restaurants, maybe we should eat here so Ed can have his cigarettes. He's a very entertaining golf partner, you know. Sort of like you, only more so. Does Jessica golf?"

"You don't remember? She was on the golf team in high school. She may actually give you some competition."

Suddenly, Henry put his paws on the table, sniffing in the direction of Steve's plate. Steve pushed him away. "God, you're such a pushy German, Henry. A real *schwein,* like the tourists we encountered in Bermuda." He smiled at Lexie. "Remember how that guy elbowed me aside as I tried to enter the elevator with you? We were still in our wedding clothes, for heaven's sake." He patted Henry's head. "And don't tell me you're still hungry, boy. You should have been adopted by a slaughterhouse." He stood up. "Time to take him for a walk, I suspect."

"I'll come with you. It's such a nice night."

5

Angry Raccoon
Tuesday, May 25, 2010

Dover Pitt had been a counselor at Northrop High School for much longer than the two-year limit he'd set for himself. Too late, he realized he wasn't cut out for this job. Maybe he should have applied to be a coach, despite his master's in psychology. After all, he'd been the top-ranked golfer on his Warsaw high school team, had won a Junior Player of the Year award in 1999, and attended Indiana University on a golf scholarship. He was almost as good at tennis. He could no longer remember what demonic impulse led him to major in psychology. Most of what he studied seemed like nonsense, but by the time he acknowledged that, he was in too deep to change majors.

Coaching tennis and golf would have suited him. At least he'd have been outside most of the time and been teaching something he enjoyed. He'd be dealing with relatively normal kids. As it was, there were days when he didn't just want to drink a cup of coffee, he wanted to drown in a tub of it. Or stroll slowly into heavy traffic. Or base-jump off the gymnasium roof. Or swallow an entire bottle of aspirin.

He'd never quite appreciated the significance of the 80/20 rule until he started this job. Eighty percent of the students didn't need him. Twenty percent -- the lost, the shiftless, the delinquent, the crazy ones -- needed far more than he could offer.

Jacintha Delamarter -- who alone accounted for eighty percent of the trouble created by the delinquent twenty percent -- gave him a headache just seeing her name on a piece of paper. She wore inappropriate clothes. She stole anything she could get her hands on. She smarted off to her teachers. She missed school at least twice a month. She either swore at him or flirted with him, almost nothing in between. He suspected she smoked. Once he'd just gotten out of his car when she rocketed into the faculty parking lot in a rusted-out Firebird, smoke billowing out of its dragging tailpipe, torn plastic flapping on the passenger window. Before she could cut the engine, he told her she couldn't leave the car there because she didn't have a faculty permit and the police would have to be called because she was too young to drive. She said something so vile he wouldn't repeat it to the principal. Then, without another word, Jacintha turned around, flew back the way she came, made a squealing turn onto Cook Road, and drove away, not to be seen again that day.

But, of course, to be fair -- and Dover was always trying to be fair -- the girl had some redeeming features. Without trying, she wrote more literate essays than anyone else and, strangely, was a member of the Astronomy Club. She was an excellent bowler and therefore an asset to the Bowling Club. And she had a natural talent for song and dance -- though she needed a lot of makeup -- as she demonstrated in the Charisma productions.

Jacintha was supposed to be in his office, but, naturally, she was late. Sometimes she skipped appointments altogether. He got up to open his door so that she wouldn't have the excuse that she thought he was busy with somebody else. Expecting to see an empty hallway, he leapt back with an explosive grunt. There she was, standing inches from him, glaring from eyes so smeared with black shadow she looked like an angry raccoon about to attack a garbage can.

"Come in," he said, composing his face and stepping back to let her enter. Be nice, he told himself; she just lost her mother. She needs sympathy, not judgment. "Have a chair."

"I don't want to sit down."

Dover walked to his desk chair. "Well, then, I guess I'll have to stand too, but I think this might go better if we both sit. I'm here to help, you know, and I can't do that in a few seconds."

She made a contemptuous noise but sat down.

"I'm sorry to hear about your mother."

She was elaborately unwrapping a piece of gum. "How original." Her crooked smile gave him the shivers. Really, how bad would it be to go back to clerking at Bobick's Golf Headquarters?

"Where are you living?"

"At home," she said, as if he were a slow child. "Cedar Grove Parke. You know where that is, don't you?"

He nodded.

"When you drive by it, you probably close your eyes, it's so, like, beneath you."

Dover extracted a handkerchief from his back pocket and wiped his forehead. *Don't get distracted.* "You don't have any brothers or sisters, do you?"

"No."

"So you're alone."

"Duh!"

"You can't stay alone at your age. The County won't take custody of you if you have a relative who'll take you in. I read that your mother has a sister."

"Half-sister."

"Where does your aunt live?"

"My half-assed half-aunt, you mean? Last I heard, she's in, like, a shelter. She's on meth."

"How about grandparents?"

She shook her head.

"You have grandparents you can't stay with, or you don't have grandparents at all?"

"They're dead."

"Has anybody from the County contacted you about where you're going to live?"

She looked away. Jen told her a woman wearing a pantsuit and carrying a briefcase had been seen knocking on the door of her mother's doublewide yesterday afternoon. She shook her head again.

"Well, I've been contacted by the County, so arrangements are going to have to be made."

"I'll stay with my neighbor."

"Who's that?"

"Jen Ricky. I babysit for her. She works at Scuttlebutt's, the same place Tawny did."

"Tawny?"

"Like, my *mother*," she said.

"*Like* your mother?" The word "like" made him physically ill. Jacintha simply stared.

"Are you two related? To the neighbor, I mean."

Jacintha blinked. "She's my aunt."

"I thought your mother had only one sister."

Pause. "My dad's sister then."

"Who's your dad?"

Jacintha popped her gum so loud Dover jumped. "Maybe Jen's not my dad's sister. I don't know how she's my aunt."

He closed his eyes for a long minute. "Jacintha. I want to help you, but I can't if you keep . . . keep telling me what you think I want to hear." *Don't call her a liar. No pejoratives. Stay positive. Boost her self-esteem.* The politically correct words he was required to use with students were like handcuffs.

"I know who my dad is."

"Oka-a-a-y."

"You don't believe me."

No, I don't, you spawn of Satan. "Belief has nothing to do with your father's identity. Facts are facts. So tell me. Who is he?" Dover picked up a pencil and pulled a notepad toward him.

"If I told you, I'd, like, have to kill you." Her big brown eyes, magnified by the strong lenses of her glasses, sparkled with anticipation.

You want to kill me. I can see it in your eyes. "Tell me about him then."

"He's a rich guy. Married. A businessman."

"Where does he live?"

"In Timbuktu."

He squinted at her.

"For Christ's sake, Mr. Pitts, where do you think? In Fort Wayne."

"Mr. Pitt, please." *Let the swearing go.*

"Whatever." If there was a word Dover hated more than "like," which larded students' conversations like fat marbling a prime steak, it was "whatever." Dover shut his eyes for a second. *She wins if I show that I'm mad.* "Has this man been paying child support?"

"No. Tawny and I argued about that all the time. We don't have to be this poor."

"Have you two -- I mean, you and your rich father -- been in touch?"

"Rich? You making fun of me?"

"Didn't you say he's rich?"

"Yah. But you used the word like I was lying."

Don't rise to the bait. "So are you in touch?"

"He doesn't know about me."

"What's that mean? I mean, how do you know he doesn't know about you?"

"My mother kept a scrapbook about him."

Dover wanted to put his head on the desk. The *non sequiturs* were giving him a headache. "I don't understand."

"Tawny said she wasn't sure who my father is when I asked, but then I found the scrapbook in the bottom of her hope chest, so, like, I think she knew it's this particular dude. He's awesome-looking, by the way."

If he's awesome-looking, then you can't be his daughter. And your mother had a hope chest? Hope for what? "The scrapbook is about just this one man you think is your father?"

"Just him. Tawny pasted in every newspaper article ever mentioning him. Plus some pictures it looks like she took when he didn't know she was around -- outside and inside."

"She worked at Scuttlebutt's, right?"

"Right."

"Are you talking about the owner of that place? Is he your father?"

"You're trying to trick me. No matter how I answer that, like, I give something away."

"Well, if your mother wasn't sure this 'dude' in the scrapbook was your father, it was only a suspicion, and of course it's a convenient one if he's a rich businessman." Had he actually said that out loud? Where was his professionalism? "Did she ever go to court or get a DNA test, anything like that?"

"No. Tawny was stubborn. She wanted to make it on her own."

Or she was less sure about who your father is than you seem to be. "Could I take a look at that scrapbook?"

"Sure. You wanna come home with me? There's like, beer, in the refrigerator."

He looked up from his notepad. He couldn't help the shiver. "No. Why don't you bring it in tomorrow?"

"Can't. I have to be at the funeral home for the visitation. The funeral's Thursday."

"Are you going to be back this week?"

"Friday."

"Well, bring it in then." He tapped his pencil on his notepad. "Meanwhile, I don't know what I'm supposed to do with this information about your putative father."

"Say what?"

"Putative. Meaning you're making an unproven assumption that he's your father. Until I get a name, there's not much more I can do. Maybe I'll know more Friday after I've seen that scrapbook. Meanwhile, would you promise to stay with your neighbor for a few days until we can get this sorted out? You shouldn't be alone, you know, and you're going to be much happier if the County doesn't get involved. And some financial arrangements are going to have to be made for you. Do you need money for food or anything?" It was against the rules to give students money, but in this case he'd make an exception. The ugly girl looked like

28

she hadn't eaten for weeks. She reminded him of somebody -- somebody famous. Some big-haired, drug-addled, raccoon-eyed celebrity who was starving herself to death.

"Whatever." She paused. "If you have a twenty, I could get a pizza."

He stood up, extracted his billfold, found a twenty and handed it to her.

"Thanks." Taking her time, she tucked the twenty into her bra. "I suppose I shouldn't mention your generosity to anyone."

Don't give the taunting bitch any ammunition. "I'm not breaking any rules. It's a gift from one human being to another in need, that's all. You can pay me back if you want." *Which we both know you wouldn't do even if you could.*

Then she removed the gum from her mouth and, looking him straight in the eye, stuck it under the ledge of his desk. She bent over to look at the underside. "There's a lot of gum under here. Did you know that, Mr. Pitts?" She smiled, stood up, and hoisted her battered messenger bag to her shoulder. It was stenciled this way and that with strings of words. "You know I'm no good" and "Tears dry on their own" were the only ones he could read as she moved around. She caught the direction of his eyes. "You like this? I stenciled it myself."

"Interesting." *Where are the words "like" and "whatever?"*

At the door she turned. "I'll stay with Jen for awhile. I'm babysitting tonight. I need the money." She pointed to her bra. "This twenty won't go far, you know, so I don't have a choice about it."

Hours later, as Dover was preparing to leave for the day, Amy Winehouse popped into his mind at about the same moment he noticed that the brass-and-marble pen and pencil set his parents had given him upon getting his master's had disappeared.

6

A Different Life
Tuesday, May 25, 2010

Dover Pitt had never been in a place like Scuttlebutt's in his life. He wished it was Halloween so he could disguise himself. If anybody connected with Northrop saw him, he'd be finished, he just knew it. But he was on a mission.

At four in the afternoon, the place was empty, brightly lit, only a cleaning crew in evidence. The poles on the stage looked filmy, the tables smudged. The place smelled like a smoky, beery bathroom. Why would anyone pay to linger in such a dismal setting?

A skinny man wearing a dirty apron was clinking glasses behind the immense horseshoe bar. When he saw Dover, he called out, "We aren't open."

Dover walked toward the bar so he didn't have to shout. "I'm not here for the show. I'd like to speak to the owner."

"Scut's in the back." The skinny man pointed toward a door angled behind the bar. "You want me to get him?"

"Is it okay if I just walk back there?"

"Okay with me. Take the hallway all the way to the end."

When Dover reached the end of the unadorned cinderblock hallway, he was confronted with a gray metal door. He knocked. Nothing. He knocked again. Then he heard footsteps. The door opened.

"What is it?" The man standing in the doorway was probably in his early thirties, dressed like a rich businessman who'd just spent the morning on a private plane -- sharply creased jeans, white dress shirt open at the neck, camel blazer, dark brown Italian loafers, no socks. By contrast, Dover felt like an overaged fraternity boy in his rumpled khakis, Ralph Lauren polo shirt, and Timberlands. The man's dark brown hair was cut short and fashionably spiked. Though the man in the doorway was a little overweight, he was definitely good-looking -- possibly making him awesome in Jacintha's world.

"Could I talk to you a minute? About Mrs. Delamarter."

"You from the cops?"

"No."

"I've got a lot to do, so if you keep it to a minute, you can come in."

"I'm Dover Pitt."

"Percy Scutter, but call me Scut. Everybody else does." He turned before there could be the offer of a handshake. "Have a seat."

Dover had no small talk. "I'm a student counselor at Northrop High School."

Scut glanced at the metal door. "We check IDs. No students ever get in here."

"That's not why I came. I'm here because one of the students I counsel is Jacintha Delamarter. You know her?"

"Tawny's girl. I've seen her a couple times when she drove her mother to work."

"She seems to be an orphan now, and if we don't find a relative she can live with, the County might put her in a foster home."

"So?"

"She's looking for her father."

"Who is he?"

"Don't know."

"So how do you think you're going to find him here?"

"She said her mother kept a scrapbook about the man she thinks is her father. I haven't seen it yet, and the girl wouldn't give me a name, but she described the man as a rich Fort Wayne businessman who gets his face in the paper a lot. A married guy. I thought I'd start with Mrs. Delamarter's employer as either . . . either involved or having some information. Maybe the woman said something . . . ."

Scut lit a cigarette. "Where are you going with this?"

"Probably nowhere. I can see you're way too young for the honor, but I just thought I'd give you and your dad a head's up. She said the guy is awesome-looking, and if you look like your father . . . well . . . ."

"My pop? You think he might be the guy?"

"I'm not making any accusations."

"Do you know him?"

"No. I don't even know his first name."

Scut laughed. "Owen -- that's his name -- isn't awesome-looking, I'll tell you that." He swiveled his chair, removed a framed studio portrait from his credenza, and showed it to Dover. "Here's my parents' anniversary portrait. What do you think?"

Dover waggled his head noncommittally.

"The joke in the family is he could pass for a buzzard. He's a good pop, don't get me wrong, but he's nothing to look at. And the last thing he'd ever do in this business is get his face in the papers. Anonymity is the way to go. Furthermore, I'm adopted because when Owen got back from Viet Nam, he couldn't have kids, so if you think I might qualify in the awesome department -- thank you very much -- that doesn't mean a thing about my father. He blamed Agent Orange, by the way."

"Did Mrs. Delamarter ever say anything about Jacintha's father?"

"Not to me."

"How about to your father?"

"He and my mother moved to St. Croix seven years ago, before Tawny ever started working here." Scut stubbed out his cigarette. "I don't get why you came here. Who are you trying to help?"

"Jacintha Delamarter isn't the most . . . ." Dover struggled for innocuous words. "She isn't a girl that a rich married businessman would want to show up on his step claiming to be his daughter. Her head's full of fantasies, so whatever she imagines about her father is probably wrong anyway, and, worse, she acts out in inappropriate ways. She wouldn't fit into a respectable man's life."

"A delinquent?"

"We don't use that word."

Scut laughed. "Of course you don't." He leaned forward. "Tawny was no better than she should be, if you get my drift, so if her daughter's a handful -- well, the apple doesn't fall far from the tree, does it? But you still haven't told me who you're trying to help."

"Jacintha, I suppose. If she's got a father that can be identified, he should provide for her. But I'd like to warn him what he's about to face."

"Let me get this straight. You want to help Jacintha find her father while helping him avoid the embarrassment."

Dover sighed. "Doing good is very confusing."

"Especially if you have no hard facts."

"Hard facts are very hard to get in my line of work."

"Mine too, believe me. The girls lie about everything."

"You asked me if I was from the cops before you let me in. I take it they've been around."

"More than once. They found a bottle that smelled funny in Tawny's car. I hear they think it was Gatorade."

"I read that she might have been poisoned."

"Personally, I think that's a little far-fetched, don't you? An overdose of Ecstasy or coke I can believe, but poisoned Gatorade? Come on."

"Mrs. Delamarter was on . . . on drugs?"

"Most of the girls are. That's why they work at places like this. They make twenty times what they could make waitressing, but they blow it. Literally. We don't let them snort or shoot up at work, of course, but I don't have eyes in the back of my head, so they probably do all kinds of things behind my back."

"You don't like the girls, as you call them. I can hear it in your voice."

"You wanna hear my theory?"

"Of what?"

"How the girls end up here. They don't finish high school, they have a kid before they're married, they take drugs thinking they can stop anytime, which they can't. They never learn a respectable skill, and they keep changing jobs. You make girls stay in school until they graduate and tell them to keep their pants on, the world would be different."

"Some of us try."

"Just so you know I'm not a sexist, I don't like the customers either. They're all losers in my eyes, guys who don't know how to relate to women other than to leer at them."

"You have a family?"

"Damn right. Beautiful wife -- we met in college -- and a boy three years old. That's what keeps me sane. But as I was saying, I give everybody what they want. The men get their jollies, the girls get a paycheck and whatever tips they can tease out of the suckers, and I make enough moola to buy out my pop. So it all works out."

"Maybe your customers shouldn't want what you give them. Maybe -- ."

Standing up and taking a step toward his office door, Scut cut him off. "Maybe, schmaybe. I didn't make this world and I'm not going to change it." He took a long look at Dover. "You look depressed, man. You want a beer before you go?"

Dover shook his head. *I want a different life. This one sucks.*

7

Morels
Tuesday, May 25, 2010

"This is definitely not a morel," Todd said, late Tuesday afternoon. He was pointing at the pasty white mushroom that, to Phyllis, looked exactly like a man's genitalia pointing straight at the sky. The head of the thing was covered with warts.

Phyllis made a face. "I wouldn't eat that if it was the tastiest thing in the world."

"Oh." Todd took another look. "Oh, you're right, I see what you mean. I definitely do. Not something for a lady to look at, am I right? I should have walked right by it except I don't want you to pick something that'll kill you." He looked at the picture he'd printed from Wikipedia. "*Amanita abrupta*, that's what it's called, toxic to the liver, found in eastern North America. Are we in eastern North America, you think? I always thought we were in the Midwest. Maybe the thing has been spreading west. You ever study Latin, Phyl?"

"No. I took a few semesters of Spanish but I don't remember much."

"How about that? *Gracias, muy bien hacienda, por favor.* That's all I remember."

Phyllis laughed. "That's the silliest sentence I've ever heard. 'Thank you, very good house, please.' It makes no sense at all."

Unabashed, Todd laughed too. "At least I made you laugh.

Anyway, we have so much in common, it just amazes me, yes, it does."

Phyllis swung her empty basket, unwilling to concede the point. "We both like morels. I think that's what we have in common. And Mizz Royce loves them, fried in butter, very simple. But I've never been in the woods to pick them before."

"You're looking at your permanent guide to mushroom-picking. I come out to this old orchard every year, nobody ever bothers me. It's a shame that it's been left to go wild again. I remember when you could come pick your own apples and then visit the cider mill at the end of the dirt lane. Last year I came out here, the way I always do, and picked over a quart of morels. Now, let's stop a moment. We're looking for black morels, so we're also looking for dying trees like cottonwoods and apple trees. Lots of apple trees here, of course, and most are dying, so just keep your eyes on the ground, no need to notice the trees at all. That's where morels grow, in the shade of deciduous trees, especially dying ones. You know what deciduous means?"

"Tell me." *You're going to anyway.*

"Trees that lose their leaves in the Fall. Stop a minute, let me show you what a false morel looks like."

Phyllis stopped as Todd put a hand on her arm and held out the Wikipedia print-out. "See this mess looks like a pile of bloody worms? That's what we don't want. They don't grow here, but I'm just sayin'. Can't pronounce the Latin though, so let's just call them false morels."

After a quick glance at the picture, she shut her eyes. "Todd, if you show me one more poisonous mushroom, even if it's just a picture, I'm going to throw up."

At his hurt look, Phyllis instantly felt remorseful.

"Maybe this isn't the thing for ladies, tramping through the woods, looking at ugly funguses. Oh, look there. There are some black morels. Do you know what they're called by the people in Appalachia?"

"I wouldn't dare guess."

"Molly moochers and hickory chickens. My mother came

36

from Kentucky, she called them hickory chickens. Isn't that funny? See how it looks like a honeycomb on a stalk. There's enough here to feed an army, that's the truth. We'll be done before you know it."

"If you don't mind, I'd like to pick an extra quart. I'm cooking dinner for my son and his wife tonight, and I know Drago likes morels."

"Drago. Now that's a name you don't hear very often. How'd you come up with it?"

"That's a long story, Todd. I'd bore you to death."

"You'd never bore me, not ever. No sir. You're the smartest woman I ever met."

"Drago's formal name is Pendragon, which comes from the tales of King Arthur. I read them in middle school, on my own. Pendragon means head dragon, but though that's the name on my son's birth certificate, it's too big to carry around every day, so I shortened it to Drago."

"Head dragon! He certainly earned that name last year when he saved the lives of Mr. and Mrs. Wright. That was brave, that was, running right straight into gunfire. I didn't even know you then, but I remember the stories in the papers. I've never met your son, but I'm looking forward to the day. I'd be honored to meet a hero like that. Here, let me take that basket."

They walked a couple of yards in silence, but for Todd silence was anathema. "I like that Sadie, by the way. How about you?"

"I do too. She seems like a hard worker." *And she can't cook and doesn't dress like a housekeeper, so she'll never take my place.*

As they walked through the orchard, heads down, looking for morels, Todd suddenly halted in front of a gnarly tree and exclaimed, "Look at this, will you. This is the target I put up last fall. Very faded and tattered, but it's still here, nailed to this old apple tree. You can see it's Bin Laden, can't you?" Todd counted the holes on the outline of the man. "Twenty-three hits right in the chest, three in the face." He looked at Phyllis with a triumphant smile. "That man's dead. Do you shoot?"

"I do. I go to H&H Firearms twice a year."

"What do you shoot?"

"A .38 caliber Smith & Wesson, five-shot."

"Now that's something I wouldn't have guessed about you. What made you take up guns?"

Phyllis hesitated. She didn't want to tell her darkest secret, that many years earlier she'd killed her husband to protect her son. "Self-defense."

"Self-defense, huh? Everyday you surprise me, Phyl, yes you do. Just when I think I've got you figured out, you surprise me. King Arthur's tales, head dragons, then a Smith & Wesson. What next? You want to come out with me sometime, do a little target shooting? We'll use some watermelons, okay? If we could find a dead pig, of course, that would be the thing. Doctors tell me they're so like humans that some people actually get pig hearts. I'm just sayin'."

"I've never shot outside, but I'll think about it." She bent to start collecting a patch of morels. Todd told her to straighten up, he'd do the bending. When they'd filled the basket, he had one more question for her. "You need somebody to taste those morels before you serve them?"

She smiled at the broad hint. "You want to join us for dinner, Todd? I have to warn you, though. Lucy and Drago have two babies, very noisy, you might hate the whole thing."

They were heading back through the woods. "I love babies," he protested. "Never had any of my own . . . not that I know about anyway." He laughed and patted her back. "A man's joke, you know. A man can't know the way a woman can, am I right? I'm just sayin'. Anyway, I never got around to getting married. I was close once, within weeks actually, but then I found out she drank, which is a story I'll tell you sometime, so it was no go. Got out of there just in time. I like a drink in the evening, but two's my limit. Family -- that's the most important thing in a man's life." He opened the car door for her. "Morels fried in butter. Should I bring wine or beer? A man's gotta bring something when he's invited to dinner. I'm no Emily Post; I'm just sayin'."

8

Honey Badger
Friday, May 28, 2010

Friday noon Steve was just getting ready to leave the model house at Gretna Green, where he had his office in the walk-out basement, when a man asked Linda, the receptionist, where he could find Sterling Steven Wright.

"Right here," Steve said, holding out his hand. "But people call me Steve. What can I do for you?"

The man smiled tentatively. "I'm Dover Pitt. Could I talk to you in private?"

"I'm just leaving. Some guests from Indianapolis came up for the weekend, and my wife wants me at home. But if it's a lot or a floor plan you want to look at, I'd recommend Luis Morales anyway. He's the guy in charge of sales."

"It's personal."

Steve cocked his head. "Personal. Does that mean you're selling something?"

"No. Definitely not."

"Do I know you?"

"I don't think we've met, but I'm not here about buying a lot or a house." Dover looked around. "I think you'll be interested in what I have to say, but it'd be better if we could talk where we're alone."

When they were seated in Steve's office, Dover pulled a

leatherette book out of his briefcase and laid it on the desk. "Take a look at this."

Steve pulled the book toward him and opened it. Bobbing his head in disbelief, he quickly flipped through the pages, then returned to the beginning and looked at each one more carefully. Finally, he looked up, puzzled. "This is all about me."

"Yes, it is."

"Do I have a stalker?"

"Can't say."

"Does this thing belong to you?"

"No. It belonged to Antoinette Delamarter, the woman who died at Scuttlebutt's."

"How did you get hold of it?"

"Her daughter, Jacintha, is a student at Northrop High School, where I'm a counselor. I've got a master's in psychology. I'd much rather be coaching golf or tennis but . . . ." He sighed deeply. "But that's neither here nor there. Her mother died, as you may have heard -- an exotic dancer at Scuttlebutt's. Jacintha is now alone in the world and the County will put her into foster care if we can't find a relative. She claims her father is a rich, married businessman in Fort Wayne, an awesome-looking guy, she said. At first, I thought she might be referring to the owner of Scuttlebutt's but I'm satisfied he's not the man I'm looking for, nor is his son. Today Jacintha brought this scrapbook to school, claims her mother made it. She's adamant that her mother knew you were the father of her child. That's why she made the scrapbook, she said."

Steve laughed. "I'm not her father. I'm not anybody's father. I don't have any children yet, though my wife and I are trying. We've only been married a few months, so . . . ." He trailed off, wondering how he'd gotten suckered into saying as much as he did. This man was a complete stranger with a ridiculous story.

Dover had a hard time looking Steve in the eye. "You have any idea why Jacintha's mother would think you were the father?"

"No."

"You never met her, I take it."

"Well, she and I both went to Carroll High School back in the

Nineties, but I never dated her, and I've never been in Scuttlebutt's in my life. I barely remember her. I hadn't heard her name in fifteen years and wouldn't have given her a thought if my wife hadn't read me the newspaper article about her death."

"What do you remember about her?"

"Not much. I hate to say bad things about the dead, but Tawny, which was her high-school nickname, had a . . . ," he paused, searching for a kind word, ". . . a reputation for generosity. Maybe she was different after high school, but since she was working at Scuttlebutt's, my guess is nothing changed."

"What year did you graduate from Carroll?"

"1994."

Dover opened a little notebook and flipped a few pages. "The girl was born in 1995, May 30 to be exact, so her father might well have been someone Antoinette Delamarter went to school with."

"I'm telling you, Mr. Pitt, without being too pointed about it, that could be anyone. Did she ever get a court order for a DNA test or file a petition for child support?"

"Not to my knowledge."

"If she knew who her daughter's father was, don't you think she would have done that?"

"I asked that very question of Jacintha. She said her mother was stubborn, wanted to make it on her own."

Steve made a dismissive sound and shook his head. "She didn't know who the unlucky bastard was, that's all, and no court would just let her cruise through the phone book."

"I don't suppose you'd be willing to take a DNA test."

"No."

Dover extracted a photo from his notebook and laid it on the desk. "Would you be interested in looking at Jacintha's school picture?"

"Not really." But, out of politeness, Steve took a look anyway. His stomach flipped over. The girl looked uncannily like his mother: the set of her brown eyes, the freckles, the thin lips, the determined chin. And she had two features he himself had had corrected a few weeks after he graduated from college: a crooked smile -- concealing bad teeth? -- and ears that stuck out through her hair. The only things he didn't recognize were the mass of curly chestnut hair, the high cheekbones, and the long eyelashes.

"Remind you of anybody?" Dover asked.

Steve pushed the picture away and sat back in his chair. "No." But his mind was stirring with buried memories. And then the last person he wanted to see was suddenly standing in his doorway. How long had she been there? What had she heard? "Lexie! What are you doing here?"

"I came by to pick you up for lunch. Jessica and Ed are in my car and Ed's hungry as a bear." She walked into the room, glancing first at the picture of Jacintha, now turned in the stranger's direction, and then at the stranger.

Dover got to his feet and held out his hand. "Dover Pitt."

"Lexie Royce, Steve's wife. I'm sorry to interrupt but my husband said he was coming home twenty minutes ago."

Steve stood too. "Mr. Pitt is a counselor at Northrop High."

"Ah." Lexie waited for the men to explain.

"He's here about Antoinette Delamarter's daughter . . . what's her name again?"

"Jacintha. Jacintha Caitlin Delamarter." Dover looked like he wanted to disappear. "Quite a mouthful, wouldn't you say?"

Lexie cocked her head, puzzled. "And this girl has what to do with my husband?"

When Dover suddenly had a coughing fit, Steve stepped in. "Mr. Pitt is looking for the father of the girl. He thought I might know something."

Lexie smiled at Dover. "Does the father have a name?"

"I'm sure he does, but nobody knows what it is, not for sure anyway, least of all me. Jacintha's one of the students I counsel from time to time." He looked uncertainly at Steve. Should he continue or not?

After an awkward pause, Steve spoke, his eyes on his wife. "Sit down, honey. This won't take long, but you might as well hear what Mr. Pitt just told me." He nodded at Dover. "Show her the book."

Dover slid the scrapbook toward Lexie. He gave her the same explanation he'd given to Steve about why he was in possession of it and what Jacintha thought it meant.

Lexie flipped through a couple of pages. "I take it every page is about my husband."

Dover nodded.

"Did Antoinette have any other scrapbooks like this about other men?"

"That I don't know, but Jacintha probably would have showed me the others if she did."

Lexie glanced at the school picture lying in the middle of the desk. "Who is that?"

"Jacintha." Dover pulled the picture so it lay between him and Lexie, who looked at the picture without touching it. Finally, in a shaky voice, without meeting her husband's eyes, she said, "The girl looks vaguely familiar, but I can't place her."

"Me either. Why Tawny made that scrapbook, I have no idea."

Lexie tried to laugh. "Sometimes women get odd fixations."

Dover retrieved the scrapbook. "I wouldn't be here except I feel it's my duty to help the girl find a relative who'll take her in. Otherwise, she'll become a ward of the County, and that isn't a fate I'd wish on anyone. She's not the age or . . . or the kind of girl that foster parents seek out."

When Dover tried to pick up the school picture too, Lexie's hand shot out to grab it. She affected the professional tone of a plastic surgeon. "This girl needs a lot of help, whoever her father is. Even if she doesn't find a home with a relative, somebody ought to pony up for cosmetic work. That smile . . . if she ever went to a dentist, I'd be surprised. And it looks like some Lasik surgery is in order so she can get rid of those horrible glasses. Not to mention her ears need to be pinned back." Her voice trailed off and she glanced at Steve. He looked so troubled she decided to change course. Though filled with a sinking feeling that there was more to this story than she knew, she wasn't about to embarrass her husband before a stranger.

An awkward silence followed. Finally, Lexie managed a smile

in Dover's direction. She'd made a decision, but she wasn't ready to tell either man what it was. "Give me your card, Mr. Pitt, and we'll stay in touch."

Dover retrieved the photo and handed Lexie his business card. Then he directed himself to Steve. "I didn't really think you ever had anything to do with Jacintha's mother, but once the girl showed me this scrapbook, I thought I'd better forewarn you that Jacintha isn't likely to let the matter drop. This scrapbook isn't evidence of anything other than her mother's wishful thinking, but Jacintha assumes it's as true as gravity. Once her mind is set on something, she has the tenacity of a honey badger. At least this way you two are prepared if you open your door one day and the girl is standing on the doorstep, ready to move in."

"How would any couple prepare for something like that?" Steve asked.

Dover stood up. "Mr. Wright, I should have an answer to that, but I don't. As I said, I wish I'd taken an entirely different direction in life myself."

"Don't we all," Steve muttered under his breath.

9

Charity

Friday - Saturday, May 28 - 29, 2010

When I saw the picture of Antoinette's daughter, I thought I was looking at a picture of Steve's mother, but of course I didn't want to say anything in front of Dover Pitt. I never actually met Laurel Ann Wright, but Steve keeps a framed picture of his parents on his office credenza, and he has a few other pictures of them in a cedar box, some taken when they were very young. His father died in an industrial accident when he was six. Then his mother died from an asthma attack when Steve was in seventh grade. I remember that day because the principal suddenly appeared in our social science class and, with a funereal face, asked Steve to step out. He didn't return for a week.

We weren't an item in those days, though I already had my eye on him because he was the cutest boy I'd ever seen -- big brown eyes that always looked mischievous, a spackle of freckles across his nose, a big shock of reddish hair, and a lopsided grin. Of course, he also had crooked teeth and ears that looked like sails, so he wasn't perfect, but his intelligence and personality, not to mention his baseball talent, made up for his physical defects.

Well, almost. We began dating our sophomore year and we were inseparable until the summer of 1994, when we graduated from Carroll High. Then one night in early August, while making out in his ancient Bel Air, he proposed that we not date anybody else in college and get married the day after we graduated. I wasn't ready for that. He said he wanted to farm; I didn't want to live on a farm. He didn't have the model looks I fancied I deserved in a man -- though I didn't either in those days, so what was I thinking? He'd grown up in a poor family with no social standing. My father was the Scrapyard King, we lived in a huge house, I had a closetful of trendy clothes, and I had everything I ever wanted from day one. The only thing I was missing was my mother, who was killed by a deer jumping through her windshield when I was three.

The defects I found in Steve weren't the whole problem. Something in me wanted to test the waters at Purdue, where I was sure I'd find someone far more worldly than Sterling Steven Wright. And, of course, I did. Unfortunately, it was Ferrell Hawke, a Brit six years older than me, a graduate assistant in the Engineering Department. He was sophisticated, traveled, voluble, with a charming accent. He claimed he was in line to be the eighth Baron of Hawkemere. Foolishly, I married him, only to discover that he was arrogant, greedy, jealous of my success, and, in his depressive moods, violent. Meanwhile, Steve married Mattie Belden, an emotionally remote, narcissistic spendthrift. Then, after we were both divorced, Steve and I met again at a dinner in Indianapolis and the rest, as they say, is history.

The moment I laid eyes on the school picture of Jacintha Caitlin Delamarter, I saw the resemblance between her and Steve's mother. But I couldn't imagine how that could be. Surely my husband was never foolish enough to date Antoinette in high school; if he had, I would have heard about it. And while Steve was a passionate boyfriend and wanted to go further than I did, he never tried to wheedle me into doing what I was afraid to do -- so how could he could have been crazy enough to bed down that skank even for a one-night stand? Perhaps, I'm thinking, Frank, Steve's older brother, is the culprit, or one of his many red-haired cousins.

The only way I survived the weekend with the Singers was to put on the shroud of denial. I wear it well. I pretended not to miss my mother when I was little. I pretended I could save my marriage to Ferrell. Now I pretended I wasn't concerned about the resemblance between Antoinette's daughter and my husband. The scrapbook was surely just the fantasy of a loser, a woman who wished she'd slept with an ambitious businessman instead of the out-of-work bum she probably did.

Steve was unnaturally subdued all weekend, and Jessica noticed. "Something wrong with Steve?" We were refreshing our lipstick in the Club bathroom after our golf game on Saturday.

"What do you mean?" I asked, stalling for time.

"He's hardly said a word all day and hasn't told one bad joke."

I pretended it was just the disappointing Tuesday afternoon we spent with the Linkermans that had gotten Steve down, and I knew what button to push to get Jessica off on another subject. I told her how Martine Linkerman bragged about her French heritage, all the way back to Napoleon, and then lectured me on giving more to charity, especially to third-world countries.

"Who would want to be descended from Napoleon, for Pete's sake, except some dirt-bag Frenchman who forgot he was a tyrant? And I thought the Bonapartes were Italian anyway."

"Martine was specific that she's descended from Napoleon's sister Caroline. But she didn't mention that part about the family's being Italian originally, so maybe she doesn't know as much as you do."

"Or she's making the whole thing up to make you, the American nobody, feel like a European castoff."

"Could be. Anyway, she and her husband have a foundation called The Link -- Linking the World. They're good friends with Bono and go around the world nagging politicians to give more money to Africa. She tried to get me to buy a table for ten at some fund-raiser luncheon at the Coliseum. The money's for mosquito nets."

"And did you buy a table?"

"Steve gave me that look -- he really wants Linkerman to buy lots here -- so I did -- a thousand dollars." I smiled at my beautiful friend. "There's a place for you next month if you're interested."

Jessica ignored the invitation. "And what do you think about her palling around with Bono, lecturing Congress and producing glamorous but useless concerts?" Jessica asked, forcefully snapping her cosmetic bag shut as a comment on people who brag about their charity.

"I prefer finding ways to give people employment here at home. That way they have pride in their own hard work. They don't need to feel grateful for somebody's largesse, and they can count on gaining something through their own efforts the next day and the day after that. But, of course, in the interests of Steve's business goals, I didn't say a thing."

"She couldn't know it, of course, but I know you're also very generous with the people around you -- Drago, Jean, Phyllis, Todd. I don't suppose you told her that."

"No. Never. There's a reason for the way I do things. I like to know my money is actually going to do some good that I can measure instead of funding a big bureaucracy I can't see and know nothing about."

"Well," Jessica said, holding the door open for me, "so did the Linkermans commit to a lot or two here?"

"No. That's what has Steve so worried." Which was true in a way, but not the whole truth. I suspected he was as unsettled by the picture of Jacintha as I was. Would he say anything to me or not?

Even at that moment, however, I was thinking of an entirely different form of charity from Martine Linkerman's. Maybe I should do something -- preferably directly but anonymously -- for the orphan Jacintha Caitlin Delamarter, no matter who her father was. She reminded me a little of myself at that age: unexpectedly deprived of a mother, and in need of minor cosmetic dentistry and surgery if she was going to hold her own in the viciously judgmental world of high school.

But I wasn't ready to confide my project, even to Jessica. And I had yet to discuss anything with Steve, who seemed unusually preoccupied.

10

Bad Old Memories
Saturday, May 29, 2010

Ed and Steve were sitting in the grill room of the new Gretna Green clubhouse, perfunctorily examining the menu and waiting for their wives to join them. Ed, a pediatrician, was talking in worried tones about the health care act President Obama had signed into law several months earlier. Normally, Steve would be interested, or at least sympathetic, but certain old memories -- bad memories -- had begun coming into focus on the golf course.

A few days after he'd broken up with Lexie before they left for college, he'd been talked into going with friends to a wild end-of-summer party in Nick Forenza's basement game room. Nick's parents had left for the weekend. The music was loud and sexy, the swimming pool overflowed with skinny-dippers, and the bar was open. Reefers were being passed around like candy. Couples -- none older than nineteen - weren't even trying to hide their amorous antics. He was angry at the world but especially with Lexie, who, of course, had left as soon as she spotted him.

He got so drunk he puked over and over and then couldn't drive home. He'd slept all night on his friend's lawn, only to be raked over the coals the next morning by his aunt, who knew what the bite mark on his neck meant. She was absolutely furious with him.

Was Antoinette Delamarter the girl that he and his unattached friends took turns with in an upstairs bedroom? He couldn't remember for sure, though the name Tawny rang in his head like a death knell. He could still hear Sheryl Crow singing *All I Wanna Do*, assuring him he was just having a little innocent fun before real life started. He thought he remembered a mass of chestnut curls and glassy eyes with smudged mascara. Before he started removing his clothes, he'd clicked off the table lamp, as if darkness meant nothing regrettable was really happening. Had either of them said a word, or did they just go at it like foxes in heat?

If it was Antoinette Delamarter he'd encountered that night, and it probably was, how unlucky was he if he was the one that made her pregnant? He hadn't lasted a minute. The girl on the bed, who was willing enough, meant nothing to him. There'd been at least a dozen other guys who'd made it up the stairs that night and, if the rumors were true, probably dozens before that in many other places. He hadn't been prepared with a condom, but he was sure he'd pulled out in time.

The chance that he'd fathered a child that night was surely a minus number. How could the impulsive, one-time act of a hormonally overwhelmed, heart-broken teenager have such permanent and irreversible consequences?

But the face of Jacintha Delamarter mocked him. Her eyes were the accusatory eyes of his mother, her smile his own at that age.

What the hell was he going to do now?

11

Terrible New Thoughts
Tuesday, June 1, 2010

The moment the interminable Memorial Day holiday was over, I wasted no time looking into Jacintha's situation. Tuesday I met Dover Pitt at Cedar Grove Parke. I wanted to take the measure of the woman with whom Jacintha was ostensibly staying and have a look at the place Antoinette Delamarter had called home. I wasn't ready to meet the girl herself, but since she'd be in school, there was no chance of that.

At a few minutes before noon, Jen Ricky was sitting in a plastic lawn chair on the deck of her mobile home, drinking a Mike's Hard Lemonade and smoking a Kools. She was dressed in a pair of bagged-out jersey shorts and a dago-t, barefoot, her mousy hair pulled into a sloppy ponytail. One of the bows on her cheap sunglasses was taped into place. A paperback, minus its cover, lay folded over on a milk crate beside her chair, and in the corner of the deck stood a pathetic little houseplant in need of water. The deck was slippery green with mold, desperately in need of power-washing. She said her twin girls were taking a nap, so we'd probably have a half hour to talk.

Once we were seated in mismatched plastic chairs, she leaned over to take the lid off a foam cooler and offered us a Coke, a beer, or a Mike's Hard Lemonade. Both Dover and I accepted a Coke. She asked if we wanted some potato chips, it wouldn't take a minute to grab some from the kitchen. We said no thanks. I almost never smoke, but I'd bought a package of Virginia Slims that morning so I'd have something to do with my hands. Surprisingly, Dover accepted a cigarette, though he assured us he never, ever smoked and menthol gave him a headache. I noticed his hand shaking.

Jen pushed her sunglasses up on her head, revealing swollen eyes, and smiled at me. "I really like those leggings. Did you get them at Walmart?"

I shook my head, ashamed to admit they were fifty-two dollar matte opaque Wolfords from Nordstrom -- and more than a little disappointed they apparently looked no better than a ten-dollar Walmart brand. The jersey tunic I was wearing was an even more expensive Puli from Susan's, but apparently it looked even less special than my leggings. In a way, I rationalized, it made things more comfortable, for Jen saw no difference between me and her. We were social equals.

"Mr. Pitt said you have some questions about Jacintha."

I nodded.

"Are you related to her or something? Or were you friends with Tawny? I thought I knew most of her friends."

How should I explain myself? I had no intention of admitting I was the wife of the man Jacintha thought was her father. I glanced at Dover, who looked expectant, like he was hoping to hear me name JonBenét Ramsay's murderer. "No relation, but Antoinette and I were classmates at Carroll. I heard her daughter might need a hand."

"Jacintha babysits for me. By the time I leave for Scuttlebutt's, the girls are ready for bed, bathed and in their pajamas. All Jacintha has to do is give them a snack, read them a story, and tuck them in. After she's washed the dishes, she can watch TV, do homework, or go to sleep. But to hear her tell it, you'd think she had to wrestle wildcats to the death every night."

"I take it you're saying she's a little over-dramatic."

"That girl feels sorry for herself, that's what I'm saying. And she never wants to talk when I get home -- ."

"What time is that?" I asked, cutting her off.

"Two, three in the morning. She pretends she's deeply asleep and I'm just a nuisance, handing her a twenty."

"Why do you wake her? Doesn't she stay here overnight now that her mother's . . . her mother's dead?"

Jen looked at Dover for help. "I know I'm supposed to keep her here, but I can't make her stay."

I nodded. "So do you make sure she has breakfast and brushes her teeth before going to school?"

Jen shook her head. "No. She won't let me in her house."

"How does she get to school?"

Again Jen looked at Dover for help, but his face was impassive and he stayed silent. "She drives to school, I think. The cops returned her mother's car."

"She's old enough to drive, I take it."

"What's the date today?"

"The first of June."

"She was old enough Sunday -- she turned sixteen. Or did I hear the law has changed? Does she have to wait another six months? I don't know. I can't keep up."

Dover finally spoke up. "She wouldn't have a license yet, and in any case she can't legally drive alone for awhile, so for the next couple of weeks maybe you can persuade her to catch the school bus. I don't want the cops to pick her up."

Jen laughed derisively. "I can't even persuade her to stop smoking or swearing, or eat something that's good for her . . . or anything." She threw up her hands. "Have you ever met Jacintha?"

I shook my head.

"Then you don't know what I'm talking about." She lit another cigarette. "I don't get why you're here, Lexie."

My name in her mouth jolted me a little. I know it's the American way, to call strangers by their first name, but I swear I'll never get used to that level of familiarity. I decided not to answer her directly; the fact is, I couldn't because I wasn't sure myself what I was doing there. "Did you know Antoinette sixteen-seventeen years ago?" *When Jacintha was conceived?*

"No. I'm from Bluffton, moved up here ten years ago. When Tawny and Jacintha moved in here, that's when I met them."

"Do you know if Antoinette was ever married or lived with somebody?"

"I'm pretty sure she was never married, but for a couple of years her boyfriend lived here. He was the thinnest man I ever saw."

"Did Antoinette ever say anything about her daughter's father -- who he is, where he lives, anything like that?"

"No."

"You think she might have told her boyfriend?"

"Maybe, but don't go looking for him. He died six months ago."

"Really?"

"He was allergic to peanuts. He ate a peanut butter cookie and died right outside, over there." She pointed down the street. "The way he gasped for breath was just terrible."

"But Antoinette must have known who her daughter's father is, don't you think?"

Jen got up, emptied our ashtrays into a bucket, then sat down again, clearly troubled. "Not necessarily."

I let the silence grow.

"My twins," she said, gesturing over her shoulder at the quiet house, "they've got a father, obviously, but I don't know who it is. I've run through the list . . . well, not a list exactly . . . a dozen times, but the fact is, I don't know where to start." She patted her tummy. "And it's all happening again. Another bun in the oven, but I don't know who the baker is." She laughed shakily at her joke.

I tried to look understanding, but frankly I never knew such a thing could happen. I probably looked like the church lady. "Your twins don't look like somebody important to you?"

This time Jen laughed grimly. "No. No man's ever been important to me, if you want to know the truth, not for very long anyway, not in the way you mean." She adjusted the scrunchy on the back of her head. "I have to make a living, you know. Sometimes you get a surprise."

It took a minute to process that. Fortunately, Dover spoke up. "I take it, Jen, you're not Jacintha's aunt."

She looked astonished. "No. What made you think I might be?"

"Something Jacintha said last week, but my understanding is that her mother only had one sister -- a half-sister -- and she's reportedly in a shelter, so I suspected Jacintha was just telling me what she thought I wanted to hear."

"Why would it matter if I'm her aunt or not?"

"Unless we find a relative for the girl to live with, the County's probably going to put her in a foster home . . . if one can even be found. It would be convenient if you were her aunt so we could keep the County out of her business."

"You wanna know the truth? I'm glad she can't live with me and we're not related. I'll miss her if she can't keep babysitting the nights I work, but she's a real handful and I don't have the strength." She shot Dover an apologetic look. "I know I said she could stay here awhile, but I can't make her stay. I can't make her do anything. She hated her mother, and I think she hates me too. She doesn't listen to a word I say, and she never has a nice word for anyone. She just wears me to a nubbin."

"That's a teenager for you," I said, intending to sound encouraging, but my words didn't have that effect.

"She's worse than I was at that age, and I was a pistol. My mother wanted to kill me." She looked at her watch, then glanced at the front door. "It's time for the girls to get up and they're way too quiet, so if it's all right with you, I'll go in now before I find out they've smothered each other."

I shivered as terrible new thoughts blotted out all reason: it wasn't unusual not to know who the father of one's baby was, Jen was so bad as a girl her mother wanted to kill her, Jacintha was worse than Jen, and the twins might have smothered each other.

12

Car Crash
Tuesday, June 1, 2010

Jen hadn't even opened the screen door when she heard Tawny's old Firebird roar into Cedar Grove Parke and then hit something. It wasn't a big crash, but metal was unmistakably crushing metal and glass was breaking. Shit. Then she heard a dog barking. What had Jacintha done now? Her twins momentarily forgotten, Jen whirled around to see what had happened.

The strangers who had come to her house were standing on the deck, rigid with astonishment. Jacintha was climbing out of the Firebird, not looking the least apologetic, but mad as hell. She peered at the three people on Jen's deck. "Who's car is this?"

"Mine," Lexie said, walking down the stairs and out to the street. The back end of her bright red Mini Cooper was crumpled, and Henry, who was inside, had his head out the back passenger window, barking like crazy. He looked like he wanted to leap out and attack the girl.

"What's your car doing here? I never saw you before. You could have pulled onto the lawn or parked over there," Jacintha said, pointing toward a long carport. Then she spit a wad of gum onto the street.

"You didn't see my car?"

"Duh! Of course, I saw it, but it was right in my path and by the time I saw it I couldn't stop. The brakes barely work on this old thing. So what was I supposed to do? I hope you have, like, insurance, because I don't."

Dover strode up to the women. "Mrs. Wright, this is Jacintha Delamarter."

"Oh, for goodness' sake." Lexie was momentarily at a loss for words. She wasn't prepared to meet the girl, especially under these circumstances.

"You aren't going to call the cops, are you?" the girl continued, hands on hips, head cocked defiantly. "I'm just a kid. It wasn't my fault."

Dover started to lay a hand on her arm but thought better of it. "Take it easy, Jacintha. Before we get into who's at fault, let me explain something. Mrs. Wright went to school with your mother."

"Yah? So?"

Dover looked at Lexie for permission to continue. "Mrs. Wright is the wife of Steven Wright."

It was Jacintha's turn for silence as she studied the woman standing before her. "So. You're married to my father. You owe me then, and you're, like, rich, so you can afford to fix my car."

If there was an attitude that sent Lexie to the moon, it was the assumption that as a rich woman she should voluntarily shoulder everyone else's responsibility for whatever went wrong in life. "I don't owe you anything, but perhaps we could sit down and talk a minute. By the way, what are you doing home this time of day? Aren't you supposed to be in school? And what made you think it's all right to drive at your age?"

Jacintha's face crumpled, though no tears escaped from her eyes. "Have a heart. I'm an orphan now." She stuffed a stick of gum into her mouth. "I need help."

Lexie nodded, trying to decide what to do next. The girl's moods changed faster than Fort Wayne weather. "Why don't you show me where you live and then I'll take you to back to school. We can stop at McDonald's on the way."

"Are you going to call the cops?"

"No. I think we're going to have to settle this ourselves."

"That's a great-looking car, by the way. Wish it was mine. Is that your dog?"

"It *was* a pretty cute car, and, yes, that's my dog. Henry."

"Can I pet him?"

"Just say hello, but I wouldn't put my hand in the window until he's forgiven you for banging up his ride, okay?"

"Whatever."

Lexie noticed Dover stiffen at the utterance of that word.

"But you don't really want to see my house, do you?"

"I do."

"You have any cigarettes?"

About to say absolutely not to the girl's insolent request, Lexie instead decided to seize the opportunity, underhanded as that was. Before they left Jacintha's house, which was a terrible, dirty mess, she furtively retrieved Jacintha's cigarette butt, placed it in a tissue, and tucked the wad into her purse.

13

Our Better Angels
Tuesday, June 1 - June 30, 2010

By the time Northrop High had discharged its students for the summer, Steve and I had made our decision about Jacintha. To get there, we had to travel a rocky road. The trip left us bruised and bleeding but determined to do the right thing.

My first encounter with the girl who claimed Steve was her father was hilarious. I didn't see it that way at the time, but the more I thought about it, the funnier it was. She smashed my car the way she was smashing my life: violently, without warning or apology, with consequences I alone had to confront. It was tragic slapstick.

The girl intrigues me. She's sassy and confident in the way of deeply insecure people. The clothes she wears are cheap but put together with a certain rocker-chick style all her own. Though her hair needs shampoo and a comb, she has plenty of coppery curls to work with. I recognize her physical defects: near-sighted eyes hidden behind out-dated black-rimmed glasses, crooked teeth, jutting ears. The little bump on her nose is just like Steve's, only it doesn't look good on a girl. Her makeup is far too flamboyant for a girl of sixteen -- or else exactly what you'd expect from a sixteen-year-old exaggerating the difference she feels from everybody else.

People now say I look like Katherine Heigl, but I didn't start out that way. And Steve didn't start out looking like a Viking version of the mischievous Prince Harry. Both of us had some cosmetic dentistry and surgery, me before college, Steve afterward. So I don't count the girl's defects against her. They can be corrected.

Neither am I very much put off by her sassiness. Well, to be honest, I am a little put off. Her attitude that the best defense is a good offense is shockingly well developed in such a young girl. But once I saw where she lived and thought about her mother and the life she'd lived, I found some compassion lurking in my heart. The doublewide mobile home she now occupies in solitude is smaller than the entryway to my new house. In fact, half a dozen doublewides would fit just in the auto courtyard of my estate. When I entered her house the day of the accident, I saw that her clothes were strewn everywhere, and they smelled; she said the clothes washer was broken. The sink was full of dishes, but there were no pots and pans in evidence, meaning she was probably eating potato chips and frozen dinners. If that. She doesn't look healthy; she has that thin, pale, consumptive look of Mimì in Puccini's *La bohème*.

That day of the accident, I took her to McDonald's before dropping her off at school. The only thing she would touch was a supersized batch of French fries and a supersized Coke. Then I went shopping at Scott's and Walgreens and returned to Cedar Grove Parke with three big bags of groceries and two of toiletries, which I left on her doorstep, together with a bag of junior-size clothes from TJ Maxx. I left a note that I'd be in touch.

My next stop was the law office of Duke Simmons. He represented Steve when he was thought to have been the last to see his murdered girlfriend, Vicki Grinderman, and Duke probably had a record of Steve's DNA, which had cleared him as a suspect.

I told Duke what I knew about Jacintha Delamarter.

"Have you talked about this with Steve?"

I shook my head. "He doesn't know I'm here. In fact, I didn't expect to be here today."

"Has he seen the girl?"

"Not that I know of, just the picture Dover Pitt had with him."

"So, why don't you just ask your husband outright if there's any possibility that he's the girl's father?"

I had no good answer for that. "Why not turn that question around? Why doesn't he talk to me about it? I can see he's worried, and he must realize I might be feeling a little unsettled."

Duke lit a cigar. Like Churchill, he's often pictured in the papers holding a great big old stogie in one hand, his other arm resting on the shoulders of the client he's just successfully defended.

I broke the silence. "He's probably ashamed that anyone could even think he ever had anything to do with that woman."

"I'm not a marriage counselor, so I can't help you on that one, but at some point you're going to have to talk this out, you know."

"I know." I reached into my purse for the cigarette butt wrapped in a tissue. "What would you think about having this tested for the girl's DNA and then comparing the results to Steve's?"

"I can arrange that."

"I'll pay whatever premium I have to shell out to get this tested as fast as possible. If she's Steve's daughter, then we're going to have to start thinking what to do."

"Why are you so composed about this, Lexie?"

"Do I look composed? Do I sound that way?"

He nodded.

"I don't feel that way inside, let me tell you."

"You're a little ashamed, I suspect."

I hated to admit he was right. "The last thing I ever wanted to do was marry a man with an illegitimate child."

"It happens, you know. More often than you might think. Unless a man lives like a monk, he can't be a hundred percent sure he's never been a father. And if a woman is promiscuous, she can't be a hundred percent sure who the father is."

It took two weeks to get the results. Steve was Jacintha's father.

The night I found out, I confronted Steve with the news. He was furious that I'd gone behind his back to have the girl's DNA tested. I was furious that he'd been so stupid as to bed down Antoinette Delamarter, the class whore. He was disappointed that I suspected he was the girl's father. I was disappointed that he actually was. He was defensive. I was mercilessly accusatory. He was sick that he'd done such a foolish thing. I was sick that he'd been so disloyal immediately after our teenage breakup. He was ashamed that his youthful indiscretion would probably have to become public. I was incensed that I would be subjected to public humiliation that I'd done nothing to deserve.

We fought like wounded children and didn't speak for several days after that. We occupied separate bedrooms. We barely spoke. We avoided each other's eyes. Our beautiful new house became a dark and drafty crypt. Our honeymoon hadn't lasted a year.

But finally our better angels made their appearance, gossamer figures at first, then gradually more and more manifest. Steve apologized for his youthful sin; I forgave him. I apologized for my stiff-necked pride; he forgave me.

With a lot of tears and protestations of eternal love, interspersed with renewed vows of honoring each other for better or worse, we made up. Carried on wings of duty and hope against a headwind of trepidation, we instructed Marty Solomon to start legal proceedings to make Jacintha Caitlin Delamarter our daughter.

The day we got word that the girl was now ours, pending some final dotting of i's and crossing of t's, we were dumbfounded at what we'd done. Jacintha, however, took it in stride, as if she'd known all along what would happen.

The very day our daughter moved into 13339 Stonehaven Lane, *The Journal Gazette* published the coroner's report on Antoinette. She had died of renal failure, probably from ingestion of ethylene glycol mixed with Gatorade and vodka, manner of death undetermined. In other words, the Coroner didn't know if she committed suicide, accidentally ingested antifreeze, or had been murdered. We made sure Jacintha didn't see the report.

Part Two

When she was good, she was very, very good

Third line of an old nursery rhyme

"You did not choose me, but I chose you . . . ."

Jesus speaking, John 15:16

14

A New Life
Monday, June 28, 2010

The irony was not lost on Dover. His professional acquaintance with Jacintha Delamarter had led him to a whole new place in life. He had thought of the wild child as a curse, but in fact she'd been a blessing in disguise. Here he was, the golf and tennis pro at the Gretna Green Golf and Tennis Club, having more fun than he'd ever had in his life, playing the games he loved every day, managing the pro shop, and meeting some of the most interesting people in Fort Wayne. He reported directly to Steve Wright, the smartest, most even-tempered boss he'd ever had. When, for example, he'd suggested adding Cutter Buck to the Nike and Adidas lines, Steve said yes. The boss listened to him.

Being a golf and tennis pro was so much fun, he'd have done it for free, but in fact he was handsomely paid -- so handsomely paid that he had bought a villa lot and was building a new house. He'd been warned that most of his neighbors would probably be old widows and retired couples, but he didn't care. He'd never live in an apartment again and, at age thirty, he'd be a homeowner.

None of his good fortune would have happened had he not met Steve Wright to warn him about the meaning of Antoinette Delamarter's scrapbook. And he wouldn't have known about the scrapbook had Jacintha been anything other than a pain in the ass. Luckiest of all, when he first met Steve, he'd mentioned something about his golf and tennis prowess. When a few days later, Steve asked him to come by the Club to talk about working there, he didn't waste a second saying yes.

His love life had changed too. It had gone from nothing to something overnight. One evening late in June at the Wright mansion, he'd met Jean Arnold, Lexie's office manager. The Wrights entertained a lot in their Tuscan courtyard, usually friends they'd developed through business, but that Monday, Jean and Dover were the only guests. It was one of those peculiar Indiana days when dark clouds hovered in the northwest, moving very slowly, keeping their distance like rumors of war, but you just knew they meant trouble. Still, while the sun shone, the peasants made hay.

Jean, who was the same age as the Wrights, was a few years older than he, but that fact only enhanced her glamor. Everything about her was different from the other women he'd dated. Her voice was a little raspy and breathy, yet she spoke with firmness as if she could not possibly be wrong about anything she said. She displayed her curvy figure with low-cut blouses and her beautiful legs with short skirts. Her red hair together with a cool demeanor promised a life of fire and ice, a combination that stirred passions he hadn't felt before.

Over dinner in the Wrights' Tuscan courtyard, he learned that Jean was an actress and world-traveler, on the rebound from a long relationship with some night nurse named Dwight. Though she smoked one cigarette after another -- a new habit, she claimed -- she never touched the delicious wine that perfectly complimented the grilled lobster tails, instead sticking to sparkling grape juice. His infatuation only increased when the dark side of the glamor gradually became apparent. She didn't make any money at acting, the gigs were sporadic, they led to nothing bigger, and the reviews never pleased her. Her world travels were confined to a few well-worn Caribbean islands and to London. She broke up with Peter-Pan Dwight because she wanted to get married and he wouldn't commit. And she made no secret that as a recovering alcoholic she deeply missed a glass of wine after work.

Still, she was upbeat, her dreams far exceeding his own. She vowed to visit every continent before she died. She wanted to star in a Nora Roberts television special. She was determined to be married and start a family within the next two years. Furthermore, though she was troubled by the disappointing course her life had taken and the difficulty of realizing her dreams, she was not afraid to admit it out loud. That was something he had a hard time doing.

What impressed him most was Jean's interest in him. Though she talked a lot, she also asked him questions -- personal but not too intrusive -- and actually responded to his answers. "Why did you take up golf?" "Did you really quit your job at Northrop?" "What was the hardest part of being a high-school student counselor?" "What can you tell us about Jacintha?"

It was that last question that exploded in his head and then froze his brain, like lava hardening across a volcanic landscape. What could he say that was truthful but wouldn't offend his hosts? When he'd been hired to be the golf pro at Gretna Green, he'd had no inkling that Steve Wright and Lexie Royce were already planning to take Jacintha as their daughter or that Steve would publicly admit he was the girl's father. In his mind, leaving Northrop meant leaving Jacintha and all the other troublemakers behind. But here he was, part of the same inner circle as the Amy Winehouse clone. He couldn't get away from the girl.

He searched for something positive to say. "She's intelligent. Her IQ is 132, almost genius level." He nodded at Steve. "She gets that from her father, I suspect." He knew he sounded like a boot-licker, but he had no intention of imperiling his new job.

"So she got good grades?" Jean asked.

Dover hesitated. "Well, no. I'm not sure she even had a B average."

"Why was that?" Lexie asked.

"Why was what?" Stalling for time.

"If she's that smart, why didn't she do better?"

"I'd be speculating."

"Well, speculate away," Steve commanded.

"Perhaps her home life stood in the way. Maybe her mother didn't encourage her, or she didn't have a suitable place to do homework. Lots of our students go home to a noisy, chaotic life that doesn't encourage reading and studying. Maybe she was bored. Some bright students are bored, you know, and the teachers really don't have the leeway to change the curriculum for them. Maybe the baby-sitting she was doing for her neighbor left her too little time to think." *Or maybe she's just too crazy and rebellious to do anything that's expected of her.* "I don't know."

"Well, I hope Steve and I can change that once she starts at her new school in the Fall," Lexie said. "She'll have a nice quiet room upstairs, and we'll make sure she understands how important it is to do well in school."

Jean smiled at Dover. "You should see the room that's being prepared for her. A suite really. A bedroom, an adjoining room for study, a walk-in closet, her own spa bathroom, a big veranda, with a separate staircase from the backyard, overlooking the pool. I'd have been over the moon at her age if I'd had a place like that to call my own."

"I couldn't have gone overboard again, could I?" Lexie asked mockingly.

"You could and you did, a little . . . well, more than a little, in my humble opinion. She's going to get a big head, you watch, going from trailer-park girl to heiress overnight. But I suppose her suite's in keeping with the house."

Dover winced. He was not used to hearing someone openly criticize a boss. Maybe the Wrights liked a little frankness in their staff. He'd have to watch Jean, maybe learn something.

Lexie gave no sign of irritation with Jean's remarks. "The rooms are really nothing to see yet, but you can take Dover up if you want. They were originally decorated for guests, but making them suitable for a sixteen-year-old won't start until Jacintha is actually here, of course. I want to be sure that whatever Jessica thinks the rooms should look like meets with our daughter's approval. A girl her age wants things her way." Lexie smiled conspiratorially at Jean. "A sixteen-year-old girl has firm ideas about everything -- room decoration, clothes, hairdos, cars. Am I right?"

"So right. And boys too." Jean turned her attention to Dover.

"Did she have a boyfriend at Northrop?"

"She never mentioned one."

"Well, from the picture I saw, she's not the prettiest thing in the universe." Jean shot an apologetic look at Steve. "Now, that was speaking out of turn, wasn't it? Forget . . . ."

"But she will be," Lexie interjected. "I think she looks like Steve's mother, who was very pretty. Granted, she needs some minor . . . adjustment. . . . I realize that's partly because she simply hasn't grown into her face yet, but the corrections I intend to have made can be done now. I shamelessly used my influence with the best plastic surgeon in Fort Wayne to get her in right away for some work on her ears and nose. Then she's booked for Lasik surgery and cosmetic dentistry. After that, she'll be the prettiest junior at Carroll."

"Have you asked her what she thinks about having surgery so soon after arriving here?"

"We've talked about it, and she's enthusiastic."

Jean shook her head. "If my new adoptive mother immediately sent me to a plastic surgeon, I'd think I wasn't good enough. You might want to let her settle in awhile before you do something so drastic."

Dover watched a multitude of looks pass across his hostess' face in a nanosecond. He braced himself for an explosion. But none came.

"I'll think about it. Anyway, it'll be a week or two after she gets here before the cosmetic work starts, so she'll have time to settle in."

"She arrives when?"

"Wednesday this week. Less than forty-eight hours from now. Then Jessica's coming up Friday to help plan her bedroom." Lexie turned her attention to Dover. "Speaking of bedrooms, have you had a tour of the house yet?"

He shook his head.

"Why don't you take him through the place, Jean, while Phyllis clears the table and sets out dessert." She glanced at the sky. "Those clouds are suddenly on the move, so we may have to finish indoors anyway."

Dover realized he should probably use the tour to gather ideas for his own new house, the plans for which were still on the architect's drawing board, but the chance to be alone with Jean blotted out rational thought. If he'd been alone, he'd have gotten lost, for the house rambled here and there; suddenly, just when you thought you knew where you were going, there were steps up or down and unexpected rooms. Turn a corner and there was a strange little nook or a glass atrium, even an indoor lap pool. Every room led outside to an enclosed garden or long terrace. He noticed oversized, luxurious furniture, probably too big and expensive for his villa, but mostly he noticed Jean.

They were standing in the conservatory when he asked if she'd been serious at dinner about always wanting to take up golf.

"I am."

"You want me to teach you?"

She laughed. "Sure. Why not?"

"I have some free time tomorrow morning. Really early, I'm afraid, but we could start then and you'd still get to work on time. If you really want to, that is."

She touched his arm. "I really want to -- but everything depends on the weather, doesn't it? Look at the storm that's blown up."

The room had grown dark, the trees outside were whipping in the wind, and the rain was sheeting against the glass. Then they heard a crash as something blew over, probably near the swimming pool. But Dover was not to be discouraged. "Everything'll be fine in the morning. You watch."

15

Secrets

Friday, July 23, 2010

Jacintha became interested in Jean Arnold very quickly. The first day she could get out of bed after surgery, she made her way to the office suite off the courtyard, where Jean and her staff managed Lexie's business life: appointments, bookkeeping, bill payment, and public correspondence. A flood of inquiries, invitations, random messages, solicitations, and threats washed through the door every day.

"Can I help?" Jacintha asked as, uninvited, she plopped down into a chair.

Jean, mildly irritated at the interruption, pushed her hair to the side and tried to look friendly. "No, but it's nice to see you up and about. How are you feeling?"

"I can't breathe," Jacintha said, pointing at her nose. Her eyes were black and blue. "And I can't wear my glasses, so I can't see a thing."

"Why can't you breathe? They didn't do anything inside your nose, did they?"

"I just can't."

"You'll see well enough without glasses when you get the Lasik treatment."

Jacintha put her hand to her forehead. "I think I have a fever."

"Well, then, you should go back to bed."

Jacintha picked up a random piece of paper, and looked at it.

Jean half stood in alarm. "Here, put that down, please. It might be confidential, and I don't like things to get out of order. If you come in here during work hours . . . ."

A long pause. "Yah? If I come in here during work hours, what?"

Jean tried smiling again. "Just be respectful, that's all."

Still holding onto the paper, Jacintha gave her an enigmatic smile. "Lexie says you're an actress."

"Amateur. A play here and there. Musicals are my favorite." Jean reached for the paper but Jacintha pulled it back. *What kind of game is this?*

"Mine too. Last year, I was the lead in *Guys and Dolls*."

Jean's eyes stayed on the paper. "Sarah or Adelaide?"

"Adelaide."

"You consider that the lead?"

Jacintha tossed her head. "I was better than the girl who played Sarah, so yes, I was the lead. Are you working on some production now?"

"I'm going to try out for a part in *White Christmas*."

"Could I go with you sometime? Especially, like, to a rehearsal."

"First, give me the paper." The girl tossed it onto the desk. Jean sighed. "That's better. You can go with me if I get the part -- and if it doesn't interfere with your school."

"School hasn't started yet."

"I know that, but I'm not sure when the rehearsals will start -- and, as I said, I don't have a part yet. Are you looking forward to school, by the way?"

"Not sure. I won't know anybody."

"But you'll be the prettiest girl there. And I hear you're very smart."

"Whatever. Since I have to change schools, I'm going to change my name. Start over, you know."

"What do you mean? Change your name to what?"

"What do you think of, like, JayCee Wright?"

"Just initials?"

"No. J-a-y-C-e-e. All one word."

"Is that better than Jacintha?"

"Way better."

"What do your parents think about that?"

"Who? Oh, you mean Steve and Lexie. I haven't mentioned it yet." She fingered another piece of paper but didn't pick it up. "Why do you think Lexie made me get this surgery right away? You think I didn't look good enough for her?"

Jean had expressed that very fear to Lexie -- that the girl would secretly think of it as criticism of her appearance. "I heard you were enthusiastic about it."

"Heard where?"

"Lexie."

"Whatever."

"I don't understand 'whatever.'"

"She thinks I'm ugly, doesn't she?"

Everybody did, if you really want to know. "You want to step outside a minute with me? I need a cigarette."

"I want one too."

"If I give you a cigarette, Lexie will have my head."

"No, she won't. She gave me one the first time I ever met her, after I bashed her car." JayCee reached into her shorts pocket and removed a package of Virginia Slims. "I just need a light."

"Good thing Lexie's in New York. Just don't tell her I condoned your smoking."

"Say what?"

"Condoned? Is that the word you're asking about?"

JayCee nodded.

"Approved."

"Okay, but you haven't answered me about, like, whether she thought I was ugly."

They settled themselves in a shady corner of the courtyard, JayCee on a lounge, Jean on a chair. JayCee looked very much the *au courant* teen in her Victoria's Secret pink jersey shorts and ribbed tank top. Was the silver chain with the heart dangle from Tiffany?

Or Juicy Couture? What was Lexie thinking, overindulging the girl like that?

Jean searched for the most positive response she could make. "Your parents just want the best for you. If you really want to know, Lexie said you're the opposite of ugly-- that you're pretty, like Steve's mother. I never met her -- Lexie didn't either -- but we've seen pictures. Lexie herself got a chin implant before she left for college, had her teeth veneered, a mole removed, probably other things, and Steve had stuff done after college. In my opinion, there's no shame in getting a little help from the experts. None of us is born perfect, after all."

"But you were. You're really pretty. I'll bet nothing's ever gone wrong in your life."

"Oh, it has, believe me."

"Like what?"

"It's too nice a day to talk about sad things."

"It's never too nice for that. Besides, it's hot as hell. Tell me a secret, I'll tell you one of mine."

"I don't have any secrets. People call me an open book."

"Then you're perfect, just like I said."

"I'm not perfect. I'm an alcoholic. It's really not a secret, and I no longer drink, but I learned in rehab that once you're an alcoholic, you're always an alcoholic. At least that's what the experts claim."

"You never drink anything -- beer, wine, coolers, nothing?"

"Not any more."

"You smoke dope?"

"No." *Not since I was in college.*

"That must be, like, really hard."

"You mean not drinking?"

"Yah."

"It is. But this job is more important to me than a glass of wine, and I'd lose it if Lexie ever found out I'd fallen off the wagon."

"What's that mean, falling off the wagon?"

"Taking another drink."

"What was your favorite drink before you quit?"

"White wine . . . chardonnay, pinot grigio, zinfandel, white burgundy. White liquor too -- gin, vodka, rum. But enough about me. What's your secret?"

"When Lexie took me shopping at Forever 21, I stole a camisole."

"You didn't."

"Wore it right out under my t-shirt."

"Why? Your mother would have paid for it. And she's never stolen anything in her life."

"Made me feel good, like I got one over on the clerk. We spent so much money that day, the shop should have given me the cami anyway. I was entitled to a gift. They owed me."

"No one's *entitled* to a gift."

"Whatever. Do you think Lexie loves me more than you, or the opposite?"

Jean suppressed a gasp. "What in the world made you ask that?"

"I want to know."

"I'm sure she loves us both in different ways. You're her daughter, I'm her friend. We play different roles in her life."

"Roles. Like in a play."

"Not exactly."

"But which one of us does she love more?"

"Jacintha -- ."

"*JayCee.* That's my name from now on."

"Okay. JayCee it is. Love isn't like that. It can't be measured the way you're thinking."

"What's love then, if it can't be measured?"

Jean felt as if she'd walked into a philosophy quiz she hadn't studied for. "Off the top of my head, I don't have a simple answer to that."

"She has to love me more, don't you think? Like you said, I'm her daughter now, and you're just an employee. She can't get rid of me, but she can fire you."

Jean tried to hide the shock in her eyes. *Who thinks like that?* "I don't know how Lexie feels about us -- we can't know her heart

-- but let's return to the stolen camisole. You can't steal things. It's wrong."

"It's not wrong unless, like, somebody finds out."

"But thieves do get found out, and then there's hell to pay. Your reputation would be ruined."

"With Steve and Lexie, you mean?"

"With them. Your friends. Your school. Everybody who knows you. You should tell your mother, promise never to do it again, and return the cami."

"No way."

"It's the only way."

"Whatever." JayCee stretched out on the lounge and closed her eyes. "You aren't going to tell Lexie about the camisole, right? Like, I know your secret, you know mine, so neither of us can rat on the other. We're like sisters now. Sisters keep each other's secrets."

It wasn't until much later at the Club with Dover that Jean tried to sort out the puzzle about secrets. "Let me tell you about this afternoon."

Dover listened to Jean's account of her encounter with JayCee without registering a bit of surprise, but Jean looked genuinely puzzled when she finished. "So what in hell secret does that girl think I told her?"

He patted her hand. "It's obvious, isn't it? You have a vulnerability she can exploit if the occasion arises. That's the Jacintha Delamarter I know, always trying to manipulate the world."

"Do you think I should tell Lexie she stole something?"

He looked thoughtful. "I'm getting into the weeds here, but as a student counselor I wasn't required to tell the principal anything I heard unless the student disclosed a plan for imminent criminal activity. So what are you going to do?"

"Tell Lexie, of course. I already left a note for her."

He laughed. "Then why did you ask for my advice?"

She laughed too. "I was hoping you'd tell me what I wanted to hear. Isn't that what people always want when they ask for someone else's opinion?"

After Jean returned to the office suite, JayCee used her brand-new iPhone to call Phyllis in the kitchen and told her to come out to the courtyard.

"Why?" Phyllis asked, irritated.

"I need some raspberry lemonade. Yours is the best in the world. The lemonade with the mint leaf in it. And I could use something to munch on. My stomach hurts, and I think I have a little fever."

"I'm sure you're fine, and I'd be glad to make you some lemonade, but it'll be a half hour or so if you want me to come out there. I'm in the middle of making a Béarnaise sauce and I can't leave the stove."

"But I need it now. Immediately."

Nobody needs anything immediately except the next breath. "If you were able to get down to the courtyard, Jacintha, you can manage to walk to the kitchen." She tried to soften her tone. "That way, you can have your drink right away. Or since you're in the courtyard, you can grab a bottle of water out of the little fridge in the outdoor kitchen."

"Lexie said -- ."

Phyllis laughed. "*Phyllis* says come to the kitchen."

Dramatic pause. "What kind of servant are you, Phyl?"

That's my last nerve. Imitating her tormentor's sinister tone, she whispered back. "My name isn't Phyl. It's Mrs. Whitlow. And if I'm a servant, I'm the kind who spits in the lemonade when I'm mad. So don't make me mad."

JayCee stayed where she was. She was sick. She was the cutest thing in the house. She was so special she'd actually been chosen to be the Wrights' daughter. How many girls could claim that? So the cook should do what she wanted.

She was still on the lounge, eyes half open, when Jean's staff left for the day. One of the women, an old lady wearing the ugliest culottes she'd ever seen, was carrying a big box of envelopes for mailing. After a few minutes Jean emerged too and locked the door. She was carrying an unstamped manila envelope.

"You're still here, JayCee?"

"I'm too weak to get up. Feel my forehead. You think I have a fever?"

Jean did as instructed. "No."

"I need water. Can you get me some from the fridge?"

"Of course. Have you asked Phyllis for a soda or something?"

"She's nasty. She wouldn't bring me, like, lemonade."

"Phyllis? Nasty?"

"Nasty. She threatened to spit in my drink."

Jean laughed before she could stop herself. "Phyllis would never spit in your drink. What'd you say to her to get that response?"

"Nothing."

Jean gave her a skeptical look. "You must have said something, Jacin -- JayCee. She was probably in the middle of something and didn't want to be bothered just then. Anyway, I'll get you the water."

When Jean returned, JayCee asked what the envelope was about. "Just a note for Lexie to catch her up on things when she gets in late tonight. Sort of like the daily reports the President gets."

Reaching for it, JayCee asked, "You want me to give it to her?"

Jean took a step away. "No. I'll take it in, leave it in the usual place."

"Where's that?"

"Her private little cubby off the kitchen. You must have noticed it."

"Do I get a private little cubby too?"

Jean laughed. "Not until you're the successful businesswoman your mother is. By the way, are you always going to call her Lexie? Why not Mom or Ma or something?"

"Like that'll ever happen."

"Well," Jean said, turning to enter the house, "think about it. It would make her happy, and if she's happy, you'll be happy too."

"The law of the jungle?"

"The opposite. You're not in the jungle any more, kiddo."

"Whatever."

16

Apology
Friday, July 23, 2010

Lexie was surprised to see Jacintha, with Henry, waiting on a stone bench near the row of garages when a little after nine o'clock Drago drove her into the auto courtyard -- and even more surprised when the girl approached the driver's side rather than hers. Drago rolled his window down.

"Who are you?" Jacintha asked.

"Drago. Watch it," he warned as he gently opened his door. "I work for Mizz Royce. I'm Phyllis' son." As he walked around the car to open Lexie's door, the girl followed him.

"I've seen you on MTV."

"Oh, yeah?"

"You're really Enrique Iglesias, aren't you?"

"Not so much." He looked at his boss as he gave her a hand out of the car. "I think this girl is a little confused."

"Jacintha," she said, giving the girl a hug. "Why aren't you in bed?"

"JayCee. That's my new name."

"JayCee?"

"I'll explain later. I've been waiting for you."

"You didn't have to do that. I'd have come up to see how you're doing."

"I missed you. I'm lonely. And I'm hungry."

"Phyllis didn't make you dinner?"

"She did, but I need some ice cream." JayCee glanced at Drago, who was now removing a suitcase from the trunk. She trotted after him as he headed to the back door to the house. "Sorry to say this, but sometimes your mother is mean."

"Watch it, girl," he said, stopping to give her his P. Diddy stare. "My mom's the nicest woman you'll ever meet. Is she still here?"

"She's in the kitchen."

"I'll just pop in to say hello."

When he returned to the courtyard, he looked at the girl. "What happened to you, by the way? Oh, wait; I suppose you should see the other guy, right?"

She wasn't sure whether that was a joke. "A little surgery. I think I have a fever."

He held the door for her. "Well then, get inside and go to bed."

"Are you going to stay awhile?"

"No. I've gotta put Mizz Royce's car away. Then I'm going right home. My wife's waiting for me. If I know what's what, she needs help getting the boys to bed. And believe me, I know what's what."

"You don't want to stay a little while? We could watch a movie."

Turning away, he shook his head disapprovingly. *This girl is trouble.* "Got everything, Mizz Royce?"

"Yes, thanks, Drago. I'll stop at the Scrapyard tomorrow, so see you then."

JayCee watched him garage the car, then walk to a corner of the courtyard, where his Jeep was parked. "He's really handsome. Where's he from, South America?"

"He's from right here. His father was black, his mother, as you know, is white."

"Wow, that's cool. He looks like a rapper."

"As a matter of fact, he isn't but he could be. Great voice."

"Do you think I could babysit for his boys sometime?"

"He and Lucy would probably welcome that. But for now

80

you'd better lie down in the family room while I get you some ice cream."

"Can I talk to you first?"

"Let me put my things down, have a word with Phyllis before she leaves, then the rest of the evening I'm yours."

When she heard Phyllis leave and saw Lexie heading toward her private cubby, JayCee took action by groaning loudly. "Mom! Come quick! I can't see, everything's going black."

Lexie whirled around in surprise and panic: surprise at the word "Mom" and panic that the girl was blacking out. She ran to the family room, where she found her daughter slumped in a chair. Henry was sitting near her, his head on her knee.

"What's wrong?"

"I think I'm fainting."

"Let me get you a cold cloth. Put your head between your knees."

"Okay," she said weakly. Henry licked her face and pressed himself against her leg.

"Maybe I should call an ambulance."

"No, no. Just hold my head, please."

After a few minutes of keeping her head tipped down and allowing a cold cloth to be placed across her neck, JayCee seemed recovered enough to move to a sofa and lie down.

"Are you feeling better? If not, I've got to take you to the emergency room."

"I'm better." She reached for Lexie's hand. "Is it okay if I call you Mom?"

Lexie was touched, though it was very strange to be called "Mom." "Of course. I'm glad. We're a family. Oh, Henry, get down from there."

"It's okay. I like him to be next to me. I want you to call me JayCee from now on. Is that okay?"

"I changed my name in high school too, so I guess there's not much I can say."

"What did you change it to?"

"Xandra." She spelled it out. "Nobody could spell it when

81

they heard it or pronounce it when they first saw it, so I thought I was sophisticated when really I was just pretentious and irritating."

"You think JayCee is pre -- ?"

"Pretentious? Uppity? Not exactly."

"I have to confess something to you."

"Confess what?" *That you didn't stay in bed all day or eat any vegetables?*

"Remember last week when we shopped at Forever 21?"

"Yes."

"I took something."

"Took? What do you mean?"

"I wore it out."

"You mean so it didn't get added to the bill?"

"Yes."

Lexie's heart sank. "How about at Victoria's Secret or ULTA?"

"No."

"What did you take?"

"I wore a cami out under my t-shirt. It wasn't expensive. In fact, I think it was, like, on sale."

"That doesn't matter, how expensive it was. Stealing is wrong."

"I know. I'm really sorry."

"But why did you do that? I'd have paid for it. Did I deny you a thing you wanted?"

JayCee whimpered. "I'm sorry, really I am. I'll never do it again. I used to steal stuff -- food, candy, lipstick, cig --." She caught herself. "Otherwise I wouldn't have had anything. You don't know how poor we were."

"But you aren't poor now."

"I guess I just have to get used to that, stop thinking the way I did then."

"Yes, you do."

"My life was a nightmare."

"I know it was. But it's better now. Tomorrow we're going to take the cami back and pay for it."

"What will you say?"

"Me? I won't say anything. It's up to you to explain what

happened."

"But I don't want to do that. It's embarrassing."

"Stealing has embarrassing consequences. That's a fact of life."

JayCee whimpered again, her face contorted with fear. "Will they arrest me?"

"I should think not." Lexie hugged her. "They'll be glad to get their money. And with me standing right there, ready to pay, the store will accept whatever you say. They may even be impressed with you."

"Can I say I forgot I had it on?"

"Did you forget? Or did you do it because you thought they owed you something?"

"I forgot."

"If that's the truth, that's what you say." But Lexie was troubled. She knew she was giving the girl an out, covering theft with a lie, but just where was the line between a positive lesson and a devastating punishment? As the poor girl's new step-mother, she wanted to stay on the right side -- the softer side -- of that line. "Tell you what. I think Henry's in the mood for ice cream, and obviously you are too, so let's have some."

JayCee wiped her eyes and giggled when Henry licked her face.

Over ice cream -- which Henry scarfed up faster than they did -- JayCee seemed to have a change of heart about the requirements of her new life. She resisted none of her mother's admonitions and counsel -- though she had a litany of complaints. Phyllis had been mean, Jean had scolded her about being out of bed, Sadie never spoke to her, and Todd talked too much. She cried. Sniffling, she said she was afraid she'd never fit in.

Lexie once again moved to the sofa to comfort her daughter. "Everything will get better with time. You'll see." She steered their confidences to a cozier place: the green VW Bug JayCee wanted so she could drive herself to school, and the belated Sweet Sixteen party to be held for her sometime before Labor Day. She'd already met a few neighbor kids, and Lexie had ideas about some other guests.

It was not until after she'd tucked her daughter into bed, just before Steve returned from a late-night dinner with the Old Stogie Club, that Lexie finally read Jean's note: "*Sorry to be the bearer of bad news, but Jacintha told me today that she stole something while you were shopping last week. She said it's a secret and made me promise not to tell you, but I thought you'd want to know. I think she must have said something to Phyllis she shouldn't have. She said Phyllis was nasty to her -- which I can't believe.*"

Rather than being shocked or dismayed by the note, Lexie was heartened. Phyllis hadn't made any complaints about the girl's behavior. JayCee -- would she ever get used to that trendy name? -- had confessed to the dreadful deed on her own and promised never to steal again. And she'd called her "Mom."

Lexie knew the girl was under tremendous pressure simply being a teenager. With the sudden death of her mother, the confirmation of her father's identity, her adoption, and the huge change in her life, she must be near the breaking point. Perhaps it was time to add some counseling to the cosmetic work.

In any case, the girl's voluntary confession and her use of "Mom" gave Lexie hope.

17

Treadmills
Saturday, July 24, 2010

Drago was not in a good mood. Usually he looked forward to dinners at his mother's house. He used to have dinner with her at least once a month, always by himself, so they could exchange secrets. But lately she wanted Lucy and the babies there too, and now Todd sometimes joined them. Todd the know-it-all talked too much. He never shut up: guns, rocks, mushrooms, you name it. Any subject that came up, he knew more than anybody else. What did his mother see in the son-of-a-bitch?

The new dinner routine wasn't the only sore point. Last year, after he'd rescued the Wrights from certain death, they'd given him Steve's beautiful house in Autumn Ridge as a reward, but while it was mortgage-free to him, he still had to pay the heftiest real estate taxes he'd ever paid, not to mention insurance, utilities and maintenance. Furthermore, though the house was more than twice the size of the bungalow they once occupied in Huntertown, it felt small. From the state of the rooms, you'd think he and Lucy had had sextuplets rather than just twins. He could barely walk through a room without stumbling over plastic and rubber land mines or knocking his shins into playpens and pumpkin seats. Did the boys do anything but poop and eat, drool and scream? At seven months, they were little more than noisy garbage processors.

And then there was his career. Well, career was too big a

word for where he was now. Last year, his best friend, Rolie, Mizz Royce's brother, had cashed in his chips. For years -- ever since high school in fact -- they'd run a profitable drug trade. When it got too risky a few months before Rolie died, Drago left and with Mizz Royce's help got a legit, safe job at the Royces' scrapyard. At first, with his new job, he hadn't missed the drug money, but now he did. The twins plowed through formula, cereal, diapers, car seats, baby furniture, toys and ear medicine like a pig through corn. Every month they needed a new wardrobe. He regretted not saving more money when it flowed so freely.

So. At the age of twenty-five, where was he going? How long would he play second fiddle to Nate Grabbendorf? When would he get another raise? Nothing either Lucy or his mother said to him provided an ounce of comfort. The treadmill he was on led nowhere that he could see.

And speaking of treadmills, he hardly ever got to the gym any more and hadn't run even a 5K since the twins were born. Between after-work diapers and feedings and a few obligatory minutes with his wife, there wasn't a moment of free time. Lucy's constant complaints about how hard it was to lose the baby weight now irritated the crap out of him. He used to find his wife's constant dieting amusing, but no more. He himself was starting to get a gut and had no idea what to do about it.

Yes, he told his friends, his ship had come in, but look at it: a tattered wreck that caught fire before docking, then sank in the harbor, taking all its treasure to the bottom of the ocean.

And Saturday night, here Todd was, bearing gifts as usual: wine and flowers for Phyllis, a rock for Lucy, bouncy balls for Luke and Phil, a t-shirt for Drago bearing the slogan "Geology Rocks." Drago planned to use it as a rag to wash his car.

"I love this thing," Lucy said, smiling at Todd a trifle quizzically. "What is it?"

"A geode. Very unusual and hard to excavate. See those tufts and sprays? They're millerite."

"What's that?"

"A delicate kind of mineral found in quartz. I hacked this

thing out of the limestone myself down by Route 37, north of Bedford. Very hard work to get the geode out of the limestone without messing up the millerite."

"You collect rocks?"

"Whenever I get the chance."

"When you're not shooting Bin Laden through the gut," Drago interjected. "Mom says you're quite the marksman." Too late, he caught his mother's warning look. They'd had coffee the morning after Todd's first visit, and she'd warned him to be nice. She couldn't afford to make an enemy of the full-time handyman, who was in any case harmless. She also scolded him for the way he was acting around Lucy and the twins. "If you don't watch out, you'll be like your father. Neglecting your wife and making your boys scared of you is no way to be a man." He'd hung his head a little, knowing she was right. But still.

"So true," Todd said, beaming. "But I spend more time collecting and polishing rocks than anything else. That's my favorite hobby. I like anything outdoors. You ever go camping, Drago?"

"Never. I like an indoor bathroom and locks on the door."

"So do I. Your mother and I are going camping next weekend." He walked over to Phyl and patted her back just before she bent to remove a pork roast from the oven. "Isn't that right, Phyl?"

She straightened up and lightly placed an aluminum tent over the roast to let the juices settle. "I'm going to give it a try." She glanced at her son. "Todd promises to bring me right back to civilization if I can't stand it."

"Separate tents, I assume?" Drago stubbed out his cigar.

Phyllis blushed. "No tents. Todd has a little Airstream we're staying in. It has a bathroom and a lock on the door."

And separate bedrooms? But Drago didn't dare ask.

Still smiling, Todd said, "We both need to get away now that the Wrights have adopted that girl. She's a handful, she is. I'm just sayin'. Have you met her yet, Drago?"

"Last night."

"What did you think?"

"She's trouble."

"My thoughts exactly." He imitated JayCee's voice. "The pool's dirty, Todd. And that tree looks sick. Could you pull this lounge over by the pool? It's too heavy for me to move and I've got a fever."

Despite himself, Drago snorted something resembling a laugh. "Last night, she ordered me to stay and watch a movie with her."

Lucy stood up and walked over to him, putting an arm around his waist. "You're kidding."

"I'm not."

"Well, I better not hear you ever did something like that. She's jail bait, you know, and even if she wasn't, I'd kill you if . . . ."

"You don't have to spell it out. I know what comes after 'if.'" In a moment of kindness, his mother watching, he bent to kiss his wife's cheek.

"At least she hasn't called any of the rest of you a servant."

"She called you that, Phyl?" Todd asked, horrified.

"She did. I told her if I was a servant, I'm the kind that spits in the food when I'm mad, so don't make me mad."

Before they all stopped laughing, Todd chimed in again. "I'll tell you a little secret. She smokes Virginia Slims and throws the butts under Sadie's window. Her balcony is just around the corner from Sadie's, so the little brat thinks she's fooling me. A girl who grows up with a mother like she had is trouble. I'm just sayin'."

"Have you told Mizz Royce yet?"

"No, Drago, and I won't, not unless she accuses Sadie of something. Sadie, after all, is a Mennonite, very disciplined. Sadie's a lady." He caught the rhyme. "Oh, gosh, listen to that. Now I'm a poet."

"Mushroom hunter, rock hound, expert marksman, poet -- what can't you do?"

If Todd caught Drago's sarcasm, he let it pass, but Phyllis didn't. She shot her son a warning look.

18

Powers Lunch
Monday, July 26, 2010

When Dave Powers invited him to lunch at Ruby Tuesday, Steve assumed it was strictly social. And at first it was. They'd been best friends since high school, where Steve had been the star pitcher for the Carroll Chargers varsity baseball team, and Dave had been the first black quarterback for the Carroll Chargers varsity football team. Neither had come from upper-class families, but their athletic caché propelled them to the top social circles. Both had married up -- Lexie, the Scrapyard King's daughter, and Sheila, Judge Wayne Johnson's daughter.

Now they played a round of golf once a week in the summer and every February escaped for a week to Arizona for spring training and golf. They were both members of the Old Stogie Club and shared a taste for black-and-white crime movies from the Thirties and Forties. Anything with Edward G. Robinson, James Cagney, and Humphrey Bogart was good.

Dave, a Lieutenant in the Fort Wayne Police Department, was now assigned to homicide investigations. And Antoinette Delamarter was on his mind. After their table was cleared, as a way of easing into his request, he asked Steve, "How's your new daughter doing?"

"Okay, I think."

Dave laughed. "There's a man's answer if I ever heard one.

The girl's mother, an exotic dancer, suddenly dies of poison, administered by unknown means. Then the girl moves from a squalid trailer to a beautiful mansion and acquires loving, generous parents and everything she could ever want. She's starting a new school in a month, and she probably has to make all new friends, neither of which teenagers want to do." He signaled the waiter for more coffee. "Overnight, Cinderella becomes the princess, moving from the dark and dirty scullery to the castle's luxurious tower bedroom, but without her biological mother and no friends. Nevertheless, everything's okay . . . you think."

Steve smiled ruefully. "Lexie's the one to ask."

"But I'm asking you, friend. You two talk, I assume, like all married people."

"We do. There have been some rough spots, I'm not going to lie. JayCee -- that's what she's calling herself now -- told Lexie she stole something from a store at Glenbrook, but my wife is satisfied she's sorry and won't do it again. Apparently, she treats our household employees . . . a little roughly. We've talked to her about that, of course. The big positive change is she's calling us Mom and Dad."

"Well, that's progress, I guess."

"It's a shock every time I hear 'Dad.'"

"I'll bet. And what's been the reaction of people who found out you're the girl's father?"

"Mixed. Sometimes I get funny looks -- ."

"Or you imagine you do."

"True. I could be a little paranoid. My aunt Maude wants to kill me. But a few people tell me I did the right thing."

"Sheila tells me it wasn't easy for Lexie."

"That was the worst part."

"I'm sure you've heard that nobody knows how the girl's mother died. They know what killed her -- antifreeze in her Gatorade bottle -- but not how it got there."

"Lexie read me the newspaper report of the Coroner's findings. We assumed it was suicide."

"But no suicide note, which raises red flags. And if she was trying to kill herself, why did she go to work that night? Suicides don't take poison and then go to work. And how and when did the antifreeze magically get in the Gatorade bottle? No antifreeze at her house, none in her car."

"I see your point."

"As luck would have it, I've been assigned to the investigation."

"And . . . ?"

"And I've interviewed everybody I can find who knew Antoinette Delamarter, lived near her, employed her, worked with her, was related to her, palled around with her -- even a few of the many men who knew her in the biblical sense. We found two sets of fingerprints on the bottle, the victim's and some unknown person's. No matches. A security camera shows Antoinette talking to a man when she got out of her car at the back door of Scuttlebutt's before she went into the dressing room that night, but he's been identified and cleared. So has Sally Redfield, one of the dancers in the dressing room, and Percy Scutter, the owner. When Antoinette got out of the car, she wasn't carrying the Gatorade bottle; we found that on the front passenger seat. Which means that by the time she got to work, she'd already ingested most of the contents, antifreeze and all. We got a search warrant for her trailer and a little shed at the end of her parking pad but didn't find any antifreeze. We checked the trailer park's dumpster, but by the time we could do that, the garbage had already been picked up, so if anybody dumped any antifreeze in there to get rid of evidence, it was already gone."

"So you're at a dead end."

"So to speak. The one person we haven't talked to is Jacintha."

"JayCee."

"Okay, JayCee."

"She isn't a suspect surely."

"Of course not. It's just that she might give us a lead she doesn't even know she knows." *Plus her neighbor saw Jacintha dump a bag in the dumpster at 4:15 am the day her mother died. Could she have inadvertently dumped something significant? Where did the bag come from?* "So I'd like the chance to talk to her, for which we'd like your consent."

Long pause. "My first instinct is to say no, but I'll talk to Lexie about it. And Duke Simmons."

"Not an easy decision, I know, but I'm sure she wants some closure in her mother's death. You too. So think about it."

19

A Mark of Civilization
Saturday, July 31, 2010

Phyllis had lived in Indiana all her life but never visited Mounds State Park near Anderson. Todd, of course, knew all about it. He'd even been there once for an archaeologists' weekend and made it sound like one of the seven wonders of the world.

They walked to a wooden stockade fence enclosing a grassy area. "What am I looking at?" she asked in a disappointed tone.

"The Great Mound."

"That grassy knoll?"

"Very mysterious earthworks, wouldn't you say?"

"What's the grassy ditch around it?"

"Part of the earthworks. Everything's overgrown now, of course."

Phyllis tried to think of something positive to say.

"Think of it," Todd said, nodding at the mound. "The Adena culture constructed this before Christ was born, it's that old. They made these mounds all over the Ohio River Valley. Nobody knows for sure what they are, but maybe they're burial sites."

"It's not as big as I thought it would be."

He consulted the Wikipedia printout. "From this bank to that one, it's almost 400 feet."

"But the mound is so small."

"I guess you're right. It's only four feet high . . . though we can't know how tall it was when the Adenas, or whatever they were called, made it. Maybe it's silted in or something. With time, whole cities get buried, you know. Everyday, the archaeologists learn something new. They don't tunnel any more; now they uncover sites one layer at a time. Technique is one thing; knowing what they've found is another, though. Every structure they find they're sure is about burying the dead or worshiping the sun, never just grain storage or a garbage pile, something simple and everyday. Frankly, I don't think the experts know what they're talking about most of the time, but I listen anyway. 'The mound might mean this, it might mean that, it could be millions of years old.' Pure speculation. I'm no archaeologist myself, but I'm just sayin'."

They stared at the mound a few minutes. "Anyway, I guess the important thing is," Todd resumed, "at least these Adenas cared about their dead enough to bury them properly. That's a mark of civilization, isn't it?"

"Depends on whether they were honoring the dead or worshiping them. If they did more for the dead than the living, I don't think they were all that civilized."

"We'll never know. A hundred years ago some pranksters scattered chimpanzee skeletons around some mounds like this just north of here in Alexandria, got the public all worked up thinking it was our little hobbit-monkey ancestors who made these things."

"You ask me, the only people who hope our ancestors were monkeys are the ones who don't want to answer to God."

It took a minute for Todd to digest that thought. "Never thought of it that way, Phyl. You are deep, yes, you are."

"Not deep at all." And then a bad thought gnawed its way into her mind. She hadn't honored her dead. Carver, the husband she'd shot in the back of his head twenty years ago, hadn't been buried in a ceremonial mound with honor. She and her sister had wrapped his body in an old quilt, carried it to the grove where Mizz Royce's new house was now situated, dug a shallow grave at midnight, and dumped his body in. No ceremony, no honor, no marker, no nothing. Then, when they dug him up, Drago wrapped his bones in plastic and disposed of them, God knows where. It didn't bear thinking about. And speaking of God, she hadn't answered to Him for her dark deeds any more than the most ardent evolutionist.

"Looking at that mound, thinking of those monkey bones, reminds me," Todd said. "Mr. Wright told me about the human bones found on the back of his property near the creek. You'll never believe what I found there a few weeks ago when I was planting some lilacs."

""What?"

"An old ID bracelet. It was black, but when I cleaned it, guess what? It turned out to be sterling silver. The surface is scratched pretty good, meaning somebody wore it a lot, but still it's nice."

"A chain or a solid band?"

"Heavy chain links."

"A man's or a woman's bracelet?"

"It's not delicate, that's for sure. And it fits me, so I'd say it's too big for a woman. Plus it's engraved with initials, plain as day."

The Great Mound faded from her sight, replaced by a silver ID bracelet. It couldn't be, could it? The personalized bracelet she gave Carver the first Christmas they were together. How could something so meaningful have slipped from her memory? When her son had dug up Carver's bones, they made sure to retrieve the silver chain he wore around his neck, but she hadn't given a thought to the bracelet then or since.

He nudged her arm. "You aren't curious about the initials?"

"No." *You're going to tell me anyway, but I already know.*

"GWCB. Very unusual, don't you think? Not many people have four names."

I knew it: George Washington Carver Bott. "What did you do with the bracelet?"

"Gave it to Miss Royce."

"Why?"

"I found it on her property, so it belongs to her."

"Did she say anything?"

"Not really, just thanked me, said it wasn't likely we'd ever figure out who it belonged to but she'd keep it awhile in case the owner turned up. Then oddly enough, she laughed."

"At what?"

"Not sure. Sorta like she knows something I don't." He took out his handkerchief. "Let me wipe your forehead, girl. You're sweating. I think the sun's too hot for you."

"Where'd she put it?"

"Put what?" He dabbed at her face. "Oh, the bracelet. Now, how would I know that? It's not worth much, so maybe she took it to a junk shop. Or even to the Scrapyard to be melted down. I hear the price of silver's going up."

Speaking of junk, there's a little junk drawer in her cubby. Maybe it's there.

"You ready to go, Phyl? Not much more to see here. We could go into town, get a bite to eat. Then I thought we could do some canoeing, spend the afternoon on the water. We'll get you a hat. What do you think?"

★ ★ ★ ★ ★

Early the next Monday morning, Phyllis went right to Mizz Royce's cubby, opened the junk drawer, and scrambled around. But there was no ID bracelet. She hoped it was gone forever.

20

The Meek
Saturday, August 21, 2010

In two days, JayCee would start her junior year at Carroll. She was fully recovered from cosmetic surgery and Lasik treatment. Her ears were perfect, the bridge of her nose was smooth, and she could see without glasses. Her teeth were capped and free of decay. Her only flaw, she thought, was her mouth -- not quite wide enough, lips too thin. But lip gloss helped that. For the first time in her life, she was smiling.

And she was ready to celebrate. She already knew a dozen kids, some her Gretna Green neighbors, some the teenaged children of Gretna Green Golf and Tennis Club members, and two from the youth group Lexie talked her into joining. What she didn't know was that Lexie had formed the nameless group explicitly to introduce her new daughter to the moral standards that would now be expected of her.

JayCee thought the youth group was lame, though she greatly admired Sheila Powers, who was leading them in Bible study. The nine kids met in a meeting room Steve made available once a week at the Gretna Green clubhouse. They were reading the Beatitudes and discussing them one at a time. "Blessed are the meek, for they will inherit the earth!" She couldn't suppress a giggle when she was made to read it aloud. Even when Sheila explained it, the sentence was hilariously nonsensical. The meek, she was sure, would inherit nothing and die alone in a place like Scuttlebutt's. She was not meek. Her father owned the clubhouse they were meeting in, and she made sure everybody knew that.

Sheila was cool, though. An African-American, she was the daughter of a judge, the wife of a detective, the sister of a State Trooper, and the mother of ten-year-old Leland, who sat in the sessions because he had nowhere else to go. During the school year, Sheila taught reading at Maple Creek Middle School, and though she led the singing of a hymn at the start of each meeting, JayCee was pleased to note that she herself was the better singer.

But Sheila's hair style was something else. It was perfect. They both had very curly hair that couldn't be straightened without a lot of effort and damage. So now JayCee wore her hair like Sheila's: a springy mass of curls ending at her chin, caught up behind her newly flattened ears with combs. The style -- a curly bob shiny with silicone spray -- not only showed off a part of herself that she'd always tried to keep covered before, but it also opened up her face and emphasized her beautiful brown eyes. When she gazed in the mirror, which she did often now that all the bruising and swelling had gone away, she couldn't believe the image that smiled back. She was just what Jean had said she'd be: the prettiest girl at Carroll.

But she probably wouldn't be the smartest or most popular.

The two kids she admired most, Mary Elizabeth "Libby" Stuart and Joseph "Joey" DeWitt, were superstars compared to any other students she'd ever known. They were good-looking, smartly dressed, and well-spoken. Libby was poised, Joey confident, even a little cocky in the most attractive way. Both were respectful of Mrs. Powers without being a suck-up or spring-arm. They seemed familiar with the Bible. And they were a couple.

Libby and Joey engaged in no public displays of affection other than sometimes holding hands, but still you could see they were as tight as spandex. They finished each other's sentences, laughed at each other's jokes, and exchanged intimate looks. They'd been best friends since sixth grade. JayCee wanted what they had.

So she started with Libby and made a friend of her. Discovering that bowling was déclassé, she got Dover to teach her golf and tennis, then invited Libby to play with her -- free to Libby, of course. The two friends spent an afternoon at the zoo, JayCee paying for everything -- entrance fee, lunch, and souvenirs. She insisted that Libby accompany her and Lexie to shop for a Sweet Sixteen dress in Indianapolis.

And a week before her Sweet Sixteen celebration, she invited Libby and two other girls to a pajama party, where they watched Emma Stone as Olive Penderghast in *Easy A,* the story of a high school girl who tells her best friend that she had sex when in fact she didn't. The "Christian" girl who overhears the confidence spreads the gossip. Once she has a reputation as a harlot, Olive decides to wear the scarlet "A" and flaunt her bad reputation. She pretends to have sex with a gay guy to change his image, accepts money from straight losers in exchange for virtual sex, and even volunteers to take the blame for spreading chlamydia to protect the adulterous guidance counselor. In the end, though, everything comes right. Olive confesses via Facebook that she lied about being "easy" and then effortlessly hooks up with the handsome, nonjudgmental boy she's always had a crush on.

"So what did you think?" JayCee asked her friends after turning off the movie. "That was, like, really fun."

"Honestly? You want to know what I really think?" Libby asked.

"Yah."

"My parents wouldn't have let me watch that."

"Why not?"

"Sex before marriage and telling lies ... they're both off-limits. Things like that get you into trouble, but you wouldn't know it from the movie."

"It was just a little white lie she told to make herself seem sophisticated. Olive was helping the less fortunate."

Libby got up to pour herself another glass of Phyllis' homemade raspberry lemonade. JayCee smiled when she saw Libby walk a bit unsteadily. What none of the girls knew was that she'd spiked the lemonade with vodka. It was very funny to watch.

Libby returned to the couch. "And I don't like the way the Christian," making quotes in the air, "kids were portrayed."

"I have to disagree with you there," JayCee said. "The lie wouldn't have gone anywhere if those self-righteous religious girls hadn't spread the rumor. They just wanted to feel superior."

"Good heavens, JayCee. Can't you see? That's the way Hollywood wants you to think religious girls are: vicious hypocrites, worse than anybody."

"Well, aren't they?"

Libby stared at her friend. "Is that what you think I am? A liar? A skank? A rumor-monger? Or how about yourself? Are you a hypocrite? Would you spread a rumor like that?"

"Of course not. You're right. I'm just, like, testing you." She involuntarily giggled as she remembered the line about the meek inheriting the earth.

Sandy spoke up. "Her clothes were fabulous, though. And I love the ending, don't you? Olive rides off on a lawnmower with Todd. Everything came out all right for her."

JayCee watched with amusement as Libby nestled into a pillow in the corner of the sofa and murmured, "Killing your reputation is just dumb. Lies have permanent consequences, you know."

"Not little white lies," Sandy protested. "It's like telling your friend her hair looks good when it doesn't."

"I'm feeling a little woozy." Libby seemed to be having trouble focusing her eyes.

"You haven't eaten anything, that's your problem." JayCee got up and passed the cupcake platter around. Then she refilled the girls' glasses. "Let's have some more lemonade. It'll give us energy."

A week later, Libby and Joey were the perfect guests at her Sweet Sixteen party. They swam in the pool and chatted up all the other kids, even those they didn't know. They danced to the rock music of American Graffiti in a huge tent set up by the creek. They dutifully complimented Todd on the grilled hamburgers and Phyllis on her red velvet cupcakes.

JayCee spent the afternoon testing Joey's attachment to Libby. She asked him to dance. She flirted outrageously and made jokes that Joey didn't understand about how much Libby liked raspberry lemonade. She asked if he wanted to take a drive with her in her new VW Bug. When she caught him emerging from the pool house, she offered him a cigarette, nodding in the direction of some lilac bushes lining the creek.

Joey wasn't entirely unresponsive. He flirted a little too. He danced three or four times with her. He pretended he'd have a cigarette with her sometime, but not here. And he said he'd never driven a VW Bug but always wanted to, so maybe that could be arranged. But she couldn't get him to say a bad word about Libby or ask what it was about raspberry lemonade that was so hilarious.

Like real adults, Libby and Joey thanked Steve and Lexie for inviting them before they left. JayCee watched them as they headed toward their car, holding hands. She wanted what they had.

21

Empty Bottles
Monday, August 23, 2010

Sadie went in search of Todd. She couldn't carry all the empty bottles she'd found in the office suite, which she cleaned every Monday morning before Jean and her staff arrived for work. He was out by the creek, watching the contractors take down the tent.

"Todd, I need help."

Those were sweet words to Todd. He loved helping. "Of course, my dear. What do you need?"

"I found a whole bunch of empty bottles in the office again."

He looked faintly amused, knowing from her expression she must have found sinful bottles. "What kind?"

"Mostly wine bottles, but this time there's a big green gin bottle too, plus one called dry vermouth and another called Grey Goose, whatever that is."

"Bottles again! How do they get there, you think?"

"Somebody's drinking in secret, I'd say."

"Not very smart of them. You'd think whoever's doing it would just take the empties home so they'd never be found. Was the door locked when you got there this morning?"

She nodded.

"Well, then, that suggests somebody on the staff is doing the secret drinking."

"You think I should tell Miss Royce? Show her the bottles?"

"Now, that's the age-old question, isn't it? If you don't inform her what's happening on her own property, you're not doing your job and you might be making a situation worse. If you do inform her, you risk offending somebody and looking like a tattle-tale. Very hard question. I'm just sayin'."

"So what's the answer?"

"I'll go find a box. Let's keep quiet for now, keep our eyes open, our nose to the grindstone, but if it happens again -- well," pointing his thumb at the sky, "let's see which way the wind blows before we decide."

22

The Princess Bride
Wednesday, September 8, 2010

JayCee paused at the tennis courts where the boys were practicing. Shading her eyes against the sun, she spotted Joey DeWitt. He was taller than most of the other boys, with wider shoulders and longer legs. He wore his brown hair just long enough to be a little edgy, and sometimes he skipped shaving for a day. The stubble gave him a rakish look she found irresistible.

She watched him toss the ball in the air, then loop down on it and serve it hard across the net, so hard that his opponent whacked ineffectually at it. When Joey returned to the serving line, she was only a few yards from him. She called his name and gave him a little wave. Though he glanced her way, he instantly looked down and pivoted away. Perhaps, she rationalized, he was just concentrating.

Or maybe not. Maybe he was signaling that it wasn't cool for her to call out to him the way she did. Or maybe he just didn't like her.

The first week of school, they both showed up at the organizational meeting for the school newspaper. She wanted to write features; he had been a photographer the year before and was ready to do it again. She took a seat next to his and scooted her chair a few inches closer, comforted by the warmth radiating from his arms and his scent, a delightful mix of male hormones and sandalwood soap. Though he smiled and nodded a greeting, he abruptly picked up his folder and moved three chairs down from her, ostensibly to make room for a trio of late-comers who'd served on the paper the year before. He knew everybody at the table. She knew no one.

Joey's snub infuriated her. They'd attended the same weekly meetings all summer at her father's clubhouse. He and Libby were guests at her Sweet Sixteen party, where Joey had danced with her, not once, but three times. He'd practically promised to go for a ride in her new car -- a promise he had yet to act on. So what was the deal? Weren't they already friends?

Her new life wasn't working out the way she thought it would. After all, she was no longer the ugly duckling. She had a family and servants. Her clothes were the smartest, her car the newest, her bedroom the most luxurious. Almost every electronic device coveted by teenagers littered her world. With the change of name had come a change of image from the trailer-park girl who bowled to the princess who played golf and tennis.

But at every turn, she was beset with enemies. Jean Arnold had tattled on her to Lexie about stealing a cheap cami; she'd found the note before Lexie got home. Phyllis acted like a boss instead of a servant and nagged her about eating. Though the handsome Drago gave her some badly needed driving instruction, he refused to stop at Starbucks for a cappuccino and a cozy chat. When Dover gave her golf and tennis lessons, he was polite but treated her no differently from anyone else. Libby had the gall to rebuke her after watching *Easy A*. Even her new mother forced her to return some clothing she'd stolen, as if she was just a common thief instead of a typical teenager. And Joey ignored her.

She prided herself on outwitting a stupid world, but discovered the world wasn't quite as stupid as she believed. At her parents' insistence, she had met alone with Duke Simmons, a criminal defense lawyer she despised for his combover, his puffy waistline, and his cigars. The dead fish mounted on the walls were the trophies of a pathetic loser. How good a lawyer could the man be if his office was so overrun with paper? Before she ever sat down in a guest chair, she was determined to hate the man.

He started off by asking her friendly questions about how she was doing. She answered them with as few words as she could manage. Then he switched the subject to the night her mother died.

"What was your mother's favorite alcoholic drink?"

"Vodka."

"Did she mix it with anything?"

"Gatorade."

"Do you know if your mother had any antifreeze in the house?"

JayCee shook her head.

"How about in that little shed next to your trailer?"

"I never went in there."

"Take me through that night after Mrs. Ricky --."

"*Miss* Ricky. She's not married."

"Take me through that night after Miss Ricky told you what happened to your mother."

"She woke me up, gave me some money, and then took me to St. Joe hospital."

"Just like that?"

"Just like that."

"Did her daughters go with you?"

"No."

"Where were they?"

"She said she was going to have her mother come over."

"Did you see her mother?"

"No."

"Why not?"

"I went home a few minutes so I could change my clothes. I'd been sleeping in them. Then I waited by Jen's car till she came out."

"Did you do anything other than change clothes?"

"No." She paused. "Well, yes. I brushed my teeth, turned on the TV because it was so quiet."

"Anything else?"

"Like what?"

"You tell me."

"No. Nothing important, anyway." Suddenly, she had a flash of memory, car lights hitting her at the dumpster. Had somebody seen something? Is that why she was being questioned? "I might have taken the garbage out."

"Strange timing."

"Not really. The next day was garbage pickup, so -- ."

He interrupted. "The next day was Sunday, wasn't it?"

She was momentarily confused. "I guess, but Monday was pickup day, so I was a little early. So what? That was my job. But I can't remember for sure. I was just thinking about Tawny, you know? My head wasn't straight. I was upset."

"You remember what time that was -- when you took the garbage to the dumpster?"

She shook her head. "Before Jen took me to the hospital is all."

"You wouldn't have thrown any antifreeze away, would you?"

She practically jumped. That word again! "What antifreeze?"

"Somehow your mother had ethylene glycol in her system. Could have come from antifreeze."

She looked away from his eyes, which were like lasers. If only she could wipe that little half-smile off his pudgy face. "I didn't look in the bag. I don't know what was in there."

"What about drugs, prescription or otherwise? You throw those out?"

"No."

"How do you know if you didn't look in the bag?"

"She didn't take drugs."

"I was told she was on methadone to ease her off her cocaine addiction."

"I don't know. How do you know so much about my mother?"

"Never ask a question to which you don't know the answer."

"Then why ask the questions?"

He ignored that. He wasn't about to explain anything. "So where did the methadone go?"

"I don't know." Suddenly, she had a brilliant thought. "You just asked a question you don't know the answer to, didn't you?"

He ignored that too. "Who put the Gatorade in that plastic sports bottle found in your mother's Firebird? You or her?"

"She did."

"You watched her do it?"

"No. But, like, who else would do it?"

"Did your mother know you smoked?"

"No." She answered automatically, before the question registered.

"Where'd you keep the cigarettes?"

"In the shed."

He smiled a little. "But you said you never went in the shed."

She hesitated, then gave him a contemptuous look. "Not all the way in. That's what I meant. I kept my cigarettes in an old mitten hanging just inside the door. I never looked around, don't know what my mother kept in there."

"Did your mother have a boyfriend?"

"No."

"Didn't she have a boyfriend who died after eating a peanut butter sandwich? I thought I heard that somewhere."

"Peanut butter cookie. That's what Tug ate when he died. He was drunk."

"Didn't he carry an EpiPen?"

"What's that?"

"A little device that injects medicine to open his airways."

"I sort of remember something like that."

"What happened to it?"

She looked away. "Mom couldn't find it."

"Because you had hidden it."

"How -- ?" She caught herself. "I don't even remember what it looked like."

"What'd you think of him?"

"Who?"

"Tug."

"He coughed all the time, had allergies to everything, didn't even work. He was a loser, drunk all the time, taking up space."

"I take it life was better after he died."

"Definitely. I could have peanut butter cookies again without having to sneak them into the house . . . not have to see him sitting around in his underwear."

"So you were the one who sneaked in the cookies that killed him."

She sighed. "I didn't say that."

Duke smiled. "And your mother didn't have another boyfriend after that?"

JayCee sighed. "Sometimes I'd hear a man's voice when she got home from work, but there wouldn't be anybody around when I got up for school, so I don't think there was a boyfriend."

"What did you argue with your mother about? The men's voices you heard while you were trying to sleep? Smoking? The money she was blowing on drugs? Or something else?"

She was puzzled. "How do you know we argued?" She spit a wad of gum into her hand and when Duke wasn't looking stuck it under his desk.

"My wife and I raised three kids, so I know all teenagers argue with their mother."

"I didn't see her that much. When I left for school, she was asleep. I didn't see her all day. When I got home, she was out running errands or getting ready for work."

"But you argued about something. You had time for that."

"Mostly why she didn't make my father pay to raise me. We didn't have to be that poor. We didn't have to live in that ugly trailer."

"That made you mad, I'll bet. It'd make me mad."

She nodded.

"I hear you were pretty sure you knew who your father was."

She nodded again.

"Tell me about that."

"Tawny kept a scrapbook about Dad. Steven Wright, you know. At the time, I didn't know who he was and had never even seen him in person, but that was the only scrapbook she made, so I was pretty sure it meant something."

"And your life is better now."

She smiled. "Lots better. Look at me. I'm the princess now."

And he did look. He stared at her so long, apparently without really seeing her, she squirmed. "Well, that's it, princess. You can go. Send your father in."

"Why am I here? I don't get it."

Though he didn't answer, she did get it. Somebody suspected her of something.

Sitting in the ugly reception room where the carpet smelled moldy and the magazines were all about fishing and duck-hunting, she anxiously watched the door for Steve to emerge. In the car, she asked him what Duke Simmons had said.

Though her father kept his eyes on the road, she could see the tension in his face. "The police want to talk to you about the night your mother died because you might have seen something you didn't even know was significant. But that seems unlikely." Finally he looked at her, a tiny little smile on his face. "At your age we don't want to put you through a session with the police, so it's not going to happen. You can relax."

She bristled. "I am relaxed. I have nothing to worry about. They can ask me anything they want."

"I didn't expect you to be worried. I just meant Lexie and I don't want you to go through one more stressful experience."

Suddenly, she began to cry, the first real tears she'd shed since Tawny died.

She felt her father's hand on her shoulder. "I'm sorry, kid, we had to put you through this. I know it's hard, probably awakens a ton of memories. You must miss your mother a lot. If you want to talk about her, I'm listening." She said nothing.

★ ★ ★ ★ ★

That night after the meeting with Duke Simmons, she found *The Princess Bride* in her parents' DVD library and took it upstairs to watch it again, all alone in her bedroom except for Henry, who cuddled against her side in a big comfy chair. And there on the screen was the answer: Inigo Montoya, the Spanish sword fighter whose life was consumed by his desire to get revenge on Count Rugen, the six-fingered man who had killed his father. All the while Inigo was killing the Count with sword thrusts, he recited his tale of vengeance. It was a thrilling scene.

Somewhere she'd heard that revenge was a dish best served cold, but the dish Inigo served up seemed pretty hot and very satisfying.

23

Pahrump

September 22 - 28, 2010

Phyllis had never been to Nevada before. She'd never expected to be loved again. And if anybody had told her a week ago that, drawing from a holster, she could put two bullets through a man's ocular-cranial cavity in 2.3 seconds, she'd have thought him mad.

But all of it had happened. When Todd suggested they take their vacation together in Las Vegas, she demurred. She wasn't a gambler. Sin City sounded dangerous. And nothing about Wayne Newton held any appeal.

But Todd persisted. First, they would spend four days in Pahrump at Front Sight, a firearms training academy in the desert west of Las Vegas. They'd learn to shoot like professionals. Then they'd spend a day rock hunting and the rest of the week exploring Las Vegas. They could play the slots, do a little shopping, soak up the sun by the pool. It was his treat. She wouldn't spend a penny and she'd never be in the least danger because he'd be right there to protect her.

The firearms training was more exciting than Phyllis could have imagined. She thought she knew how to load a gun, sight the target, and pull the trigger, but the fact was she didn't know shit. She learned the value of dry fire practice and how to align the sight. If her gun malfunctioned, she knew what to do. She learned to aim at the center of the mass, shots not too wide, not too narrow. Todd too was astonished at what he learned, and even more astonished that on the four-day defensive handgun skills test, Phyl did as well as he did.

The days of firearms training were exhausting, but in the evenings, sitting in folding chairs with Todd outside the Airstream, Phyllis felt like a teenager again, flabbergasted at her new knowledge, thrilled with her stamina and concentration, feeling muscles she didn't know she had. She had dared to try something new, and she was good at it.

She didn't even mind the day of rock-hunting in Virgin Valley, though all she did was watch Todd work and sweat. It was pleasant just to be outside in the sun, to have nothing to do, to experience his joy at finding a rough black opal.

"I'm going to polish this up for you," he said, putting it into her hand so she could admire it, though it didn't look like an opal to her. "Notice the flash of blue. You want a ring or a pendant for a necklace?"

"Aren't opals bad luck?"

"Now, that's just a myth. In the Middle Ages, opals were thought to bring good luck because they reflect every color under the sun, so everything good about every stone on earth was possessed by the opal. Then something bad happened."

"What?"

"Sir Walter Scotland -- ."

"You mean Sir Walter Scott?"

"How do you know that?"

"A young girl's taste for historical romance."

"You're a wonder, you are. Well, anyway, he wrote a popular book where a magical opal that allowed people to be invisible turned into nothing but a colorless stone when a drop of holy water fell on it. That's when everybody started hating opals. That's what I read anyway."

She tried to hand the rough opal back to him. "It's beautiful, but you should keep it for yourself, Todd. Or give it to somebody who's special to you."

He impulsively kissed her hand, startling her. "You're the

woman who's special to me, Phyl. Nobody else would be such a good sport."

The next afternoon, they left the Airstream at the RV park and drove his Navigator into Las Vegas. As a surprise, he'd booked half a day at a spa for her while he tried his luck at blackjack. Then, after a little window shopping, they made their way to the Mandalay Bay Resort, where Todd had made reservations at Fleur, a restaurant featuring "globally inspired small dishes," whatever they were. They only had to wait a half hour for a table on the patio.

"Don't you love this," Todd asked, marveling at the menu. "We get to share the food, just a taste of this and that, try things we'd never find at home. I won a few hundred dollars, so the sky's the limit. See anything that looks good to you?"

"I could look at palm trees every day for the rest of my life. How about you?"

He looked up at the trees, clicking in the breeze, then shook his head. "They're nice, they're different, but they're not the trees I'm used to at home."

Phyllis closed her menu and took another sip of her Tom Collins. "Everything looks good to me. Why don't you order?" For once, she wasn't in charge of anything. She didn't have to think for herself, let alone a dozen other people. She hadn't been on her feet all day, and she was dressed in her Sunday best, with a manicure and pedicure to show off. Todd looked good in his red plaid short-sleeve shirt and khaki shorts, freshly shaved and smelling like Old Spice. Even his chubby cheeks looked adorable. Life was good; it hadn't been this good in over twenty years.

She watched Todd's face as he ordered half a dozen dishes. Then, as she half-listened, he talked some more about black opals, their geologic origin, their mystical meaning. He was a puzzle to her. She'd always distrusted men who were attentive to her, who seemed to like her more than she liked them. She distrusted their motives. Real men were remote and kept their distance, she knew that, so she only wanted real men. Her father had been a gruff, quiet man she could never quite please. Her one and only high school boyfriend unceremoniously dumped her after bowling a bad game, berating her with vile words as if his defeat was her fault. His attempts at reconciliation were angry and demanding, not loving. Carver had kept her at arm's length at first, but she had persisted and finally won him. Walking down the aisle after marrying him had felt like a triumphal march through Rome in the days of the gladiators. Finally, she was good enough to be loved.

But Todd was altogether different. He liked her as she was. The more she tried to shoo him away, the more attentive he was. Wherever they were, his attention never strayed to other women. Nothing about her displeased him; nothing she said was stupid or boring. She was not allowed to pay for anything, though he probably made no more money than she did. Even the fact that she was at least five years older than he was, had a grown son, and was already a grandmother seemed to carry no weight.

"Ah," he said, leaning aside as the waitress began setting dishes on the table, "here we are. Is that the lobster mac and cheese?"

The waitress nodded and pointed. "And that's the veal schnitzel, the braised Thai duck, and the brick dough wrapped prawns. Anything else?"

Todd looked at Phyllis, who was smiling, then back at the waitress, who wasn't. "Looks good for now, but come back in twenty minutes. Leave a menu here. We might need a few more dishes. And we both need more drinks, another beer for me, another Tom Collins for the lady."

He prepared Phyllis' plate for her, putting a little portion of each dish on it so that no preparation touched another.

With no warning, after they'd begun tasting each dish and commenting on it, he suddenly said, "I like your son."

"You do? Why?" *He's treated you pretty badly, so there's no reason for you to like him.*

"He's very young to be married with two kids, working five days a week, half-days on Saturday. That's a lot of responsibility for a guy his age."

"Oh, that. I was younger than he is when I had him. And I was working too."

"So it runs in the family. Like me. I've been working since I was ten, mowing lawns, shoveling snow, delivering newspapers." He paused. "You've never told me about your husband. I've told you about my life, but you've hardly said a word about yours. I take it you're divorced."

"No. He's dead."

"How did that happen?"

Now here was the chance to test Todd. She not only wouldn't try to please him, she'd reveal the worst about herself. "I killed him," she whispered. "I shot him in the back of the head."

Todd put down his fork and looked at her. "Now, there's a story to bend the mind. I ask a simple question, you astonish me with your answer, yes, you do."

"Aren't you going to ask me why I killed him?"

"It's on my mind, of course, now that you say you shot him, but it's up to you to decide what to tell me."

She told him the story of how Carver beat Drago so badly he had to be hospitalized when he was only six years old, why she was afraid her husband would eventually kill the boy if she didn't kill him first, and what happened afterward -- the burial and the exhumation.

"So you were protecting your son."

"That's my excuse. I could have left, but I didn't. I'm not a good person, Todd."

He reached for her hand. "Oh, but you are, Phyl. You're the kinsman avenger. Some call it the kinsman redeemer, but I like avenger."

"The what?"

"The man who redeems his family's land or avenges a murder. Like Boaz in the story of Ruth. Except you're not a man, of course, no, sir." He signaled the waitress for another round of drinks. "Never really heard of a woman avenger before, but it could happen. I'm no expert on the Bible, but I always liked that story of Boaz and Ruth. What the law won't do for you, you have to do for yourself. It's only right. I'm just sayin'."

"The only other people who know about it are my sister

Ruth, who helped me bury him, and Drago, who dug him up, so I hope you can keep a secret. The bones Mr. Wright found were my husband's, and the bracelet you found belonged to him too."

"He had four names?"

"George Washington Carver Bott, but he always went by Carver."

"I've heard of that guy he's named for. Didn't he invent peanuts or something?"

She laughed. "No. I'm pretty sure God invented peanuts, but George Washington Carver found lots of new uses for them."

"And your sister's named Ruth?" He smiled. "How about that? Now that's a coincidence for the books." He pulled a zipper over his mouth. "But don't you worry. That secret's staying right here, I can tell you that." He looked at her with admiration. "The kinsman avenger! Now I know why you got so good so fast at Front Sight. You were picturing -- well, let's not spell it out. The less we say, the better. You're my steel magnolia, yes, you are."

Phyllis couldn't help laughing again. "We don't live in the South, Todd, so magnolia doesn't sound right."

"My steel hydrangea, then. How about that? Maybe you should think about buying a .45 semi-automatic, some hollow-point bullets, just in case something like that ever comes up again. A woman's gotta protect herself."

Phyllis dabbed at her eyes, wet with tears both from sorrow and amusement. "I'd like to get that bracelet back. When you found it, I wish you'd showed it to me first."

"Now that I know what it is, so do I. I'll have to think about getting it back. Maybe there's a way."

Silence fell upon them like a weight.

"I don't understand why you don't hate me, Todd, why you aren't running out of this restaurant screaming."

He looked down at his empty plate, then back at her. His voice was uncharacteristically shy. "Because I love you. That's why."

24

Miss Trouble

Saturday, October 2, 2010

Miss Trouble had followed Drago around the Scrapyard all morning and he was both pumped with flattery and uneasy at her intentions. She flirted, touched him, fawned about his physical strength. "Gosh, all the guys really look up to you," she said more than once. It was flattering for a girl as young and pretty as JayCee to find him awesome, and he couldn't help but enjoy the good-natured ribbing from the workers when they noticed her infatuation. Still, he reminded himself, girls like that are trouble.

In particular, she slipped in some very personal questions about the women in his life, which made him deeply uncomfortable. Maybe he looked like a player, but he wasn't. He'd started dating Lucy his junior year in high school and never strayed, not because he wasn't attracted to other girls or thought a bachelor shouldn't play the field, but because even as a teenager he liked the security of commitment, of not being rejected. Scrambling around for a girlfriend was just boring when other things were more interesting, like keeping at least a C average and making some pocket money. But admitting he had no real experience with women wasn't in his nature. It sounded pussy. And he wasn't a pussy.

In short, reveling in JayCee's girlish admiration while trying to maintain his cool P. Diddy persona was a struggle.

JayCee was supposed to help Trude Weide, the bookkeeper,

with paperwork, but she refused to stay in the office. She wanted to be outside, she said, learn everything she could about what really happened at the Yard. He told her to follow Nate Grabbendorf around if she really wanted to learn something since he was the manager, but she made a tearful face and said he was *so* gross. She had to be with somebody she knew. Somebody who had all his teeth and didn't carry a toothpick in his mouth. She laughed. She wanted to be with somebody nearer her own age.

JayCee told him she was writing a feature story for the school newspaper about high-school students who had jobs. He knew that was a lie -- or at least a partial lie. His mother had overheard Mizz Royce telling the girl she had to get a job to pay for some clothes she'd stolen, and if she wanted an iPad, she'd have to earn the money herself, learn the value of money and how hard it was to earn it. Something about the girl wanting an iPad really ticked him off. Lucy wanted one too, and though both of them were working -- Lucy part-time in her parents' liquor store, he more than full-time at the Scrapyard -- they couldn't afford it, so what was this girl thinking that at sixteen she was entitled to whatever expensive gadget caught her fancy? Spoiled brat.

He gave in to her demands, though. He wasn't about to tick off Mizz Royce.

JayCee was especially interested in his confrontation with a driver whose battered old pickup was filled with bronze vases. Drago asked the man to remove a few so he could have a closer look. The man explained that his father owned an old cemetery and these were leftovers.

"And these beer kegs. Just layin' around an alley, were they?"

The man nodded.

"Tell you what, pull into that shed, I'll be with you in a second."

As the driver pulled ahead, Drago told JayCee to write down the license plate, then signaled a worker to pull a pallet truck in behind the pickup. While that was happening, he turned his back and speed-dialed someone on his cell phone. "Dave? Drago Bott here. I hear you're not in property crime any more, but I think I found that cemetery thief the cops been looking for -- you know, the one who steals bronze vases off of graves. I've had him pull into a shed, we'll box him in until you can get somebody here."

Watching the cops arrive, talk to Drago, then question and handcuff the driver was the most exciting thing JayCee had ever seen. It made for a great story, but she didn't understand its significance until later, when Drago explained that the vases had been stolen from cemeteries for the copper they contained. "Why did you report that instead of just taking the vases?"

He looked at her as if she were crazy. "Because Mizz Royce don't want stolen goods here. She'd tie my skinny ass into a knot if I let stuff like that through."

"But didn't you just cost the Yard a lot of money?"

He shook his head. "Right is right. Know that."

At one o'clock, he clocked out for the week, ready to go to lunch with Nate and Trude, as they always did on Saturday. He looked forward to those lunches. With time, Nate had become more talkative, mostly about his experiences in Viet Nam. Trude, who openly adored him, talked about the Shelties she raised on ten acres near the Canyons. She was trying to talk Drago into adopting a puppy -- preferably two so they'd have each other as companions. She tried to persuade him that his twin sons would learn life lessons she knew were vital: responsibility, compassion, and respect. So far, he'd resisted adding anything to his household that ate and pooped, but his defenses were being worn down, one Saturday after another.

"Where are you going, Drago?" JayCee asked as he headed for the office to get his comrades.

"Lunch."

"By yourself?"

"No. With Nate and Trude."

"Can I go with you?"

"You won't learn much for that article you're writing."

"But I want to interview you. Make it personal. Give it the human element readers like. Otherwise, it'll just be a boring story. And if I don't write a great story, I'll never get another chance. You can't believe how smart the kids are at Carroll."

"Yes, I can. That's where I went to school."

"Then you know how hard it is to be there, especially to be the new kid. This is really important to me, Drago. To Mom too. She expects me to do well, you know."

It was not the pleading face but the mention of her mom that got him. He'd do anything for Mizz Royce.

"Where do you want to go?"

"Buffalo Wild Wings, the one on Dupont. We can sit on the patio."

He looked at her skinny arms. "You actually going to eat something, put some flesh on those bones?"

She sounded astonished. "You think I'm -- what? Too thin?"

"Real women have something you can hang on to. Know that."

As it turned out, the only thing she really wanted to talk about was whether he'd ever killed anybody before shooting the man who threatened Steve and Lexie's life the year before.

"Where'd you hear about that?"

"Tawny -- my real mother -- kept a scrapbook about my dad. I saw the articles about what happened at the Lodge in Michigan."

"Creepy place, bats and bears everywhere. Don't know why people like places like that. Anyway, the man that went down didn't die from my bullet, so technically I didn't kill him."

"But you tried, Drago."

"I wanted to kill him, believe me."

"Why?"

"Why? Next to my mother and my wife, Mizz Royce is the best woman I ever met. Scary smart about business, but she's got a big heart. Luckily, I got there just in time. Your mother wasn't more than a few gasps from death by the time I did what I did." He pointed at the sky without looking up. "The man upstairs was working overtime that night. Know that."

"You believe in the man upstairs, as you call him?"

"Yeah. Don't you?"

"Not really."

"I admit I don't understand him, but he's there."

"You think it's natural to want to kill somebody?"

Yes, you silly girl. It is natural. But it's wrong. Just like buying bronze vases stolen from cemeteries is wrong. "Now what kind of question is that?"

"I think it's a good one."

You're nuts, girl. "I don't see what killing has to do with the article you're writing. And I'm not saying anything more about it. On that subject I don't want to see my words in some damn school paper, know that. Ask me whatever you want about the Scrapyard, but that's it."

She pushed her basket toward him and grabbed his hand. "You want some of my wings or fries? I can't eat them all."

He had no idea they were being watched from inside the restaurant by Cricket Grinderman and Trent Senser, two of Lucy's good friends. For them, gossip, not bread, was the staff of life.

25

Obi-Wan Kenobi
Saturday, October 2, 2010

Because Saturday morning broke clear, with occasional sun, a light breeze, and none of the rain predicted by the local weatherman, Steve and Lexie played nine holes of golf with Dover and Jean, then retired to the Club restaurant for lunch. When the only thing Lexie would order was tea and wheat toast, Jean gave her a suspicious look. "Now what's that all about? No appetite?"

Lexie glanced at her husband, who raised his eyebrows but said nothing. "I think I'm pregnant."

"What do you mean, you think? You don't know?"

"I've never been pregnant before, so I'm not sure what this is, but I'm a little nauseated at unexpected times, and nothing but the blandest food tastes good to me. Except, for some reason, cheese and apples."

"How far along?"

"Not sure."

"You haven't take one of those home-pregnancy tests?"

"No." Lexie glanced at Dover. "Are we embarrassing you?"

He blushed but shook his head.

"Well, I'm late about six weeks, so that's my best guess. I have an appointment next week with my Obi-Wan Kenobi to find out for sure."

"Your what?" Dover laughed.

"Ob-gyn. Obi-Wan Kenobi is just a silly euphemism that rolls off the tongue. We haven't told anybody else, by the way."

"Why?" Jean reached out to touch her friend's arm. "We won't tell anybody, of course, but I'm just curious."

"I read somewhere that you should wait until the third month to be sure the pregnancy's all right. Most miscarriages happen in the first trimester, or so I'm told, and from what I've read, I'm awfully sick for being only a few weeks' pregnant."

"Doesn't that mean it's a boy? Maybe the hormones have kicked in, making you sick. Or is that an old wives' tale?"

"I have no idea. In any case, we're keeping quiet because I just don't want to explain if something goes wrong."

"Have you told Jacintha yet?"

"No. And I won't for a few months."

Steve spoke up. "She's under so much stress as it is, we just don't want to add to it. We're going to try to figure out how to prepare her for a sibling."

"Speaking of stress," Dover said, "I assume you read in the paper that Hal Linkerman died in Egypt a few days ago, whitewater rafting with his wife and her daughter, who also died."

Lexie gasped. "That's horrible!"

"What a fool!" Steve said. "He managed to kill two wives and four kids and finally himself."

"Imagine the loss to the friends and relatives they leave behind!" Jean added.

And to me, Steve thought without saying so aloud. The Linkermans hadn't closed on the lots they reserved. "What do you suppose makes people keep doing something they know is dangerous and they're not very good at?"

"The rush," Dover said. "I see it in sports all the time. And pride, the inability to admit you aren't as good as you think. One of my golf students is a guy who's sure if he swings hard enough, he'll get the ball to the green in one shot. He'd rather lose showing how powerful he is than win with a little finesse."

Jean looked at Steve. "Enough! Let's talk about something more fun. I take it you're going ahead with the Halloween party here at the Club."

"We are. Adults only," Steve said. "It'll start after trick-or-treating ends around 8 so the parents can be home for that, take their kids on the rounds, but then they'll have a chance to kick back, do a little celebrating themselves afterwards, grown-up style. I'm looking to hire a party planner."

"Oh, let me do it," Jean exclaimed. "I'll do it in my spare time."

"You have experience with that?"

"Not exactly, but I love costumes and games. I'll do it for free."

"You think people will want to wear costumes?"

"For sure. But we don't have a lot of time, so let me put a plan together. Can I talk to you next week, Steve? Oh, this is too exciting."

Dover glanced at Steve. "What are you going to do for the teenagers like your daughter who are too old for trick-or-treating but too young for an adult party?"

Steve looked inquiringly at his wife. "Hadn't thought about it."

"I think most teenagers make up their own celebrations. JayCee can have a sleep-over with some of her new friends. How about that?"

"Jean told me you've put JayCee to work," Dover said to Steve.

"We don't want to take time away from her studies, but once a week she has to work at a real job. In fact, this morning she went to the Scrapyard to do some filing for Trude. Dupont Animal Care has agreed to let JayCee assist Nadine groom Henry next week. Our friend who owns a pizza joint is going to let JayCee work the counter, and we've got some other gigs set up."

"We're killing two birds with one stone, so to speak," Lexie explained. "She has to pay us back for the thing she took from Forever 21 and pay for an iPad herself -- which fits with a feature she's doing for the school newspaper on students who work."

"I can't imagine JayCee -- ." Dover stopped when he felt Jean's knee under the table. "I can't imagine she won't learn a lot. That's good parenting."

★ ★ ★ ★ ★

Afterwards, driving back to his apartment, Dover said, "Thanks for the warning knee. I was about to say I can't imagine that girl working at a real job. And the whole setup is a little artificial when you think about it. She didn't have to apply for the jobs and risk rejection, so the work isn't authentic. And I'll bet anything she's not getting paid by the employer. How valuable could she be?"

"What? You think Steve and Lexie are shuffling money from their pocket to each place JayCee works back to her in the form of a paycheck?"

"Exactly."

Jean laughed. "Never thought of that. But you're right. I can't imagine her working. At home, she acts like a princess, ordering everybody around, expecting the world to kneel at her feet, fetch and carry everything. Imagine what she'll do at the pizza joint -- either ignore the customers or throw deep-dish pizzas at them."

"I wouldn't want to be the one to tell the princess she's about to be replaced by a baby. How about you?"

"She won't be replaced, Dover."

"I'll bet you anything that in her mind it'll feel like that. She just grabbed the brass ring, after all. I don't see her letting a brother or sister grab on too. She'll pry its little fingers off, one by one."

26

Black Nights
Saturday, October 2, 2010

About once a month I have a night where I simply cannot sleep, no idea why. It's been that way since I was a little girl. Phyllis once told me the occasional sleepless nights began after I was told my mother was never coming back. Sometimes in those days I had night terrors too, but they have passed -- sort of. When I was little, Dad would sometimes come to my bedroom and hold me; later, it was Phyllis, or if she wasn't there, my step-mother, Matilda. Now, I sit up in a chair, alone in the dark, longing for the oblivion of sleep. Before I thought I was pregnant, I'd drink hot chocolate with whiskey in it, but, of course, that's not possible now.

On these blackest of black nights, I cannot think of one good thing. I cannot concentrate on a book or a movie. I cannot count my blessings or even pray. I cannot imagine a bright tomorrow. My mind roils like a storm cloud slowly, inexorably transmuting into a tornado.

Tonight, I'm sitting in the glass-enclosed atrium I copied from a New York hotel, comfy in an overstuffed lounge chair, reveling in the rain splattering on the roof. I could turn on a table lamp, but the darkness suits my mood. So does the cup of tea that's grown cold. At least I have Henry's company, but even he's subdued.

It's always been this way, these random little attacks of dolor. After graduating from college, when I first started Junk in the Trunk and Without a Shred, my waste collection businesses, the dark thoughts were mostly about making the next payroll, managing my credit line, keeping old customers happy and finding new ones, not embarrassing my father. Some were also about my crazy husband and how to keep from provoking him into a rage -- an impossible task. I would tell myself there was nothing I could do about my problems at three in the morning, so worrying was stupid, but nothing I told myself helped me sleep.

Now the dark clouds are about something else. This pregnancy, if that's what it is, doesn't feel right, though I can't explain why I think that. I have no idea, after all, how it should feel. I have nightmares where I've given birth to a thing that's sort of human, sort of not. Sometimes it's a doll, sometimes a real baby but with a weak neck and a head that keeps falling off. The most frightening nightmare was a baby made of wires with a wolf's head. It bit my breast.

In my rational moments, I know I'm just worried about what everybody else is worried about: holding onto the money I earned by the sweat of my brow and the freedom I always took for granted. The political *Zeitgeist* scares me. Because I pay taxes, own guns, go to church, support the Constitution, and distrust most politicians, I'm now described as an enemy of the people, tantamount to a terrorist. The declining stock and bond markets make it hard to find a decent investment. Thank God that last year I added North Dakota land and oil wells to my portfolio.

So the unnatural baby in my dreams might not really be the baby I'm carrying, but me, Lexie Royce, either as an uncertain investor or an unprepared mother. As an adoptive mother, I'm a failure. JayCee has been here almost four months and I don't feel I know her at all. I have no control over her, nor any idea what I'm doing.

I admire people who are generous enough to adopt a child, but I was never inclined that way. It always seemed too risky to me. What do you know about the DNA of a stranger? What if the sweet, innocent baby is hard-wired to be stupid or mean or violent? Can a child over six be molded, or is its character already set in stone? If it had been up to me, I would never have adopted a child, even if it turned out that for some reason Steve and I couldn't have our own. I'd have accepted it as God's will and moved on with my life.

But Steve's teenaged indiscretion changed all that. I was prepared to help Jacintha Caitlin Delamarter even before I knew who she really was, mostly because in some ways she reminded me of myself at that age, but I wasn't prepared to involve myself in her life the way I am now.

I do not understand her. I don't trust her glib assurances of reform. I don't know how to help her. Trying to toe the line between generosity and discipline, I feel like a drunk careening down an alley, stumbling into one wall and then crashing into the opposite one, accomplishing nothing but making a fool of myself and an enemy of her. For once in my life, I'm out of my league. I can't help but wonder if my uncertainty about how to be a mother stems from my own motherlessness.

It hurts to know that my friends think I'm doing a bad job. When Jessica came up to help decorate JayCee's bedroom suite, I could see she thought I was crazy to let her choose periwinkle walls and black curtains, demand a huge television set for herself, and insist on the most expensive furniture and closet fittings. That three thousand dollar antique French chandelier and the zebra print duvet JayCee insisted upon almost undid Jessica.

When I asked Sheila how JayCee was doing in Bible class, she stumbled around, finally saying it was probably a good experience for the girl. We should definitely do it again next summer and meanwhile she could recommend a Christian psychologist specializing in family dynamics.

When at lunch today we talked about JayCee's little part-time jobs, Jean and Dover looked like they were on the verge of laughing, and I saw Jean nudge Dover under the table when he was about to say something about her working. What was he going to say? Something negative? I know Jean was trying to be helpful a few months ago when she told me JayCee had confessed to stealing, but I took it as a rebuke for my blindness.

Phyllis says nothing about JayCee, but it's plain as day she's irritated with the girl, and Sadie avoids her. Even Todd acts different around her, less jolly, more wary. Though Henry still waits for her to get home from school, he's stopped sleeping outside her bedroom door. They spend less and less time together.

Steve does his best. He went along with every idea I had for JayCee's Sweet Sixteen party. He took her to see Duke Simmons -- though he was vague about what Duke told him. All I know is that we're not going to let the girl talk to the police about the night her mother died, presumably because it would be too stressful. If she knows something that would help the police -- stress or not -- I think she should talk, but I'm deferring to my husband on this one. He's taken a big role in finding little jobs for JayCee and in many other ways tried to act like a normal father. But when I try to talk to Steve about my fears and misgivings, he downplays them, saying give it time, things will work out. Guilt is written all over my husband's handsome, amiable face.

I don't know what to do.

27

The Watchman on the Wall
Monday, October 4, 2010

Todd was in his element, getting the house and grounds ready for Halloween. Miss Royce had spent an hour with him, outlining what he could and couldn't do. There would be no cheesy lighted figures, no assemblage of fake gravestones, no smoking cauldrons, no scarecrows, no banners. Yes, he could hang gauzy ghosts in the trees and line up carved pumpkins, skulls, and feathered crows along the outer courtyard walls. Well, okay, tie a few scarecrows to the coach lights with some dried Indian corn and raffia. And, yes, he could scatter some hay bales and deformed gourds, drape giant spider webs over the boxwood, put orange bulbs in all the coach lights, and train black spots on the walls. Anything else?

"If I get another idea, I'll run it by you first, okay?"

Lexie smiled at Todd's enthusiasm. "It's a deal, but keep in mind, I don't want to overdo it. I don't want people driving by just to see how we've decorated. By the way, Sadie told Phyllis she won't help decorate or be around for any celebrations. It's against her beliefs."

"I heard. In fact, I talked to her about that. I said I know it's a pagan holiday, but we're not worshipping the dead or honoring Satan or anything like that. She wasn't havin' any of it, though. I think she's missing out on a lot of fun, but you gotta respect her views. I'm no Mennonite, of course. I'm just sayin'."

"I take it you and Phyllis have become good friends."

He ducked his head. "That we have, yes, ma'am, we're good friends. She's the smartest woman I ever met -- 'cept you, of course. I like everything about her. She's a brave woman, she is. I admire bravery in anybody, but especially a woman. Did she tell you what a good shot she is now? Those four days in the desert were a wonder, let me tell you. Don't sneak up on that woman, try to break into her house or anything, when she's all alone at night is all I'm sayin'." He laughed as if he was joking. "She's Annie Oakley now, for sure. By the way, did you know that Annie Oakley could split a playing card, edge on, at ninety feet with a .22 caliber rifle? Now there was a sharpshooter. I'd like to have seen her show. Even I can't do that, and I'm a man."

Lexie laughed at his innocent assumption that any man by rights should be better than any woman at anything. "I was surprised, Todd, when Phyllis agreed to ride half way across the country to spend a week in the desert, learning to shoot a gun and living in an Airstream. I couldn't picture her doing that. You must be quite a man to get that done."

For a few seconds, Todd was speechless. He'd never been called "quite a man" before. "I don't know about that, but Phyl didn't learn to shoot out there. She already knew how." *Can't go into that.* "She learned a lot, of course. So did I. We had fun, let me tell you. The best vacation I ever took." He was suddenly very nervous. "Miss Royce, do you remember that silver ID bracelet I found out by the creek?"

Lexie squinted as if trying to remember. "That was months ago, but I think I do."

"Have you found the owner yet?"

She shook her head.

"Do you still have it?"

"I don't know what I did with it, Todd. Why?"

"I'd just like to have it back if it's no use to you."

"It's got the wrong initials for you, doesn't it?"

The right ones for Phyl, though. "I can take it to a jeweler, get them changed."

She smiled enigmatically. "I take it you don't think we'll ever find the owner."

He did his best to sound like his old jaunty self. "Maybe, maybe not. There must be a statue of limitations, don't you think? I'm no lawyer, you know. I'm just sayin'."

"You mean a statute? A statute of limitations."

"Yeah, what I said, like in robbery. So many years pass, you can't be charged. Anyway, I'm thinkin', it's been a few months, so finders keepers."

"And losers weepers. Frankly, I can't remember what I did with the bracelet, but if I find it, I'll let you know."

When Todd started to rise out of his chair, Lexie motioned for him to stay put. "I only have one more request about Halloween night, Todd. I'd like you to come over after the trick-or-treaters have stopped coming, around 7:30. I'm letting JayCee invite some boys and girls over to play pool and watch movies, but I want the boys and all the girls except Libby Stuart to leave by eleven. No stragglers. When the five boys and three girls have all left, you can go home. I'll pay you overtime, of course."

"How do I keep an eye on them without . . . without . . . ?"

"Without being conspicuous? I have a monitor in the family room so you can watch the gates and doors, keep an eye on the party while watching television on another screen. The kids will either be in the media or game room, or on the adjoining terraces. I'm not asking you to spy on them exactly; I just don't want them sneaking in pairs off to the pool house or leaving the grounds altogether. Can you handle that?"

"Of course, Miss Royce. I'd be glad to do it. Sort of like the watchman on the wall, that's what I'll be. The watchman on the wall."

28

The Note

Saturday, October 30, 2010

By seven o'clock Saturday evening, JayCee and her nine friends had assembled at St. Vincent's Halloween haunted castle. Though masks and costumes were deemed to be too juvenile, they'd decided all would wear only black and orange clothes. The girls chose the tightest outfits they could find; the boys wore cool leather jackets and slim jeans.

There was much laughing and bumping of bodies and general horseplay as they made their way, like a supersized, hormone-fueled amoeba, through the maze. Jokes flew about the old cemetery a few yards away. "Why are cemeteries fenced? People are dying to get in." Crazy epitaphs provoked guffaws. "I always liked it hot, but this is ridiculous." "Here lies an Atheist, all dressed up and no place to go." "I *said* my feet were killing me."

Some girls pretended to have seizures in the room where black lights blinked on and off, momentarily revealing a frightening face here, a skeleton there, costumed bodies running helter-skelter. The boys had an excuse to enhance the threat and then offer the girls manly protection. The girls had an excuse to simulate great fright and then grab the boys for security. It was adolescent play-acting at its most raucous and innocent.

Libby Stuart was no stranger to the haunted castle, having toured it every year since she was eight, but this night she was unhappy. She and Joey had had a bitter fight over his pairing up with JayCee to photograph her bathing her dog at Dupont Animal Care, weighing pets at Pine Valley Veterinary Clinic, and working the counter at Buster's Pizza. Joey and JayCee even returned one Saturday morning to Summit City Metals to take pictures of Drago and her posing in front of the auto crusher.

Joey protested that as the school photographer assigned to JayCee's feature story, he had no choice but to spend time with her. They were, so to speak, nothing but professional partners. "We aren't even friends," he claimed.

"Sandy saw you at Dawson's Dogs Saturday afternoon, getting out of JayCee's new car, then disappearing into the shop."

"We ate lunch, Libby." His tone was gradually becoming more sarcastic. "Stop being so jealous."

The word "jealous" sent Libby over the edge. She was definitely not a jealous girl. She was confident and poised. She was an A student and captain of the varsity cheerleaders' squad. She certainly couldn't be jealous of JayCee, who was nothing but jumped-up trailer trash with rich parents, oodles of sass, and bad morals.

The moment such dark thoughts beset her, she was remorseful. JayCee had been nothing but kind to her. JayCee paid for all their fun times: golf, tennis, movies, the zoo, bowling (which Libby enjoyed far more than she wanted to admit). JayCee effusively admired everything Libby wore without going out and buying the same clothes. She let Libby drive her car to the mall and opened her parents' magnificent mansion to Libby several nights a week. JayCee humbly took makeup lessons from Libby. She never even hinted at any personal interest in Joey except as a good photographer, an awesome tennis player, and Libby's steady boyfriend.

Still, Joey's answers were far from satisfactory. She wanted to believe he had nothing but a professional interest in JayCee, but her instincts told her otherwise. He was spending far too much time with her. He smiled too much when JayCee's name came up.

Now, here they were, at the Haunted Castle, but not as a couple.

For the first time in years, Libby and Joey had arrived separately at an event and then kept their distance, trying to see what the other was doing without being obvious about it or accidentally locking eyes. It was very strange not to be half of a pair. She felt like a comet that was being sucked into a black hole whose existence she hadn't even suspected. Libby was so upset -- so sure she'd crash and burn -- that she felt like throwing up.

In the room illuminated only by flickering black lights, she thought she saw Joey put his arm around JayCee but the images were confusing and disjointed, the noise of overexcited teenage voices shattering. Was Joey kissing her? Libby couldn't be sure. Then she felt an arm around her own waist, her hip bumped. Was it Joey? Surely it was. She leaned into the body beside her and reached for a hand, but as quickly as the body had materialized, it disappeared.

It was not until she reached JayCee's house that she discovered the note in her jacket pocket.

29

The Stone Bridge
Saturday, October 30, 2010

Libby practically ran to a bathroom so she could take the note out of her pocket and read it in private. The paper was a lined page roughly torn out of a small spiral notebook and folded in quarters. "Meet me at the stone bridge, midnight. xoxoxo." It wasn't signed. The handwriting looked vaguely like Joey's but wilder, as if he'd been drunk when he wrote it. When did he start drawing little circles over the i's? The author had to be Joey.

She smiled at herself in the mirror, then refreshed her lipstick and combed her hair. Joey wanted to make up. She pictured the two of them at the bridge, maybe running into each other's arms. She rehearsed words of indignation, then words of forgiveness. She vacillated. What tone should she assume? What look should she give him? How could she humble him and still get him back? What proof should she demand that his only love was her?

When she emerged from the bathroom, JayCee was waiting for her. "What took you so long? You okay? You have a headache again?"

Libby laughed, a little hysterically, and pulled JayCee back into the bathroom, carefully locking the door. "I want to show you something." She took the note out and unfolded it.

JayCee looked up after glancing at it. "It's not signed."

"It's Joey's handwriting."

"If you say so."

"He wants to make up with me."

"You sound surprised."

"I knew it would happen, just not this way."

"Well, it's really romantic, Libby. I wish I had a boyfriend."

"You're so pretty, so . . . so different from the other girls, it will happen to you too."

"What do you mean, different? How am I different?"

"I just mean you're pretty and smart and have an air about you . . . ."

Libby paused so long JayCee wondered what was on her mind. "An air of what? Tell me. Tell me something nice."

A knowing air. You're a little scary, if you want the truth, as if you have a lot of secrets. As if you know a lot more than the rest of us. "If I believed in reincarnation, I'd say you're an old soul."

JayCee smiled. "If I believed in souls, I'd agree with you."

When Libby looked shocked, JayCee punched her arm and laughed. "Just kidding. I wanted to make you laugh, you look so serious."

"I have a favor to ask."

"About what?"

"Joey."

"Tell me the favor." *Before I make any promises.*

"Would you tell Joey sometime before the boys have to leave that I'll meet him at the stone bridge. Be sure, of course, nobody else knows about it."

"Let me see the note again. Oh, yeah, he said midnight. I suppose he means the bridge over the creek at the back of our house, right? The one that leads to the Sixth Tee."

"Is there another stone bridge out here?"

"Not stone. There's a wooden bridge near the clubhouse and another before the Seventeenth Tee, but no other stone bridge. I'll tell him."

★ ★ ★ ★ ★

Todd was bored to death in the family room. Early in the

evening, he'd walked with Lucy as she wheeled the twins in their dinosaur costumes around their Autumn Ridge neighborhood. He did his best to walk Louie and Freddie, the Sheltie puppies Drago had finally adopted, but they were so frisky and out of control it was exhausting. Lucy, he believed, was the sweetest woman he'd ever met, so patient with her little boys, constantly talking to them. At that rate, they'd have the vocabularies of five-year-olds by the time they celebrated their first birthday. After trick-or-treating, Phyllis was waiting for them at Lucy and Drago's house with hot apple cider and his favorite cheese ball and crackers. Then he'd reluctantly left to report for duty at Gretna Green.

It was a mild night for the end of October, so JayCee's guests spent as much time milling around on the terraces as playing pool and watching music videos, but he could spot no hanky-panky -- nobody slipping off to the pool house or trying to get into an office suite, the locks of which he'd earlier checked as a precaution.

Promptly at eleven, he told the boys and girls the party was over and counted them off as they left. At eleven-fifteen, he admonished JayCee and Libby to be good, said his good-byes, set the alarm, locked up, and left the house. Lexie had assured him it would be all right for the girls to be alone a few hours because she and Steve would be at the clubhouse, two minutes away. Besides, at sixteen, JayCee was old enough to be alone in the house even if she didn't have a friend with her.

Todd headed to Huntertown, easy in his mind and happy in his heart. Phyllis was waiting for him.

30

Never Be Your Stepping Stone
Sunday, October 31, 2010

Joey was enjoying himself. The boys who'd been at JayCee's party retired to his house on the other side of Gretna Green. His parents were at the clubhouse, celebrating Halloween adult-style. With all of Sunday to recover, the boys were feeling reckless. They were playing pool, drinking beer -- lots and lots of beer. Racking balls led to jokes about the racks on the girls they'd left behind at the Wright mansion. They bragged about their athletic skills and compared biceps. They outshouted each other. If they'd been deer, they'd have butted heads over who had the biggest antlers.

When he finally remembered to look at his watch, Joey saw that it was already 12:30, a half hour later than he was supposed to meet Libby at the stone bridge. Damn! He didn't want to go. He hated scenes and "we have to talk" moments. Maybe she'd already left.

But what if she hadn't? What if she was waiting for him?

When JayCee took him aside on the terrace to tell him Libby would meet him at midnight on the stone bridge, just as he'd commanded in the note, he was puzzled. "I didn't write her a note."

"She thinks you did."

"Why? Who signed it? I didn't."

"There's no signature, just a lot of x's and o's, but she recognized your handwriting."

He shook his head. "That's impossible. Let me see it."

"I don't know what she did with the note, but I saw it, so I know what it says. I don't know what your handwriting looks like, of course, but I recognize the paper from that little notebook you carry around when you're photographing stuff."

"I didn't write her a note, I swear. She must have written it herself."

"So what do you want me to tell her?"

When Joey didn't answer, JayCee put her hand on his arm and said, "She loves you, Joey. Meet her. What can it hurt? Maybe the two of you will make up." She stood on tip-toes and unexpectedly kissed his cheek. "I want the best for you, Joey. We're buddies, right?"

He looked at her appraisingly. Was she coming on to him? He thought so, but this was no place to do anything about it.

Thank God he didn't have to drive anywhere. His head was way too fuzzy for anything like steering and braking. He left his friends, saying he'd back in fifteen minutes, then walked out into the thickest ground fog he'd ever seen, with no moon to light it. It was like walking through a heavy cloud. He was reminded of his mother's joke that in Fort Wayne, having one's head in the clouds simply meant one was standing up.

Fortunately, he could follow the golf cart path; otherwise, he'd never have found his way. The little LED flashlight he carried with his house keys didn't penetrate the fog more than a foot. By the time he reached the stone bridge, he was soaked, the air was so saturated.

Just as he anticipated, Libby wasn't there. She probably thought he'd stood her up, or got spooked by the fog. Well, if he ever wanted to get back together with her, he'd have a lot of explaining to do.

He glanced at the Wright mansion. The floodlights along the walls barely penetrated the fog, and so far as he could see, all the windows were dark. He knew Libby was staying overnight with JayCee. Should he walk over there and see if she was waiting outside? If she wasn't, would he dare knock on a window -- if he could figure out what window to knock on -- or ring a doorbell at this time of night?

He leaned against the stone wall of the bridge, wrestling with his conscience, wishing he had a cigarette. Suddenly, his eye was caught by the fluttering of gauzy ghosts in the lilacs along the creek and his heart took an extra beat. It took him a second to remember that they were part of the Halloween décor.

Reflexively, he speed-dialed Dan, his best friend who was still at his house. When in doubt about what to do next, call somebody. "She's not here."

"You sure?"

"Yeah."

"Libby stood you up?" Dan snorted. "She's pulling your chain, dude."

"Why?"

"Because she could. Get your ass back here, forget about her. The night is young."

Deep in thought, Joey turned around to hang over the bridge, stretch his back, clear his mind. Libby wasn't the kind of girl to pull her boyfriend's chain. What was she up to? As he peered at the water below, a piece of orange cloth near the bottom of the bridge caught his eye. He leaned over as far as he could, puzzled, then tugged at it. The cloth, which was snagged on something, ripped as he freed it. It was long, edged with ball fringe. When he brought it to his nose, a fruity concoction assailed his nostrils, reminiscent of the perfume Libby wore. Had Libby been wearing an orange scarf at the party? He couldn't remember for sure. He hadn't exchanged a word with her all night, tried not even to look at her. If she was going to accuse him of flirting with another girl, then she'd have to make the first move to heal the breach. She'd have to apologize.

Then he heard the strangest thing from below the bridge, Duffy singing "But I will never be your stepping stone. Take it all or leave me alone." Libby's cell phone. What the hell was it doing under the bridge? "I will never be your stepping stone. I'm standing upright on my own." He leaned over and directed his flashlight where he thought the sound came from but couldn't see anything. The song kept playing. He walked to the end of the bridge, made a u-turn, and started scrambling down the steep bank through weeds, wet leaves, and slime. Before he found the phone, he saw a dark shape floating in the water. Too big for a raccoon or even a fox, too small for a deer.

He froze. He trembled and began to sweat as the hair rose on the back of his neck. The orange scarf smelling like Libby, the sound of her cellphone -- she'd been here. Then he sensed what the shape really was. Horrified, he wanted to scramble back up the bank, run home, pretend he'd never been here, but something held him. Reluctantly, fearfully, he waded into the water and shone his flashlight on the body in the water.

Though the creek had a slight current, the body was not moving downstream but merely bobbing gently next to a pylon. It must be snagged on something. Should he touch it or not? Every molecule in his body was revolted at the thought, but what if it was Libby? He gingerly reached out to touch the body and instantly knew from the texture that he was indeed touching cloth, not fur. So it was a person. He grabbed a handful of cloth and began to pull but, suddenly losing his footing on the slimy creek bottom, fell back, shocked by the cold water. He struggled to his feet and again tugged on the body, finally dragging it to the bank. Reluctantly, he turned it over.

It was Libby. Her eyes were half closed as if she were just a little drowsy. He called her name and slapped her cheek. Nothing. Finding her wrist, he felt for a pulse. Again nothing.

He realized he should try mouth-to-mouth resuscitation, but he didn't know how, and besides he was revolted by the mud and weeds on her face, the blankness in her eyes. He scrambled back up the bank, trembling with cold and horror, and followed the golf cart path home as fast as the fog allowed. His father would know what to do.

31

Swingpack

Sunday, October 31, 2010

Even though I'd pulled the curtains in our bedroom, I was awakened by red lights strobing outside, intermittently making the curtains glow as if on fire. I had just fallen asleep and was very tired from the party at the Club. I lay there a few seconds, willing the light to stop. But it didn't. Maybe I should have installed blackout curtains, just as Jessica recommended. I thought about waking Steve so he could find out what was going on, but I knew he was probably even more tired than I was. So I got up, pulled the curtain aside, and had a look.

The revolving light came from the direction of the creek. Through the fog, I couldn't make out exactly what the source was, but I thought I saw the vague shape of a fire truck. A fire truck! Where was the fire? Why hadn't I heard any sirens? I opened the window and heard engines and voices.

I went to the bathroom and turned on the light. It was 2:42 in the morning.

I shook Steve's shoulder. "What?" he mumbled.

"I think there's a fire truck out near the creek. Somebody should . . . ." Before I could finish, the bell rang on the auto courtyard gate.

It was Dave Powers. As soon as he told us that under the stone bridge the body of a girl had been found, tentatively identified as

Libby Stuart, I ran back up to JayCee's room to be sure she was all right. She wasn't there. Her bed hadn't been disturbed. Panicked, I ran back down to the media room. There she was, wrapped like a mummy in a blanket, sound asleep on one end of a long leather couch. At the other end of the couch was another blanket, half balled up, half draped over the edge, but no Libby.

The rest of the night is a blur. Joey DeWitt's handsome face, rigid with fear, haunts me. So does JayCee's face. At first, she looked blank, too stunned to react, but then the story gradually tumbled out of her mouth. The note she described was found in the dead girl's pocket, the ink runny, the words indecipherable, but JayCee remembered what it said, word for word. She was sure it was from Joey, even though it wasn't signed, because it looked like the notepaper he carried around when he was photographing her for the school newspaper. "Besides, Libby told me it looked like Joey's handwriting." JayCee said she tried to talk Libby out of going to the bridge, but she must have failed. In any case, she fell asleep minutes after the party broke up and didn't hear Libby leave the house.

After we saw Joey leave in the back of a police car, I asked JayCee if she wanted a cup of cocoa and a peanut butter cookie. She said yes, she couldn't go back to sleep anyway, she wanted to talk.

"What do you think happened? Do you think Joey could have done something to her?"

"No. He's way too nice."

"So you believe he found her in the creek, the way he said he did."

JayCee nodded.

"So then what? What in the world could have happened?"

JayCee looked scornful. "She was drunk, Mom. I didn't want to tell the cops that, ruin her reputation. Let them figure out whatever they can. I'm telling you, she, like, drank all night. She probably went out there and stumbled around and fell over the bridge. She was so out of it, that's why I told her not to go out there."

"Drunk? Where'd she get alcohol?"

"She brought it with her."

"I don't believe it."

She was instantly defiant. "You think I'm lying?"

"I didn't mean it that way, JayCee. I just mean I'm surprised. Libby isn't -- wasn't -- the kind of girl to drink."

"Look in her purse if you don't believe me."

"Her purse?" I looked around the room. "The police took her backpack. I thought that was everything she brought over here."

"She always hides her purse in the DVD cabinet."

"Why didn't you say so before?"

"God, Mom, like, I didn't want to tattle on her. Don't you know anything? Girls don't tell on each other. Anyway, I'll bet you my entire CD collection there are some little liquor bottles in there. You know, the kind you get on an airplane."

She was right. Dave Powers was back in fifteen minutes after my call to pick up Coach's signature chainlink swingpack in gunmetal gray, bulging with little vodka bottles. He had a lot more questions for Steve, me, and my daughter.

32

Poor Joey
Monday, November 1, 2010

Dave Powers wasn't sure who he admired more, Peyton Manning or Tony Dungy, respectively the star quarterback and the retired coach of the Indianapolis Colts. It was a pleasant conundrum. Despite missing three key players, the Colts were beating the stuffing out of Houston. When right off the bat Manning took his team 78 yards and then threw a two-yard touchdown pass to Tamme, making it 7-0, he knew it was going to be a good night. It made him feel a little more hopeful about his own daunting task.

During halftime, he muted the television and picked up a folder from the side table to study his notes. The Coroner's report wasn't ready yet, so he didn't know precisely when or how Mary Elizabeth "Libby" Stuart died or whether she'd been drinking vodka, as JayCee Wright claimed. Had she died from the impact from the fifteen-foot fall, or drowning when she hit the water, or alcohol poisoning, or an unknown medical condition, or some combination of them? Or instead, had she been killed? In other words, was it an accident, a natural death, a suicide, or a murder?

There was no blood on the girl, none on the bridge. Though nothing was tied around her neck, there were bruises suggesting strangulation and a ripped orange scarf at the scene that might have been used to kill her. The DeWitt boy said he'd spotted the scarf when he leaned over the bridge wall but couldn't remember whether his girlfriend had been wearing it earlier. It was snagged low on the creek-side of the bridge wall, so when he pulled it up, it ripped. If he used it to strangle the girl, it was a good story. The handwritten note in the dead girl's pocket was illegible, but given the torn left edge, it appeared to have been taken from Joey DeWitt's notebook, which the boy readily turned over to the police once they visited his house.

If it was murder, Joey DeWitt was the obvious suspect. He and his girlfriend had had an argument days before and hadn't spoken since, at least according to him. He'd been drinking. He denied inviting her to a midnight rendezvous where they'd be alone in the dark, several hundred feet from the nearest residence and thus where there were no witnesses. He claimed that he hadn't written the note JayCee said she saw. "Libby must have written it. I told JayCee that. I didn't write it, I swear. I never even saw it. In fact, I never spoke to Libby all night."

Nevertheless, he showed up at the bridge, allegedly because JayCee urged him to, a claim JayCee confirmed. He was less clear about why he showed up not at midnight but almost an hour late. When asked why he was late, he said, "Because my friends and I were partying and, frankly, I didn't want a scene. I thought about not showing up at all. I wish I hadn't."

When asked why he didn't leave when he didn't find Libby on the bridge, he said he wasn't sure. He admitted that because of the fog he couldn't see the body in the creek fifteen feet below, but he claimed that just as he was about to leave, he heard her cell phone ringtone sounding from somewhere below the bridge. Dave frowned. Finding her like that would have been a clever and convenient story if the police hadn't found the phone in the water, as dead as the girl herself.

In short, the boy had the opportunity, means, and motive to kill his girlfriend. He couldn't be eliminated as a suspect based on the time of death unless the Coroner could pinpoint precisely when she died, which was unlikely, especially given the short interval between 11:15 pm, when the party ended, and 2:04 am when the boy's father called 911. There were witnesses as to when Joey left his house but no corroborating witnesses as to what he did once he reached the bridge other than the call he had supposedly made to his friend, Dan Winter, when he didn't find Libby. Dan confirmed the call but the cell phones still had to be checked. Joey's claim that Libby must have written the note to lure him to a rendezvous was laughable. The note was written on paper that looked like it had been torn from his notebook, and Libby reportedly said it looked like his handwriting. Instead of calling 911 on his own cell phone, Joey claimed he ran home to his parents because he was scared, not because he hoped to hide his involvement. He made no attempt at mouth-to-mouth or other resuscitation because he could tell she was dead, though he couldn't explain how he knew that. He'd changed his clothes because they were wet and dirty, not because he was trying to conceal what he did in the creek.

Still, the evidence, taken together, was circumstantial and the boy didn't act guilty. At the scene, he trembled and cried and, though obviously distressed, was composed enough to answer questions coherently. He threw up. He kept asking what could have happened to Libby. Over and over, he said she was his best friend, he couldn't believe she was gone. Despite emphatically denying that he wrote a note to meet him and at least once saying he wished he'd never gone to the bridge, he blamed himself for not getting there sooner to prevent whatever happened.

Most telling, he acted like a boy who had nothing to hide. Neither he nor his parents resisted an inspection of his body, a breathalyzer test (which he failed spectacularly) to confirm suspicions that he'd been drinking, a search of his bedroom and car, the surrender of his cell phone, the provision of fingerprints and a DNA sample, the release of records, or the recording of a statement chronicling his actions that night. He agreed to take a polygraph exam in a few days.

JayCee Wright, on the other hand, was less emotional. She claimed she'd fallen asleep by the time her friend must have slipped out of the house so she didn't have any idea when the girl left other than to say it had to have been after 11:15 when the party ended and all her guests had gone home. She hadn't told the cops about the vodka bottles or Mary Elizabeth's hidden purse because she didn't want to ruin her best friend's reputation. She had nothing bad to say about Joey DeWitt and in fact expressed the firm belief that he couldn't have had anything to do with his girlfriend's death. Still, she provided three important pieces to the puzzle. Dave wasn't ready yet to call the pieces "facts."

One, the dead girl had been drinking (to be confirmed by the Coroner), though she herself had not touched any strong liquor or provided any. Two, she remembered what the note said word for word and was the person who recognized the notebook paper as the kind Joey carried around when he was taking photographs for the school newspaper. She said Libby had recognized the handwriting as Joey's. Three, the dead girl had been wearing the orange scarf all night; JayCee was certain of that because she and Libby had been together and both tried it on when they spotted it at Forever 21. Libby bought it, knowing it would be perfect for the Halloween party.

Todd Fingerhutt confirmed that at 11:15 Mary Elizabeth was present in the Wright media room and very much alive. He couldn't remember if she'd been wearing the black North Face jacket that was found on her body or the orange scarf snagged on the bridge. In his hearing, she never said anything about planning to meet someone at the stone bridge. He'd reminded the girls to keep the doors locked and had set the alarm before he left, so if JayCee didn't hear the alarm when her friend left, he didn't know why. Steve and Lexie were puzzled too because the alarm was armed when they returned a little after midnight. JayCee admitted she knew the security code but was adamant that she hadn't touched the control pad that night.

Joey admitted to having drunk at least five beers, but since he was on private property, he wouldn't be charged with public intoxication; and he hadn't been driving, so he couldn't be charged with driving under the influence. The only charge laid against him was therefore the knowing consumption of alcohol by a minor. In light of the fact that the boy had no criminal record and had cooperated fully in the investigation, Joey's lawyer, proposed alcohol counseling and deferred prosecution, with the charges to be expunged in a year if Joey broke no other laws. The plea was likely to be accepted, not just for him but the other boys at his party as well. Nevertheless, Dave heard Gilbert DeWitt tell his son that he wouldn't be driving a car any time soon. Charges against Steve and Lexie Wright for allowing underaged drinking in their home were unlikely if the bottles in the dead girl's purse could be shown to be hers. Charges against the DeWitts for the same thing were still under review. He disliked the laws about underage drinking in private homes, but the law was the law.

Dave sighed. Even if Mary Elizabeth Stuart's death was just an accident, it was deeply disturbing. The untimely death of the young always was. So was the suspicion poor Joey DeWitt was now under. If he was telling the truth that the girl was already in the water and already dead when he arrived at the bridge, then being treated like a suspect doubled the pain of losing his long-time girlfriend.

Dave closed his folder and put it aside as Sheila entered with a plate of sandwiches and a couple of beers. He smiled at Leland, who, as an aspiring quarterback, was eager for the third quarter to start. He wished he could solve the Stone Bridge case immediately, but the evidence just didn't allow it. Meanwhile, he had an exciting game to watch, good food to eat, and a happy family. He was a lucky man.

33

Magical Thinking
Friday, November 12, 2010

Joey felt his life had been ruined. He vacillated between feeling aggrieved at the unfair suspicion he was laboring under and the loss of Libby Stuart. One minute he was angry at her for engineering a midnight rendezvous with fateful consequences, and the next minute he mourned her. She'd been a pivotal part of his life since he was eleven years old. Her absence was palpable.

He was even more aggrieved when Libby's mother came to his house, unannounced, and tearfully accused him of stealing the ring he'd given Libby on her sixteenth birthday. It was a thin 10K gold band set with his birthstone and hers, a ruby chip and an emerald chip. Not an expensive ring but meaningful. "She always wore it. You must have taken it right off her hand. How could you do that, Joey?"

"I didn't," he protested. "I never touched her the whole evening . . . except when I . . . ." Picturing the horror of wading into the creek and wrestling his girlfriend's inert body to the slimy bank in a dense fog, he couldn't complete the sentence. The fact that they hadn't made up their quarrel before she died lay like a lead weight at the bottom of his soul. Nightmares had disturbed his sleep every night since Halloween. What could possibly have happened to her?

More of Mrs. Stuart's hot accusations followed, met with more of Joey's fervent protests of innocence. Her parting words stung the most. "God forgive you, Joey DeWitt, because I can't. I don't know whether you had anything to do with her death, but you broke her heart, you were the last to see her, and now I don't even have that ring to remind me of her dreams."

At school, every hour was devastating. Even his best friends avoided him. He'd been popular, a winning athlete, a skilled photographer for the school newspaper, a solid B student. He'd always been a little cocky, but that only enhanced his standing with other boys who wanted a leader and his attractiveness to girls who wanted to be the leader's favorite. Until now, that is. Now, he was a pariah. His cockiness, which had transmuted into rigid defiance, repelled everyone. And he'd been suspended from all sports for the remainder of the year.

The hypocrisy, he thought, was ridiculous, for what student hadn't consumed alcohol -- or worse? Who hadn't quarreled with a best friend? Who wasn't vulnerable to bad luck?

The only friend he had now was JayCee. Without her, he wasn't sure he could have forced himself to go to school at all. Because his father had suspended his driving privileges for six months, he would have had to ride the bus to and from school if JayCee hadn't volunteered to take him everyday. She stood up for him too, arguing passionately for him to remain as the paper's photographer -- to no avail, though she defiantly ignored the school's decision and took him along to photograph her features anyway. She sat by him in all the classes they shared. She urged him to join an indoor tennis club and played with him twice a week. Every Friday night they went bowling, then watched a movie at her house.

If that wasn't puzzling enough, her demeanor was even more confusing. She wasn't flirtatious. She didn't try to replace Libby. In fact, she never talked about Libby unless he mentioned her first. She was a pal, the buddy he no longer had.

One Friday evening, a few weeks before Thanksgiving, after watching *When in Rome,* JayCee suddenly said, "Don't you wish you could pick a coin out of a fountain and the person who threw it in would fall in love with you? If only it could be that easy."

"I'd wish for something else."

"What?"

"Undo Halloween night. Libby didn't die, I didn't go to the bridge."

"Were you in love with her?"

"I loved her, put it that way."

"But were you *in love* with her, Joey?"

"I was once, I think, but we'd kind of grown used to each other."

"Would you have made up with her if she'd lived?"

"Probably."

"And then what? Marriage? Kids?"

He made a face. "Way too far in the future to think like that."

"By the way, do you have any idea what happened to that ring you gave her?"

"No."

"But it's missing, isn't it?"

"Where'd you hear that?"

"Mom told me Libby's mom lit into you about it, accused you of taking it. So she must think you killed Libby."

"No, she doesn't."

JayCee didn't acknowledge his denial. "Libby and I were both born in May, so the emerald is my birthstone too."

"So what?"

"What if the ring showed up some day? What would you think then?"

He laughed. "I'd think you're into magical thinking, JayCee. It's probably at the bottom of the creek, deep in mud."

"So she was wearing it the night she died."

"No. I mean, I don't know. I didn't look. But that's a thought. Maybe she *wasn't* wearing it that night. Maybe she'd been mad enough to take it off and hide it somewhere after we had our big fight. Somebody should tell her mother to take another look in her bedroom."

"What did you fight about?"

He blinked. "You."

"Me?" JayCee tried to hide her smile.

"She accused me of hanging out with you too much. I told her we were just friends, working on stories together, but she didn't believe me."

"I told her the same thing."

"She talked to you about us?"

"Of course. What do you think girls talk about? But she never mentioned the ring and I hadn't seen it for at least a week. I'll bet she threw it away."

"So why did you ask if she was wearing it Halloween night if you knew she wasn't?"

JayCee smiled. "Just, like, testing your powers of observation."

"Why would she do that, throw it away?"

"Girls get mad enough, they lash out, do things like that."

"Are you telling me that's what you'd do?"

JayCee gave him a look he hadn't seen before. "If you gave me a ring, I'd keep it forever."

34

The Neon Armadillo

Wednesday, November 17, 2010

Many times in the past, especially on Friday nights when ladies got in free, Lucy Bott had met her girlfriends at The Neon Armadillo, the only western bar in Fort Wayne where even single girls could dance the Watermelon Crawl and Tush Push without looking obviously dateless. But that was before she had the twins. Now, she rarely had a moment to herself, and she missed her friends.

"Crappy Wednesdays" at the Armadillo were special -- long-necks only 98¢ -- and this Wednesday night was really special because it was Lucy's 24th birthday. In previous years, she celebrated with her family, but for once she wasn't in the mood for family. She had them twenty-four hours a day, either at home alone with the kids or at her parents' liquor store, where she worked part-time, the boys corralled in a playpen in the storage room. She needed a getaway with friends, a chance to dress up and wear makeup, perhaps an innocent flirtation with the young men who flocked to the Armadillo on Crappy Wednesdays to drink cheap beer and stir up a little action.

When there was a break in the loud music, Trent Senser asked, "Where's Drago? Why isn't he celebrating your birthday with us?"

"He's got his chauffeur's hat on tonight."

"Meaning what?"

"Mizz Royce is out of town and Mr. Wright has a meeting tonight, so they asked Drago to drive JayCee to The Civic Theatre. Their friend Jean is singing in *White Christmas*, and JayCee can't drive at night, so Drago has to do it."

"Is he going to go in with her or sit in the car?"

"Mizz Royce gave him a ticket too."

"But not you?"

"Oh, yeah, she said she'd give me a ticket, but I wasn't in the mood to be with that girl on my birthday."

Trent and Cricket Grinderman exchanged meaningful looks. Cricket nodded almost imperceptibly.

"He's been spending a lot of time with that girl," Trent said, taking Lucy's hand. "You know that, don't you?"

"You mean the article she did about the Scrapyard? They weren't *together* for that."

"How about the lunch they shared. She was all over him."

"They were definitely together *then*," Cricket added.

"What lunch? And what do you mean, all over him?"

"Buffalo Wild Wings, last month. They were sitting on the patio, sitting close, leaning into each other, whispering, laughing, holding hands."

Lucy pulled her hand away from Trent's. "I don't believe you."

Cricket looked at Trent for confirmation. "We were inside, in a booth next to a window, with Sally and Alan. Ask them if you don't believe us."

"That makes no sense. The girl is jail bait, and so skinny -- not Drago's type at all."

Cricket caught Trent's glance. Time to change the subject. "If we didn't already say so, Lucy, you look good. How much weight have you lost?"

About twenty pounds, which still makes me a size eighteen, and thanks for asking. The gift card Trent and Cricket gave her to Victoria's Secret was the last straw. There wasn't an item in that store that would fit her, and they knew it. If it was meant to be an incentive to keep dieting -- well, it was more like a rebuke than a gesture of hope, a confirmation that she was hopelessly competing with a rich, pretty, and very slim young girl.

That night, when Drago got home, Lucy lit into him about JayCee Wright. The twins were staying the night with her mother, so finally she could do some yelling, call him ugly names, without being labeled a bad mother for fighting in front of her kids. The puppies were so scared they ran to their crate.

Drago didn't yield an inch. He denied everything -- once -- without explanation but refused to go over and over the same ground, as Lucy clearly wanted to do. He avoided her accusatory eyes, apologized for nothing. Though beyond angry, he was mindful of his mother's disgust with men who hit their wives, so he didn't lash out, either with words or fists, though every inch of him felt like it. If it hadn't been so cold and so late at night, he would have gone for a run. Instead, he went downstairs, ran on the treadmill awhile, then, with the help of a couple of beers, watched a NatGeo program where a pride of lions stalked and killed an old elephant. He rooted for the lions.

He hated his life. He hadn't gotten a raise in over a year and was always short of money. The twins reminded him of ravenous baby birds, their mouths locked in open position, chirping their constant demands. The baby-proofed house was unfit for a man; in particular, the lock on the toilet lids sent him into paroxysms of rage. His pretty wife was perpetually too tired to fool around and most days didn't even comb her hair. How the hell had his life taken this turn?

If I'm going to be accused of doing something bad, why not actually do it? With that question in mind, he made a temporary bed on the couch.

35

Evidence
Friday, November 19, 2010

Todd was not without feelings. The death of that poor girl was a terrible shame. Her parents must be suffering the torments of hell. But still, a mystery was always exciting.

With a twinge of guilt, he recalled the exhilaration he felt that night when questioned by the police about what the girl was wearing and how she was acting minutes before she must have died. If he'd known the girl was so near death, he'd have taken more notice of her. His exhilaration at being so important to the investigation was tempered by his realization that he'd make a very bad detective, who he'd read once continually memorizes every little detail of his surroundings just in case something is important later. But he couldn't even remember what the girl had been wearing at the party. He knew two things for certain, however: she hadn't said a thing about meeting a boy at the stone bridge at midnight, and he had very definitely set the alarm, so if it didn't go off when the girl slipped out of the house, he had no explanation.

Still, he was more upset by the damage that the emergency vehicles had done to the Wrights' property than anything else about that terrible Halloween night. He would have to wait until Spring to restore the grounds to their former glory, but on a mild November day he decided to see if rolling the ground near the creek was a worthy undertaking. The ground was not yet frozen but it wasn't malleable either. With distaste, he also noticed the damage done to several of the lilacs he'd planted earlier in the year. What a clumsy bunch the emergency workers were, like an invading army heedlessly trampling other people's property into a muddy mess.

It was an unusually clear, sunny, windless day in Fort Wayne. He wished he was out pheasant hunting for a change. He looked up, where dozens of jet contrails hung motionless in the air, painted in criss-crossing patterns across the blue dome of the sky. Just then the Parkview medical helicopter rattled overhead on its way north, and he heard sirens in the distance. Damn! Why couldn't tragedies stop for a few minutes?

He got down on his knees to examine the deep ruts near the golf path leading to the stone bridge, when he saw something glinting in the weak autumn sun. He took off his canvas gloves and dug into the mud with bare fingers.

It was a heavy silver chain. At one end was a bow, at the other a loop from which hung a puffy heart engraved with a crown. The puffy heart was damaged, smooshed on one side. Had it been here in the dirt Halloween night? If it had, the cops could be excused for overlooking it because it would have been buried under truck tires.

He got to his feet and looked back at the house. He should take it to Miss Royce, or even the police. Given the place he'd found it, maybe the chain had something to do with that poor girl's death. Had she been wearing it? What if it was evidence of something?

He looked at the chain again, pushed the bow through the loop to see how the necklace would be worn. He thought he'd seen it somewhere before, but where? Or was he just imagining things in his zeal to help the police? More than likely, the necklace had nothing whatever to do with the events of Halloween night. It had probably been lost by a lady golfer months ago. Perhaps he should check with Mr. Pitt to see if anyone had reported lost jewelry.

On second thought, maybe he shouldn't be so quick to show

it to anybody. He'd made a fateful mistake, after all, with the ID bracelet that belonged to Phyl's dead husband.

Phyl would know what to do.

36

It'll Turn Up
Friday, November 19, 2010

When Sadie walked into JayCee's bedroom Friday after lunch, she was appalled at the mess. There were so many clothes tossed on the furniture, so many garments hanging out of dresser drawers, so many hoodies and sweat pants heaped on the floor of the closet, so much underwear on the bathroom floor, she didn't know where to start. Which items were clean, which were dirty? To be on the safe side, she'd do what she always did: gather everything up for the laundry. How could the girl be so careless with her treasure-trove of fine clothes?

The floor and furniture were littered with other stuff too: stray shoes and boots; shopping bags still containing tissue, sales tags, and receipts; gum wrappers; sticky glasses half-full of raspberry lemonade; smeared bowls that once held popcorn; cookie crumbs; spiral notebooks with dog-eared pages; crumpled Kleenex and soiled cosmetic pads; open tubes of hand cream; nail polish bottles not screwed shut; and a few dog treats. Animal-print throws were dropped in odd places, remote controls half-hidden by seat cushions. Clearly Miss Royce's threats to suspend privileges if the girl didn't keep her room clean had no teeth.

Miss Royce had instructed Sadie to make another thorough inspection of the bedroom, study, and bathroom to find a Juicy Couture silver necklace that JayCee was frantic to find. Miss

Royce had given it to her new daughter the day she arrived in early July and the girl had hardly taken it off after that.

Neither Miss Royce nor her daughter was sure when it had gone missing, and the girl couldn't remember ever taking it off. Because the clasp was just a toggle, the necklace might have snagged on something and come off without JayCee ever noticing. The necklace might be found tucked under a seat cushion or caught on a drapery or jumbled up with sweaters in a dresser drawer, even caught on a muffler. Sadie was to leave no stone unturned. She was to poke her nose everywhere.

The inspection and cleaning were going to take hours. The mirrored shelves in the bathroom held a jumble of bottles -- perfumes, body sprays, bronzers, body washes, things Sadie had never heard of -- each needing to be wiped clean. The bookshelves in the study were heaped with books, DVDs, CDs, stacks of paper, and knickknacks, all needing to be dusted, sorted, and repositioned. The desk drawers were stuffed with paper clips, pens, rulers, cords, instruction manuals, and discs. The dresser was overflowing with wadded-up undergarments, t-shirts, camisoles, and sweaters.

How the girl had had enough time to assemble so many possessions in just four or five months was beyond Sadie. And why she didn't take better care of them was a puzzle. But bringing order out of chaos, cleanliness out of filth -- well, that was what Sadie loved best.

Hours later, prone on the floor, Sadie began her inspection under the girl's four-poster bed. There, after removing stray shoes and empty shopping bags, she found a messenger bag stenciled with strange phrases, like "Wake up Alone." For goodness' sake, how else should a girl her age wake up but alone? What were teenaged girls thinking of these days? She pulled the bag toward her, got up, and laid the stained thing on the bed. Though she'd been instructed to leave no stone unturned, it went against the grain to open up someone else's bag. Still, with a frown, she pulled up the flap, opened the zipper, and dumped out the contents.

A marble pen and pencil set, sporting a little brass plaque, badly scuffed so only a couple letters were legible. A one-quart plastic bag of bottles -- Advil, Excedrin, Midol, Aleve, aspirin. Why were they not in the medicine cabinet? she wondered, but decided against removing them from the messenger bag. A rabbit's foot key chain with three keys and something called an EpiPen attached. A half pack of Juicy Fruit gum. A crumpled tissue. A spray bottle of lens cleaner. A tube of mascara still in its package, unopened. Two pennies. A linty piece of hard candy. An uncapped ballpoint pen and a heavily chewed yellow pencil with a broken lead. Some rubber bands and a scrunchy. Two blank pieces of lined paper torn out of a spiral notebook. Some loose plastic beads. But no Juicy Couture silver necklace.

Sadie replaced the contents, closed the zipper, folded the flap, and knelt to tuck the bag under the bed, then realized she had to dust the floor first. Finally, the last thing she did before leaving the girl's bedroom suite was to tuck the messenger bag back under the bed, as close as she could remember to the spot where it had originally been.

After putting away her cleaning supplies, she found Mrs. Whitlow in the butler's pantry, polishing a copper frying pan. Todd was sitting on a stool in the corner, apparently doing nothing. Sadie knew they'd been talking before she entered, but they went silent the moment she appeared. "I turned the girl's room upside down. If that silver necklace is there, it's invisible."

Mrs. Whitlow smiled. "I'm sure you did your best, Sadie, so don't worry about it. If you say it's not in her room, then it's not in her room." Glancing at Todd, she put her hand in her apron pocket. "Someday, it'll turn up at the most unexpected time, you watch."

37

Puppy Training
Saturday, November 20, 2010

On the Saturday afternoon before Thanksgiving, Trude Weide was thrilled that Drago was bringing Louie and Freddie to her house near the Canyons for some puppy training. When Drago had first appeared in her life at the Scrapyard over a year ago, she was wary, prepared to dislike him, maybe teach him a lesson or two about who was the real boss. He was too young for the job, too cocky to be an apprentice. He knew nothing about scrap. If he'd been working for Rolie Royce ever since high school, as Nate Grabbendorf said he had, then Drago Bott was no doubt a shady character, streetwise, shifty, selling dope, collecting debts, using muscle instead of brains. She'd have to watch him like a hawk.

The first couple weeks had indeed been rocky. Drago argued with Nate and ignored her. He strutted around the Yard as if he owned it, arguing with everybody. He entered her private little office without knocking, as if he had every right to invade her space any time he pleased. He pissed off her boss so much that Nate ditched him as often as he could.

Then, suddenly, things were different. Something must have happened in his private life, because one day, out of the blue, Drago was a different man. He deferred to Nate. He brought her treats from Dunkin' Donuts, drank coffee with her before going out to the Yard, humbly listened to her instructions on checking driver identification, recording license plates, and inventorying loads of scrap. He acted grateful for her tips on how drivers tried to cheat the scales when scrap was weighed, how he could tell a load of copper wire had been stolen rather than bought or found. When Nate started calling him Pup, he acted as if it was a compliment.

Trude had been engaged once, many years ago, but never married, never had any children -- in fact, never wanted any. Her Shelties were her children. Thus she surprised herself by discovering that with Drago she felt like a mother. The feeling was deeply comforting. On the surface he was angry and rebellious, but at heart he was good. And when she learned of the abuse he'd once taken at the hands of his father, she was moved.

Lately, though, his anger had surfaced again, expressed in a tightly clenched jaw and curt words. He was impatient with everything and everybody. His morning conversations with her were larded with complaints about every aspect of his life. He did more talking than listening. Looking back, she thought his new, more cynical rage had made its appearance shortly after the twins were born.

Adopting the Sheltie puppies, she was sure, was a good thing. Perhaps a turn-around was in the works. To her way of thinking, dogs were God's gracious gift to mankind -- loyal, smart, ready to serve. They were healing companions. Just petting a dog, she'd read somewhere, lowered a person's blood pressure, and if anybody needed lower blood pressure, it was Drago.

He'd warned her that the Wrights' new daughter, JayCee, would be accompanying him, together with another student to take pictures for a feature story the girl was writing for the school newspaper. Being a very private person, Trude was hesitant to accept that much public attention, but because it was Drago requesting her indulgence, she said to come ahead.

When the boy with the camera introduced himself as Joey DeWitt, Trude took a second discreet look. She recognized the face but not the name. She'd seen him with Drago and the girl at the Scrapyard the day he took pictures of the auto crusher. The boy didn't say much, didn't look her in the eye. She'd read about him in the newspapers after he found his girlfriend dead under the stone bridge at Gretna Green on Halloween. He didn't look like a boy who would do violence to a girl in the heat of the moment, though that very possibility had been broached by Drago when they discussed the death over their morning cup of coffee.

"I'll bet the girl said something nasty and he lost it."

"What makes you think that, Drago? Do you know the boy?"

"No. But I know women. Their tongues are like knives."

"Oh, come on. You're too smart to think like that. Is your mother's tongue like a knife? Or mine?"

He'd smiled sheepishly, said he guessed not, and changed the subject.

Twice before at the Scrapyard, she'd met the girl, JayCee Wright. At the Scrapyard, she'd been wearing blue jeans, torn at the knees, a distressed denim jacket over an off-white Henley, a Colts bill cap, and lace-up work boots. Perhaps she thought she was blending in with the Yard workers. Today, however, she was dressed in a fringed suede jacket and brown western boots, her wild red hair partially hidden by a cowboy hat. Her leather pants were so tight her skinny legs looked like they'd been painted. Were those her normal clothes, or was that a costume she'd adopted for an afternoon in the country? She was like an actress, dressing for each part as it came up. What normal woman did that? Or was that how adolescent girls did things these days?

The girl was perfectly charming, shaking Trude's hand, admiring the dog kennel (though she wrinkled her nose at the smell), asking if she could pet Lord and Lady MacDuff, her breeding pair.

What really struck Trude, though, was how the girl flirted with both Drago and Joey, playing one off against the other, as if trying to make one of them jealous. The girl touched both men every chance she got, talked too much, laughed too loudly. Though JayCee clearly liked being the center of attention, she merely watched from the sidelines as Trude put Drago and the puppies through their paces. At the end, however, the girl shamelessly insisted on posing with Drago and one of the puppies as if she were the dog trainer.

Trude was torn between admiring the girl's feminine chutzpah and alarm at Drago's response. She knew some men, like Isaac Royce, her old boss, were true-blue, but many, like her former fiancé, were dogs at heart. Much as she loved dogs, she hoped her darling Pup, vulnerable as he was, wasn't one of them.

38

Never a Lush
Monday, November 22, 2010

Sadie couldn't believe it. For the third time in a few months, she found a stash of bottles in a Walmart plastic sack under Jean Arnold's desk. At least there were only three big ones this time, maybe half a dozen little ones, so she didn't have to find Todd to carry them away, but still. Why didn't the woman hide each bottle in the paper trash when she finished it off? Or take it home? Then no one would know she was drinking at work.

As she was leaving the office, the plastic bag in one hand, her cleaning supply caddy in the other, Miss Royce appeared in the courtyard.

"All done in there, Sadie?"

"Yes, ma'am."

Miss Royce smiled. "What's all that clinking I hear?"

"Bottles."

Miss Royce looked skeptical. "From the office?"

Sadie nodded.

"Let me have a look."

Sadie set her caddy on the ground, then opened up the plastic bag.

Miss Royce took out one of the bottles and read the label. "Clos du Bois." She took out another bottle. "Grey Goose." Then the third bottle. "Bacardi White Rum." She shook the sack. "And five tiny bottles of vodka." She looked at Sadie. "I buy all these brands. I keep little bottles in the guest suites. Is someone stealing from me?"

"I don't know."

"What are these doing in the office?"

"Don't know that either."

"Where did you find these bottles?"

"Under Miss Arnold's desk."

"Has this ever happened before?"

"Several times, but I only found three big bottles today. Last time, I found lots more."

Miss Royce looked stunned. "Why didn't you tell me before? Wine and liquor don't belong in an office."

"They don't belong anywhere, you ask me, but live and let live."

"So I take it you never told anybody."

"Just Todd. Once there were so many bottles he had to get a box to carry them all out."

"Is he here?"

"In the garage, I think."

Miss Royce looked at her watch. "Tell you what, Sadie, put that sack back where you found it. And don't lock up. I'm going to find Todd, then I'm coming back to look at some papers, so I'll clear up this mess once Jean gets here."

When Jean arrived at eight-thirty, she wasn't surprised to find Lexie already in the office, seated in her guest chair, but she was startled by her boss' expression. "Something wrong?"

"Not sure. Take your coat off, get yourself settled."

"If you're wondering if I've got your plane tickets for tomorrow's trip to Toronto, I do." Jean hung her coat on a hanger in the tiny closet, then put her briefcase on the desk and sat down. She reached for a folder. "Your passport's in here too, plus five hundred dollars in Canadian currency, just in case. You'll be picked up at Toronto Pearson International by . . . ."

"I'm not worried about Canada. I'm worried about that bag under your desk."

"What bag?"

"Have a look."

Jean rolled back her chair and ducked her head. "What's that?"

"Open it up."

Jean scrunched down to retrieve the bag, then put it on her desk and opened it. She almost jumped. "Wine bottle. Vodka bottle. Rum bottle." She looked at Lexie, dumbfounded. "What are they doing here?"

"Somebody in this office appears to be drinking at work."

"Well, it's not me, you know that."

"No, I don't know that, Jean. Unless there's another lush in here."

"I'm not a lush. I was never a lush."

"Before Hazelden, you were."

Jean waggled her head noncommittally. "Whatever I was then, I'm not now. I admit I have an occasional drink, but only when I'm with Dover and never more than two." Lexie's silence hurt her to the core. "You don't believe me?"

"I thought alcoholics weren't supposed to take a drop."

"It's complicated, but I don't think I'm really an alcoholic. I can handle a few drinks and stop. And I never drink during the day, or alone, and certainly not on the job."

"I'd like to believe you, Jean, but the bottles suggest you drink in secret, in here, and a lot more than you're claiming."

"I don't know where these came from."

"Todd tells me this is the third time since July that Sadie has found empty wine and liquor bottles under your desk. A few months ago there were so many he filled an empty wine case with them."

"I don't know what you're talking about. Honestly."

"I need some time to think this through, Jean, but out of caution I'm suspending you today, without pay."

"For how long?"

"Until I get to the bottom of this."

Jean jumped when Todd suddenly appeared outside the glass door and knocked. "What's he doing here?"

"He'll escort you to your car."

Jean was astonished. "You mean you already decided I was guilty before talking to me?"

"I don't think there's any mystery here. Empty out your briefcase, take your coat, and leave. We'll be in touch."

"You're firing me, just like that?"

"No. I'm suspending you without pay."

"Lexie! This isn't like you. You're leaping to conclusions."

"I'm protecting myself and my family and all my other employees. You lied to me about staying on the wagon. I wouldn't have paid for Hazelden on any other condition. Now, if I were you, I'd start thinking about how you can prove to me you're still on the wagon and those bottles never touched your hands. I don't know what that proof would be, but I'm sure alcoholics are good at that kind of thing."

Todd felt very important, escorting Jean Arnold to her car, acting as Miss Royce's security guard. But he felt sad too. Though he saw Miss Arnold almost every day, he didn't really know her. Still, she was always pleasant, a hard worker. The poor woman was crying so hard he was afraid she couldn't see out the windshield.

He watched her car until it was out of sight before closing the gate to the auto courtyard. When he'd started working for the Wrights just before Christmas last year, it was a peaceful, well-ordered place. The greatest excitement came from Henry's depredations to the landscape or a late furniture delivery. Now the drama just kept coming, one mystery after another. It was like living in a soap opera.

39

Gambles

Tuesday, November 23, 2010

Staying in a perfectly appointed suite at the five-star Hazelton Hotel in Toronto should be a treat. The balcony allows a breath of fresh air. The art is stunning. The food at One is superb. The bathroom gleams, the fireplace warms, the furniture invites lounging.

But the hotel's name reminds me of Jean's rehab, a very sore subject. Nothing in either my professional or private life is going well.

The investment I've made in TransCanada might not pay off the way I thought. The presenters at the investors' conference said all the right things about the Keystone XL Pipeline, but the rumbling just below the surface is that the project might get stopped on the high plains of Nebraska, of all places. I'd never heard of the Ogallala Aquifer before, but now I've heard more than I ever wanted to know about it. Everything seems to depend on how Prime Minister Harper's meeting with President Obama goes. Well, not everything. I guess we'll just have to deal with the Chinese if everything goes to hell in the lower forty-eight, but that's not even remotely what I had in mind when I made the investment.

If anything, my private life is more of a gamble than the pipeline. JayCee's best friend is dead and her next best friend, Joey, labors under a cloud of suspicion that just won't go away. Jean Arnold is drinking again. Physically, I don't feel like myself at all, though my Obi-Wan Kenobi says this pregnancy is progressing just as it should be. And, worst of all, my husband is furious with me.

It wasn't an hour after I suspended Jean that Steve called me. "You fired Jean?"

"Not exactly."

"But you accused her of drinking on the job and booted her out. You had her marched out to her car like a criminal."

"Again, not exactly. Let me explain."

"She and Dover are in my office, sitting right here in front of me. She's hysterical, which I don't blame her for."

It was my turn to be furious. "She ran to you? You're taking her side without hearing mine?"

"Who else would she turn to? I don't go off half-cocked."

"I'd say you just did," I yelled as I ended the call.

We continued arguing last night. In my opinion, my husband's position is entirely selfish. He doesn't want trouble with Dover, who is very protective of Jean. I pointed out that a golf and tennis pro isn't all that vital during the winter months, so if Dover wants to resign over this fracas, fine. There are plenty of men in Fort Wayne who'd take his job, probably for less money. But Steve argued that Dover's athletic skill and attractive personality bring in members, he's in the middle of complicated plans for next year's golf outings and tournaments, and the pro shop, under his management, actually makes money.

"So I'm supposed to sacrifice my operation for yours, is that it, Steve?"

But the worst accusation Steve leveled against me was that I've been unfair. Jean might be telling the truth. Give her the benefit of the doubt. Start by assuming the best about her, not the worst. Anybody could have put those bottles under Jean's desk, he said.

At that stupid statement, I scoffed. I pointed out that the only people who have access to the office are the people in our household. Just which one of them did he suspect of something so irrational and under-handed? Of all the people in our household, was it reasonable to believe the culprit was the alcoholic who admitted she was drinking again or someone else? He had no answer to that.

I am so sick of alcohol I could scream, not just because it smells bad to me at this point and I can't drink it anyway lest I harm the baby, but because twice in the last month it's surfaced as the source of a major problem. A couple weeks after Libby was found dead under the stone bridge, her mother asked if she could meet with me. I told her that of course I'd meet with her, though I dreaded talking to her. The girl had been drinking in my house, after all, and though I hadn't provided the vodka, I felt responsible.

My dread was wasted energy. To my astonishment, Mary Stuart apologized to me! "I don't know where Libby got the vodka, but I know it's caused you trouble. I hope everything works out with the police. I told them I don't know where she got it but there's no reason to think you provided it."

I assured her my troubles were nothing compared to the loss she'd suffered. She talked for a long time about how blind she was to Libby's drinking, how she thought she knew her daughter but obviously didn't. "Once, in August, after she had a sleep-over with your daughter, she came home the next morning and wasn't herself. She was pale and trembly and had a terrible headache. She slept all day. I suppose I should have realized then that something was very wrong, but she said she was getting her period, so . . . ."

"Pardon me for asking, but since I've not been a mother very long, I need to know what's normal. Did you ever go through her room to see if there was anything in there that gave you pause?"

"I didn't. I wanted a relationship based on trust. Her father and I did everything we could think of to raise her right, and at some point you just have to assume you've built your house on rock rather than sand. But a week ago, I decided I had to clean up her room. It took everything I had to just to go in. The room smells like her. You can't imagine how bad I felt . . . ."

"No, I can't," I murmured.

"Anyway, I found nothing out of the ordinary. No little liquor bottles. No cigarettes. No drugs. No condoms. Nothing."

"Most adolescent girls keep a diary, don't they? Did you -- ."

"Find one? Yes, but I can't bear to break the lock."

Why? There might be a clue in there. "How about her computer? Was she messaging anybody? Or her phone? Did she have a Facebook page?"

"I'm no good at all with electronics and haven't touched her computer. We let the police take her phone but if they found anything, we haven't heard."

"How about the ring I've heard about?"

"The one Joey gave her?"

I nodded.

"It's not there."

"Do you really think Joey took it?"

She teared up. "No. I already called his mother and apologized. I should never have accused him of taking it. I was just angry, lashing out. It's probably at the bottom of the creek, don't you think?"

"Why is it so important to you?"

"It was something she treasured, that's why. It signifies the good times in her life. Joey was very good to her, you know. I never knew what broke them up -- Libby wouldn't talk about it -- but I was sure they'd get back together someday, even if it was just as friends. He must feel so bad, poor boy, for things to end the way they did."

"Have the police given you any hint of what they think happened?"

"No. Rob calls every other day to just to make sure the case doesn't get put on the back burner, and they assure him it's front and center, but if there's progress, they're not telling us."

We parted with mutual assurances that we'd do what we could for each other, but in fact we haven't talked since.

Before I went to bed, I called JayCee to see how she was doing. She said that Dad had taken her to the Club for dinner.

"You two ate by yourself?"

"No. Dover ate with us."

"Really?"

"Yah. It was boring."

"Where was Jean?"

"Mom, you're getting senile. She's in the show at the Civic, remember?"

"Oh, right. So what did Dad and Dover talk about?"

"You."

"I don't suppose they had anything good to say about me."

"I, like, stuck up for you."

"Well, thank you. I suppose Dover's sure Jean hasn't been drinking and I'm just way out in left field, thinking those bottles Sadie found in her office mean she's hitting the wine again."

"Dover's in denial, big-time. I reminded him that Jean's a good actress."

"You didn't."

"He's a turd, you know. I wish Dad hadn't hired him and I'm glad Jean's gone."

"JayCee! It isn't nice to call people names. And despite everything, I'm not glad Jean's gone. I can't bear to think of trying to find someone to replace her."

"Whatever."

"So, are you getting ready for bed?"

"I'm going to go downstairs first, make myself some cocoa. It helps me sleep."

"Well, sleep tight and dream good dreams."

I couldn't sleep myself, so, after ordering some tea to be sent to my room, I wrapped myself in a blanket and sat on the balcony for an hour, mesmerized by the lights of the city.

★ ★ ★ ★ ★

But JayCee did not make cocoa for one or go right to sleep. She was not alone.

40

Thanksgiving
Thursday, November 25, 2010

★★★Among Lexie's friends and employees, the only home in which Norman Rockwell's Thanksgiving took place, roughly as he pictured it, was at Drago and Lucy's house in Autumn Ridge. Drago inserted every leaf he found in the basement into the dining room table the Wrights had left behind; now it seated twelve in relative comfort. Lucy set the table with her wedding china and glassware. Phyllis and Ruth roasted the biggest turkey they could find. Ruth's oldest son, a carpenter, carved it perfectly. Lucy's mother brought a homemade cranberry relish that nobody but her touched. Todd brought pumpkin pies he made himself; the twin boys liked the filling so much they had it in their ears and between their toes before they were done. Lucy's father brought a case of sweet Zinfandel, half of which was gone by evening.

The conversation was light and pleasant. There were no fights. But Lucy and Drago never spoke a word to each other, never looked at each other. Phyllis watched them out of the corner of her eye, wondering what had happened. She'd seen the pillow and crumpled blanket on the sofa in the downstairs media room and knew what it meant. It wasn't like her son not to tell her what was going on in his life.

★★★Dover and Jean drove to Warsaw so she could meet his

parents for the first time. It was awkward, as all such introductions are. It would have been boring as well except that Dover's father, a fireman, tried out a new turkey fryer on the deck. He hadn't been back in the house five minutes when Mrs. Pitt smelled smoke.

"Oh, my God, Rufus, the deck's on fire."

Rufus ran out, found a shovel, and pushed the fryer over onto some juniper bushes lining a wooden fence extending from the garage. The fire grew hotter and hotter, spreading in a flash from the fryer to the deck to the junipers along the fence and then to the garage. Swearing and sweating, Rufus finally called 911 for help.

Not only was the turkey destroyed, but so were the deck and the garage, not to mention Rufus' pride when his firehouse buddies showed up to put out the conflagration. The whole house smelled so bad the Pitts couldn't stay in it and had to leave for a motel room.

On the drive back to Fort Wayne, Jean said, "That was the most spectacular fire I've ever seen. I bet the smoke could be seen from Highway 30. They're lucky the whole house didn't burn down."

Dover smiled grimly. "Usually we don't provide that much entertainment with dinner. I wonder if Applebee's is open."

★★★At two in the afternoon, the Gretna Green clubhouse was crowded with families who wanted the day off rather than a day slaving in the kitchen. The Thanksgiving buffet was lavish, the table decorations redolent of old-fashioned Thanksgiving themes -- gourds carved into horns of plenty from which spilled colorful mums, apples, and cranberries. The wait staff was dressed either as Puritans or Indians. Steve had hired a string quartet to play selections from Vivaldi, Vaughan Williams, and Copeland.

At JayCee's insistence, the Wrights were dining with the DeWitts. She knew Joey would refuse to eat in public any other way, she said. "With me, he feels safe. He's sure everybody's looking at him like a murderer."

"Nobody really thinks that, do they?" Lexie asked. "Even Libby's mother doesn't think that."

"You ever heard of the Untouchables, that caste in India that everybody avoids because they're the only ones allowed to shovel shit?"

"JayCee! Language."

"Well, have you heard of them or not?"

"Of course."

"That's what Joey is at school. He's, like, the shit-shoveler."

Lexie didn't know whether to laugh or cry at that colorful, if crude, description. But now, on the actual day of Thanksgiving, as a good hostess, it was her duty to keep the conversation light and entertaining. It was uphill work -- like shoveling shit, she thought ruefully.

JayCee couldn't help tweaking Steve about the classical music. "Dad, could you have chosen more boring stuff for them to play? We're not dead, after all. It's so, like, morgue music. Can't they play some show tunes or something with a beat? And the costumes the waiters are wearing are *so* lame." She picked at the food. "The turkey's dry and the ham's salty, Dad. There's nothing here to eat. Next time, let's serve some veggie pizza."

Steve and his daughter argued amicably until Steve gave in about the music. Right after dessert, to the sound of *Moon River,* Lexie excused herself on the pretext of needing a nap.

It wasn't a pretext. She was tired of her husband's unwillingness to take her part against Jean. Even without that, she would have been exhausted by the DeWitts' joylessness, Joey's silence, and JayCee's uninformed criticisms of everything she saw, heard, or tasted.

41

Good Friends
Saturday, November 27, 2010

Saturday was a fine day for pheasant-hunting, so as they did every year, Steve and Dave Powers spent the day walking through fields of corn stubble, flushing out ring-necked pheasants to shoot for dinner. They were accompanied by Leland, Dave's son, who was embarking on his first hunting expedition, and Klaus, Dave's German short-haired pointer, the proud veteran of many such shoots. Klaus was wearing a canvas vest and a satisfied expression on his face as he returned a dead pheasant to his master.

Steve laughed. "Look at that boy. Klaus thinks he's in charge."

Dave took the pheasant from the pointer and put it in a net bag. "Well, he is, isn't he? You try finding a dead pheasant and carrying it back in your mouth. I bought him his own game stamp just so he'd know how important he is. Next year I'm teaching him how to shoot a shotgun."

"You are?" Leland asked.

"Just kidding," Dave said, ruffling his son's hair. "But I swear Klaus could do it. He's been eyeing the car keys a little hard too. One of these days I'm going to have to explain why the dog was driving."

Very late in the afternoon, after bagging their limit of two birds apiece, they headed toward the Club, where Steve had a chef waiting to clean and cook the birds. Their wives would join them for a pheasant dinner in a private dining room. Then they'd retire to Steve and Lexie's house to watch a movie.

It was the women's turn to choose the movie and they had decided on *film noir*, the first Nick and Nora Charles movie, *The Thin Man*, based on a 1934 Dashiell Hammett novel first published in *Redbook*. When Leland saw that it was in black and white, he asked if he could go to the game room, and Lexie said of course he could. She told him she was sorry that JayCee was out with friends; otherwise, he'd have company.

All through the movie, Lexie and Sheila kept pointing and whispering about the clothes and jewelry, the hair styles, the grand décor, the posh supper clubs. Asta the wire-haired fox terrier was a hit. Everyone laughed at the repartee. Their favorite exchange was when Nora said, "I read where you were shot five times in the tabloids," and Nick replied, "Not true. He didn't come anywhere near my tabloids."

But it was the alcohol that caught Dave's attention. "That film is set during Prohibition, yet Nick not only drinks privately -- a lot -- but has no trouble ordering martinis in a club and even offering a cop a drink. The cop doesn't say a thing."

"You're thinking there might have been some hypocrisy in that era?" Steve asked.

"Not just that, but I'm thinking how prissy we're getting again. Now, you can't even let your underaged kid have a sip of beer in the privacy of your own home."

Sheila elbowed him. "Oh, right. Sorry," he said, with an apologetic look at Lexie. "I wasn't commenting on the vodka bottles in Libby Stuart's purse."

"Or maybe you were, Dave, but in the nicest way possible. I didn't supply them, they weren't lying around here, yet they were found here. Even if I'd supplied them, which I assuredly didn't, it shouldn't be anybody's business but ours and the girl's family since everything happened in this house, not in public. Who's in charge here -- me or the State?" Lexie paused. "I don't know if I'm allowed to pry, but are you satisfied as a detective that we didn't provide alcohol to Libby?"

"I'm satisfied that at this moment I can't prove where the bottles came from. The Stuarts are tee-totalers and they're just as puzzled as you are. None of the bottles had the girl's fingerprints on them. They were all clean as a whistle. But since the girl's alcohol blood level was very high, she either drank the contents or found some other strong drink."

"Would she have been considered drunk when she went into the water?"

"You could say that, I suppose. With that much alcohol in her, she would have been staggering and slurring her speech."

"Was she dead when she hit the water?"

"No."

"No?" Lexie was shocked.

"She'd been strangled, probably with her own scarf, but that apparently didn't kill her because there was water in her lungs."

"Had she been sexually . . . ?"

"Molested? Raped? No."

"Robbed?"

"Probably not, unless you assume she was wearing a gold ring her mother claimed she always wore and is now missing. No cash or credit cards on her; they were in the purse she left here, according to her mother. We found her cell phone in the water. She was still wearing stud earrings and a watch, and though neither was expensive, a robber desperate for, say, drug money might have taken them anyway, just on the off chance they were worth something. So robbery isn't a likely motive."

Steve glanced at Lexie. "We were sort of assuming it was a sexual crime. Maybe a crime of opportunity."

Dave grinned at Steve. "Not a bad guess. I don't know if you know this, brother, but there are two registered sex offenders living at Gretna Green, but both have alibis for Halloween and both alibis checked out."

Steve looked astonished. "You're kidding. I mean, about sex offenders living here."

"I'm not. Get on the computer if you don't believe me. But don't get too alarmed. Some guys get on the registry merely for urinating in public or bonking their underage girlfriends, so you have to find out if the registration means anything."

"You mean when we peed in the tree line today, we were breaking the law?"

Dave nodded. "We were. That's what I mean about getting more prissy. Ever since humans were human, hunters have been relieving themselves behind a tree without worrying about jail time. Once upon a time being a little pissy was normal, now being very prissy is. So, this afternoon, if I'd had my cop hat on, I could have arrested you."

"And yourself."

"Awkward."

"But what else could we have done, Dave? Cornfields aren't stocked with Port-a-Potties."

"Blown our bladders to pieces, I suppose. Lawmakers like to see a good bladder explosion from time to time. Convinces them they need to make more laws."

"So," Lexie said, "returning to Libby, the suspect is still Joey DeWitt?"

Dave shook his head. "I suppose that's the word civilians use, but to us he's a witness -- maybe, depending on your point of view, a person of interest. Nothing more. Not now, anyway."

"But some people apparently think he's guilty. What will it take to clear him?"

"Finding the person who tried to strangle Libby Stuart and probably pushed her over the bridge. If it was a random act, that's going to be tough."

"Any reason to think it was random?"

"No. It's just a possibility we have to keep in mind."

"Well, it scares me," Lexie said, "to think anything that violent could occur so close to our house, random or not. I'm having more cameras and motion detectors installed."

"I hear Joey's being shunned at school," Sheila said.

"I guess you could call it that. But JayCee keeps him company. She's practically defiant about it. Drives him to school, sits in classes with him, takes him along on her newspaper work. He's tutoring her in chemistry. Outside of school, she plays tennis with him, takes him bowling, makes sure he gets out of the house. He and his parents actually ate Thanksgiving dinner with us at the Club. She said Joey wouldn't have eaten in public any other way."

"I'd call that being a good friend. She's suffering with him."

"You're right, Sheila."

"You know who else turned out to be good friends?"

"Who?"

"Henry and Klaus. Look at them. Sleeping on either side of the fireplace, like living andirons, peaceful as can be. Can you believe it? Two big alpha dogs like that -- I was sure one of them would have to kill the other."

Lexie sighed, glancing at her husband. "Peaceful co-existence. Everyone should experience it."

42

Everything's a Blank
Thursday, December 23, 2010

Two days before Christmas, during the school break, JayCee was scheduled to help Sherill and Cathy wrap gifts at Christopher James, the menswear store in Covington Plaza. Joey would go with her, as usual, to take pictures for her feature article. But at nine o'clock, the girl still hadn't appeared downstairs. Her toast and hot chocolate were growing cold.

Mizz Royce was in her courtyard office, so Phyllis went upstairs to see if the girl was ready to leave. The room was surprisingly cold. She pulled aside a curtain on the four-poster, but seeing no head on a pillow, moved to the bathroom, where she knocked on the door. When there was no response, she gently pushed the door open. The bathroom was empty, the shower stall dry. Moving to the study, she noticed that the French doors to the veranda were slightly ajar. She walked out and looked around. Then she reentered the study.

Phyllis was puzzled. "JayCee, are you here?"

No response.

Returning to the bedroom, Phyllis stumbled over a panther statue. She picked it up and replaced it on the dresser. Seeing a tiny movement in the bed, she lifted the zebra-striped duvet. The girl was lying there, naked and curled into a ball. She didn't open her eyes or speak.

Phyllis was shocked at what she saw: a dark bruise on the girl's upper arm, more bruises on her hip and long scratches down her leg. When Phyllis gently pulled the girl's hair aside, she saw a goose egg near her temple very near her eye. She shook the girl's shoulder gently, and when the girl moved, she breathed a sigh of relief. JayCee was alive. She replaced the duvet and ran down the stairs and across the house to the courtyard office.

"Mizz Royce, come quick. Something's happened to your daughter."

"What do you mean, something's happened?"

"I don't know. She's got bruises everywhere."

Her heart racing, Lexie bolted up the stairs behind Phyllis.

"Where is she?"

"In the bed."

When Lexie removed the duvet, JayCee groaned but didn't open her eyes. "Oh, my God, you're hurt. What happened, JayCee?"

No response.

"Call for an ambulance, Phyllis. I'm going with her to the hospital. Call Steve, tell him to meet me at Parkview North."

For the twenty minutes she was alone in the waiting room, Lexie paced, terrifying scenarios racing through her mind. She was relieved to see Steve walking toward her.

"What happened?" he asked, hugging her to him.

She recounted the horror of discovering their daughter in her bed, naked, shivering, bruised, unresponsive. "The room was cold but otherwise it looked normal. The usual mess, but it didn't look like a fight took place there. Phyllis said the door to the veranda was open, though."

"So you think somebody entered the house last night?"

"I don't think anything." She wiped her eyes. "That's not strictly true. I think all kinds of things but nothing that makes any sense. Phyllis is checking right now to see if anything's been taken."

"If it wasn't robbery, then what was the point? Just to beat up JayCee?"

"Somebody should check the security cameras."

Steve pulled his phone out of his jacket pocket and said, "I'm calling Dave now. Did she have friends over last night?"

"No."

A woman in uniform appeared in a doorway and signaled to them. "We're being called in, Steve."

"Give me a few seconds." He returned to his call.

A few minutes later, Dr. Mueller introduced himself outside one of the cubicles, where the curtain was drawn.

"How is she?" Steve asked.

"We don't have a full report yet, but so far her injuries appear to be bruises, a sprained wrist, some lacerations, but no broken bones."

"So she can go home now?"

"We have some things to get sorted out first."

"Can we see her?" Steve asked as he reached for the curtain.

Dr. Mueller reached out to stop Steve. He looked at the couple appraisingly. "So long as someone else is present."

"What do you mean?"

"Sorry to be this frank, but until we can be sure she has nothing to fear from her family, that's the way it's going to be."

"You think we . . . ?" Lexie was stunned. "Good heavens, you don't think we hurt her, do you?"

"I have no opinion one way or the other. I'm accusing you of nothing. But until I know the facts, I have to protect her and the hospital."

Steve's face was tense with anger. "We want to see her, now. We don't know any more than you at the moment, but I've already called Lt. Dave Powers. He's a cop friend of ours, a detective with the Fort Wayne Police Department. He's heading to our house right now with our permission to do what he wants when he gets there. You want me to get him on the phone? Maybe he can come over, or send someone."

"Until we're done here, until I know what I need to know, it wouldn't make any difference what he or anyone else says. You're not going in right now. We'd like you to step into that room over there a few minutes," Dr. Mueller, said pointing past the nurses' bull pen to a door across the room.

"Why?" Steve asked.

"We need to talk to you."

The short walk to the little room was a walk of shame, knowing that the nurses probably suspected them of child abuse.

Once they were seated, Lexie looked around the little room, then pointed at the ceiling. "There's a camera up there. And that mirror looks suspicious. We're being watched, aren't we? And I'll bet somebody is listening to every word we say."

"Probably right. Whenever child abuse is suspected, this is probably the routine."

"You don't really think we're suspected of hurting her, do you? How could anybody think that?"

"Unless JayCee can tell somebody what happened, I'm sure we're going to be under the microscope."

Fifteen minutes later, an older woman walked in and introduced herself as Mrs. Swanger, a domestic violence counselor. Before either Steve or Lexie could object that no domestic violence was involved, she said, "I've just talked to your daughter. She seems to have lost her memory, at least temporarily, so I'd appreciate it if you'd tell me what happened."

"I can tell you how I found my daughter," Lexie said. "But I can't tell you how she got those bruises and scratches."

"Well, tell me what you can. You might start by telling me something about yourself."

Twenty uncomfortable minutes later, Dr. Mueller entered the room and signaled to Mrs. Swanger that she could leave. He sat down in her place. "Sorry we put you through this. Your daughter finally said something that throws new light on her situation. She told a social worker she'd been raped, strangled, and thrown off the veranda. She blacked out for awhile. The scratches on her leg are from the bushes she landed in and the stone steps she crawled back up once she came to. Then, she says, she blacked out again."

For a few seconds, neither Lexie nor Steve could get a word out. "Raped? Strangled? In our house?" Steve asked.

"We're preparing a rape kit right now."

"Did she describe the man?"

"No. She says she never saw him before."

When Lexie and Steve, accompanied by Dr. Mueller, were finally allowed to visit their daughter, she was awake but silent. Though the lights in the room had been dimmed, Lexie could see the girl's face better here than she had at home. She looked like she'd been beaten. There was a red welt around her neck.

"JayCee, we're so sorry. Where did this welt come from? What in heaven's name happened?"

"I don't want to talk about it."

"We can't help you unless you do."

"I'm thirsty."

Lexie pressed a button to change the position of the bed. "Let me help you." The girl took a few sips of water. "Whatever happened, it's not your fault. You shouldn't feel ashamed."

"I don't."

"Then talk to us. We need to find out what happened so we can catch whoever did this to you."

She stared at Lexie in silence.

"What do you remember?"

Silence.

"How did the veranda doors get opened?"

"I don't know."

"Did you let someone into your room last night?"

She closed her eyes. "Joey," she whispered.

"Joey?" Lexie repeated.

"Put the bed back down. I'm tired. I want to go to sleep."

Lexie stepped out of the cubicle and called Dave Powers.

★ ★ ★ ★ ★

Todd examined the broken holly hedge with irritation. Some kind of cloth was snagged on the branches. Some of the hedge would have to be pulled out and replaced. Then he noticed some spots on the steps that might be blood. As an investigator rounded the corner, Todd signaled that he had something to show him. This time, he was pretty sure he could demonstrate some great detective skills.

43

Twice the Victim
Thursday, December 23, 2010

Joey was relieved. Ever since Thanksgiving, his life had been on the upswing. His suspension from sports and a place on the school newspaper had suddenly been lifted. His father relented, restoring his driving privileges. He still had a shot at an athletic scholarship to college. His buddies gradually gravitated back to him and the atmosphere at school had warmed. If the cops continued to think he had something to do with Libby's death, they hadn't done or said anything about it. And he'd finally had the guts to tell JayCee he wasn't going to be her boyfriend.

And then, like an asteroid streaking out of the farthest reaches of the universe on a direct path to his head, JayCee changed his life. Thursday evening, when he was alone in the house, Detective Powers and two uniformed officers appeared at the door.

"Are your parents here? I'd like to speak to them."

Neither one was. Joey explained that his father, a corporate airline pilot, was away and wouldn't be back for several days. His mother, an emergency room nurse, was on duty at Parkview North.

Dave took a step forward. "May I come in? I need to talk to you."

"About what?"

"The events of last night."

"What events?"

"I'll get to that. I want you to come to the station with me."

"Do I have to?"

"It would be best."

"Why? What could you want with me?"

"We'll get to that."

Upon seeing the little gray interview room for a second time, Joey became nervous. What events of Wednesday night were on the detective's mind? Surely breaking up with a girlfriend wasn't a police matter.

"Where were you Wednesday night?" Dave asked.

"Am I under arrest?"

"No. You're free to leave at any time. I just want you to help me out. You don't have to talk to me at all, of course, but you might know something that would help our investigation, so your cooperation is important."

"What investigation?"

"About what happened to JayCee Wright last night."

"What about her?"

"Where were you last night?"

He hesitated. "At home."

"The whole night?"

"Yah."

"Doing what?"

He looked off into space. "The usual stuff. Watching TV. Playing video games. Texting friends."

Dave opened a computer and turned it toward Joey. "Let me show you something." He inserted an SD card. "Watch the screen."

"Why?"

"Just watch. Here goes. . . . Now, I'll pause here. That's you entering the front door at 13339 Stonehaven a little after eight o'clock last night, isn't it?"

"Looks like me."

"And that's JayCee opening the door and you walking in?"

"Yes."

"Was anybody else there with you and JayCee?"

"No. Her parents weren't home. At least, that's what she said, and I never saw them."

"Why'd you lie about being at your house all evening?"

"It's nobody's business where I was. I didn't think it was important."

"Did you know JayCee just got home from the hospital?"

Joey was genuinely shocked. "She was in the hospital? For what?"

"She was strangled and raped."

"Strangled? But she's alive?"

"Fortunately."

"And raped? When? Where? Who would do that?"

"She tried to protect you at first, wouldn't give a hint, but finally she told her mother it was you -- her boyfriend."

"Me? I'm not her boyfriend. Never was."

Lt. Powers gave him a skeptical look.

"Call me whatever you want, but I didn't rape her! I've never raped anybody in my life."

"But you had sex with her last night, isn't that right?"

Silence. Joey squirmed.

"When we get the DNA results back, we'll know. You gave us a DNA sample when we investigated Libby Stuart's death, remember? The comparison will be easy."

"We had sex."

"Was that the first time?"

"No."

"Did you force her?"

"No. What do you think I am?"

"That's what I'm trying to find out. What did you two argue about?"

"What do you mean? Who said we argued?"

"You did argue, didn't you?"

"It wasn't an argument exactly. It didn't start out that way anyway. I told her we had to break it off, stop seeing each other like that. I didn't think it was anything big. Kids our age break up all the time. We could still be friends, I said. I just didn't want to do . . . to do that any more."

"You told her that after you had sex?"

"Yah."

"Was that your original purpose in going over there, to break up with her?"

"Yah."

"Then why did you have sex with her if you didn't want to see her any more?"

"I don't know." He blushed, remembering what she'd done. "Ease into things, I guess."

Dave snorted. "Ease into things, huh? You forced her, didn't you?"

"No, I didn't. I'm not like that."

"So tell me what you're like."

"I felt dirty doing what we were doing. I never did anything like that with Libby -- or with anybody else. I wasn't acting like myself, sneaking around with a girl like JayCee. I felt -- ."

Lt. Powers cut him off. "'A girl like JayCee.' What do you mean by that?"

Joey closed his eyes. "She's very aggressive. Whatever she wants she's going to get or die trying. . . . Anyway, I felt like I was betraying Libby. I know Libby is . . . is dead, she's not coming back, but that's the way I felt. It was like Libby was always hovering in the air, watching me. The stuff I was doing with JayCee . . . if Mom and Dad found out, they'd kill me."

"Did you use a condom?"

"No."

"Why not?"

"She told me not to."

"Come on, Joey. Isn't your story a lie from start to finish? JayCee told you she didn't want sex, she tried to push you away, but you forced her."

"Oh, man, you don't know that girl."

"When she tried to push you away, you got mad and hit her. Or did you wrap that silk scarf around her neck first?"

"She started hitting me as soon as I told her we had to stop seeing each other like that. I put up my arms to defend myself, then I grabbed her wrists, but I didn't hit her. And I don't know what scarf you're talking about."

"What did you use to hit her? More than fists were involved because the bruise on her temple has a very distinctive shape, so you must have taken a weapon with you."

"I didn't hit her with anything."

"What did you say to her exactly?"

Joey tried to remember. "Exactly?" He shook his head. "I can't remember exactly. She started talking about going to the Winter Formal and Spring Fling, going to Daytona for spring break, stuff like that. She was making plans for me I didn't want, never agreed to, never would have suggested myself."

"Is that when you told her the relationship was over?"

Joey nodded.

"So you didn't go there with the intention of breaking it off. That idea came later after the sex."

"No. I did want to break it off, that's why I went there. But I couldn't get a word in until . . . until afterwards. The moment wasn't right until she started planning a future I didn't want any part of."

"Then you wrestled her outside and shoved her off the veranda."

"No, no. I never shoved her."

"You left her, naked and freezing in the bushes, not caring how badly she was hurt or what happened to her."

"She was in the bushes? How'd she get in them? She never left the room while I was there."

"So your story is she threw herself off the veranda, is that it?"

"I don't have a story about that. I don't know anything about her and the veranda and the bushes."

"That's a strange phrase -- 'I don't have a story about that.' You're telling me stories, aren't you?"

Joey was confused. Where did the idea of "story" come from? "I'm telling the truth. You gotta believe me."

"And you did the same thing to Libby Stuart -- argued with

her, tried to force her to have sex, strangled her when she resisted, then pushed her off the bridge."

"She was dead when I got to the bridge, you know that. . . . You've got to know that. Tell me you know that."

"Why didn't you rape Libby?"

"Quit saying that! I didn't rape anybody," Joey cried. "Nobody. Not ever."

"So you'll take a lie detector test?"

In a moment of bravado, Joey squared his shoulders. "Bring it on."

A couple hours later Joey DeWitt and Dave Powers were back in the same little room.

"Look at me, Joey."

He brought his head up. "Okay."

"You passed. No deception."

He closed his eyes. "Thank God." He started to rise out of his chair. "I can go now, right?"

Dave put out his hand. "Hear me out, Joey. I'm not done. You also passed a polygraph when Libby was found dead."

"Because I'm innocent!" he cried. "I was innocent then and I'm innocent now."

"Or because you're a cold-blooded, pathological liar. A sociopath can beat a polygraph every day of the week. That's why the exams aren't admissible in court." *Well, one of the reasons anyway.*

Dave let the silence grow. Finally, he resumed. "Why should we believe anything you say, Joey? You weigh what, at least sixty pounds more than JayCee Wright, stand eight inches taller? You forced her to have sex. When she tried to fend you off, you choked her with her scarf and hit her more than once. When you were done with her, you pushed her over the veranda railing. Then you left her, naked and bruised, in the cold, not caring how badly she'd been hurt or what happened next. She could have frozen to death out there. You never checked to find out what happened to her. The crime was practically a repeat of what you did to Libby, except this time the victim survived."

Joey closed his eyes.

"You know what makes me the sickest, Joey? You made JayCee the victim twice by impugning her reputation, claiming she willingly had sex with you, she hit you first, then she threw herself off the veranda. She's a slut, she's violent, she's self-destructive. In fact, she's so vile she's framing you for rape and battery. But you, of course, are pure as snow."

"I never said any of that. I can't explain what happened after I left. It's my word against hers."

"There's more to it than that, believe me."

"I'm so confused. I don't want to talk any more. I've probably said too much already. I want my dad. He needs to call a lawyer."

The interview was over. Dave Powers left the room to confer with his superior officer, Captain Schmoll, who had watched and listened to everything from an adjoining room on a video feed. "Well, what do you think, Captain?"

"You've identified the alleged rapist. You have a victim who's willing to testify."

Dave interrupted him. "You think? The only person she gave Joey's name to was her mother."

"She'll testify -- but if she doesn't, the DNA will tell the tale. The boy lied about being at the Wrights' house, then changed his story when he saw the security tape. He lies about one thing, what else is he lying about?"

"On the other hand," Dave said, "he aced the polygraph."

"You know the answer to that. He's a sociopath, a cold-blooded killer."

"We won't be able to confirm the sexual assault or match the DNA for several weeks."

"We know it's going to match."

"We have no evidence he took a weapon with him or used one when he got there."

"That's still an open question. Somewhere there's a very strangely shaped weapon that matches the mark on her temple. Once we discover it, we'll up the charges."

Dave sighed.

"What's that sigh about, Lieutenant?"

"I hate 'he said-she said' cases, especially when they involve a kid like Joey DeWitt. She says it was rape, he says it wasn't. If we believe her, his life is ruined."

"On the other hand, if we fall for his lies, she gets no justice." Captain Schmoll stood up. "It's not our job to decide whether we believe Joey or JayCee, Lieutenant, though frankly there's not a lot of doubt about what happened, if you ask me. . . . Think of it this way. What girl throws herself off a second-story structure? Or hits herself in the temple with a blunt object? In my mind, that fall to the ground is the clincher."

"Crazier things have happened."

"We have no reason to think she's crazy, Lieutenant. As I said, you have enough evidence to arrest the boy and let the court sort it out. We need to get a warrant to search the DeWitts' house, find that odd-shaped weapon."

Dave Powers returned to the interview room, where he read Joey DeWitt his Miranda rights, informed him that he was under arrest for sexual battery of Jacintha Wright, and put the cuffs on him. Then he allowed the boy to call his father. Joey spent the night in custody.

44

A Special Christmas Present
Friday, December 24, 2010

This Christmas Eve is the saddest Christmas Eve ever, except the year my mother died. I didn't expect it to be sad. A week after Thanksgiving, I had Todd put up live evergreen trees in three different rooms and wrap every banister in garlands. The atrium is filled with poinsettias, dwarf evergreens, and lilies. The fur tree in the family room, lit with the politically correct LED bulbs JayCee demanded, towers over a big pile of beautifully wrapped gifts. I'm roasting prime rib according to the detailed instructions Phyllis left behind, and the food aromas wafting through the house are as divine as if I actually knew how to cook.

But the three of us are alone. We aren't going to the Club, and I cancelled our open house scheduled for Christmas Day. By now, Phyllis and Todd are in Dollywood to celebrate Christmas Smoky Mountain style; they're probably drinking cocoa, riding the Polar Express, and thinking life is good. I have no idea where Jean and Dover are. Ed and Jessica Singer flew to Fort Lauderdale to visit his parents. Sheila wrote me a note saying they'd be busy until the New Year; the real reason, Steve suspects, is that in light of the investigation of our daughter's claims against Joey DeWitt, Dave would feel awkward in our company.

JayCee spent the day in bed, watching movies, but agreed to come down to the family room after dinner to open presents.

I've bought everything on her long, detailed list: Victoria's Secret loungewear, Marc Jacobs *Daisy* perfume, a Smashbox makeup kit, Betsey Johnson tights, a Kate Spade wallet, Tory Burch wedge sandals, MCM's backpack, an iPad, a variety of skins for her computer, and on and on -- way, way too much, the guilt offerings of an adoptive mother. And Steve bought her a ridiculously expensive music recording system and a Casio keyboard as if she were a dedicated musician instead of an adolescent dilettante who will probably abandon the whole thing in a month.

JayCee won't talk about what happened Wednesday night. When I tried to talk to her, she said, "I told that social worker all I want to remember. If I don't start thinking about something else, I'll kill myself."

"Don't talk like that, JayCee. Don't even think something so terrible."

"Get off it, Mom." Her look was pure scorn. "Did your boyfriend ever almost choke you to death?"

I was momentarily at a loss for words. I wanted to tell her that my first husband did exactly that, but this wasn't the time or place. I wanted to keep the focus on her. But she wasn't done scoring points. "Or did anyone ever rape you?"

To that question, I could truthfully answer no. "No. But that doesn't mean I can't empathize with you."

"Say what?"

"Put myself in your place. Had Joey ever done anything violent before?"

"I don't want to talk about it."

"If he had, I wish I'd known. I'd never have let him anywhere near you."

"I thought he loved me."

"You did?"

Scorn again. "You think I'm not, like, lovable? Well, I am."

"I didn't mean anything of the kind." I tried to give her a hug, but she stiffened and pulled away. "I simply meant that Libby died only a few months ago. People don't switch affections that fast."

"He hated her. He started hating her long before Halloween."

I was shocked. "Hated her? What makes you think that?"

"He said so. He was sick of her goody-goody ways, pretending to be better than everybody else. What's that saying, butter wouldn't melt in her mouth? I was pretty sick of her myself. She was always putting me down, treating me like trailer trash."

"Give me an example."

"She was over here one night with Sandy and Aila to watch *Easy A*. I liked the movie. Libby said her parents wouldn't have let her watch it because it was about sex and lies. She even defended the religious girls who spread gossip, and when I said they were skanks, she asked if I thought that's what she was. I was this close to saying yes, but I didn't."

"You thought she was putting you down?"

"God, Mom, you don't get anything."

I let the insult hang in the air as my conversation with Libby's mother came back to me. "Was Libby sick that night?"

JayCee smiled. "She was drunk, Mom. She was always drinking."

"Her parents don't drink, so where she'd get the alcohol?"

"I don't know, but maybe from Joey's house. His father's a pilot, remember? He probably has cases of those little bottles you found in her purse."

"He's not a commercial pilot where he could just duck into the galley to take a few bottles out of the drink cart, and I doubt most pilots do that anyway."

"Whatever."

"So, if Joey was violent toward you, what do you think now about whether he had anything to do with Libby's death?"

She gave me an odd little smile. "I was protecting him."

"Meaning?"

"I wasn't asleep when she left the house. I had to turn the alarm off, you know. I stood in the doorway to the media room, watched her walk out through the back to the bridge. Joey was waiting for her."

"But you couldn't have seen that far in the dark through the fog, so how do you know he was at the bridge?"

"I heard their voices. You know how sound travels through fog."

"How do you know you were hearing Joey's voice instead of someone else's?"

"I just do. He was the one wrote that note. Why don't you ever believe me?"

I decided to press on. "What did you hear, exactly?"

"Not much." She looked off into space. "I heard voices, not words, but I could tell they were arguing. I even heard Libby scream. I went -- ."

"What do you mean, you heard her scream? Why didn't you call 911? Or call us at the Club?"

"It was just a little scream. I didn't know what it meant. Anyway, I went right back in the house and pretended to be asleep. I didn't want to hear or see anything they were doing. They made me sick."

"I don't understand. What made you sick?"

"Pretending to be so lovey-dovey all the time. At least things got real when they started fighting."

"What were they fighting about?"

She smiled again. "Me."

"What about you?"

"Libby thought Joey was in love with me because we were spending so much time together."

"Did you tell any of this to Detective Powers?"

"It's none of his business."

"The truth about Libby's death *is* his business."

"Whatever."

"Well, let me think about this. How are you feeling? Do you need another pain-killer?"

"No."

"Why don't you take a shower and put on something nice. We'll eat dinner, then open our gifts. Tomorrow morning we'll go The Chapel for the Christmas service."

"I'm not going to church."

"It's a wonderful service -- live camels and lambs, beautiful music, the baby Jesus -- a real baby with his parents."

"I hate babies."

"JayCee! I hope that's not true."

"Why?"

I hadn't planned to make my announcement just then but there was no avoiding it. "We're having a baby."

"You are? You don't look pregnant."

"I will soon."

"When are you having the baby?"

"Sometime in June."

"Why?"

"Why?" I asked, laughing. "Because we want a baby. Don't you want a little sister or brother?"

When she frowned, I expected the kind of tearful response I gave Matilda, my step-mother, when she told me she was expecting Rolland, but JayCee simply said, "I like being the only kid."

"You'll like having a brother or sister even more. Think of it as a special Christmas present."

She said nothing.

"We should start thinking of names. What are your favorites?"

She turned her head away. "Call it no-name for all I care."

"JayCee!"

She patted Henry, who was lying beside her. "I'm just kidding." When Henry suddenly barked and leapt to the floor, she laughed. "Call it Barker."

I laughed too.

Then, unexpectedly, she slid down in her bed and pulled the sheet over her face. "I want to sleep."

45

Not Even a Full Moon
Friday, December 31, 2010

The emergency room at Parkview North was a busy place on New Year's Eve. It always was on the weekend, especially a holiday weekend, but typically not with the kind of gurney-crashing, anthill drama depicted on television. In her fifteen years as an emergency room nurse, Erna DeWitt had never seen a construction worker impaled on an awl or an equestrienne who'd fallen from a galloping horse while texting. Mostly the admissions could be classified, in the irreverent lingo of the staff, as pains and strains, crashes and slashes, aches and breaks that could be handled in a doctor's office if one was open.

The orderly quiet suited Erna. Her personal life was in a shambles. She was deeply worried and needed time to think. Distress at work was the last thing she needed.

Her son had been charged with rape and battery. Out on bail, he was so depressed he'd had to see a psychiatrist, who put him on Prozac. He shambled around like a zombie, refusing to eat or talk. He slept during the day and wandered around the house at night, muttering to himself.

Her husband, Gil, a retired military pilot, was keeping a stiff upper lip, but Erna knew he was worried too, not only about Joey but about his own job. The corporation he served as a pilot was planning to sell its jet in the wake of political pressure to shame "soulless" jet owners and remove the tax breaks that were allegedly ruining seniors and children. The DeWitts' savings were already gone as a result of bailing out their son, hiring a criminal defense lawyer, and undertaking a psychiatric regimen for him. They'd taken out a second mortgage on the house, canceled plans for a spring break vacation, posted their RV and Joey's car for sale on eBay, and depleted Gil's retirement account. Her job was safe enough, but her income wasn't adequate to support the family.

Erna was staring at a chart, trying to focus her mind, when the emergency room suddenly erupted like Vesuvius. Strange, there wasn't even a full moon.

First came two crash victims, a young man and a woman in her thirties. The young man, whom Erna didn't recognize, possessed a powerful Ducati but apparently not the common sense to wear a helmet. He had to be rushed to surgery.

Erna recognized the second victim, a pretty redhead with minor injuries, the kind women often suffer from inflating air-bags. She was the former girlfriend of her colleague, Dwight Perkins, a night nurse. According to the officer who accompanied the injured woman to Parkview North, Jean Louisa Arnold ran a red light leaving the Carmike theater on Dupont west of I-69. She, however, protested that the light was yellow. Furthermore, she claimed that she didn't hit the motorcycle; why the driver ran into a light pole, she couldn't explain. She made no objection to being breathalyzed; she hadn't been drinking, a claim confirmed by her companion, a man Erna recognized as Dover Pitt, the Gretna Green golf pro, who said his girlfriend was under a lot of stress and a ticket for running a red light was the last thing she needed.

A half hour later, Alexandra Royce Wright, the wife of the Gretna Green developer, was wheeled in. She was unconscious. It was quickly discovered that she'd sustained a concussion. She was suffering from cardiac arrhythmia and was having seizures. Her husband, Steve Wright, could give no explanation for her condition. She was not taking any medications and had no medical problems that he knew about. Because she was pregnant, she had not consumed any alcohol; he was sure of that. Food poisoning was unlikely because both he and his daughter had eaten the same meal and neither of them was sick. He didn't know how or when his wife sustained the concussion. He'd found her on the stone floor of the atrium in their house just before he went upstairs to go to bed. Despite the best efforts of the staff, Mrs. Wright soon began to hemorrhage.

While Erna was busy attending to Mrs. Wright, a fourth patient was rushed in. He was alive, but just barely, having apparently shot himself in the jaw in a suicide attempt gone awry. He was rushed to surgery before she saw the man.

Hours later, just before Erna's shift was over, she reviewed the charts. The biker was out of surgery and doing well. Miss Arnold had been treated and discharged.

Alexandra Royce Wright miscarried. A quick drug screen indicated there was methadone in her system. What had she been addicted to? Erna looked off into space, remembering Thanksgiving dinner with the Wrights. She hadn't even realized Mrs. Wright was pregnant, though she thought it odd that the woman ate only a few slices of turkey and a dinner roll and then left right after dessert. Had there been any signs of a drug addiction? She didn't think so.

And then Erna almost fainted. The man who shot himself in the jaw had died. His name was Gilbert P. DeWitt, 12241 Aberdeen, 42, married, a corporate pilot.

46

Humiliation

Saturday, January 1, 2011

Steve could not bear to leave his wife's bedside. For a few hours of pure hell, he wasn't sure she'd live. He was filled to the brim with remorse for the distance that had grown between them. Fear that Lexie would suffer permanent effects from the concussion or the cardiac arrhythmia overwhelmed him. And he knew that once she regained consciousness, she'd be devastated at the loss of the baby. How would he comfort her then?

The questions he'd been peppered with about what drugs Lexie could have consumed were puzzling and humiliating. He protested to the doctors that there was no way she had voluntarily taken any drugs, legal or illegal. Neither of them had ever taken drugs, not even as teenagers, and the only pills his wife took were vitamins and other supplements recommended for expectant mothers. He demanded that his wife be given a quick drug test so they didn't have to wait for a more elaborate drug screen to know what they were dealing with.

On New Year's Day, Lexie's Obi-Wan Kenobi, Dr. Ann Peterman, took him aside and said, "Your wife has methadone in her system."

"Methadone?"

"As you probably know, it's given to addicts to wean them off a drug like cocaine."

"She isn't an addict. Never was."

"I'd like to check with her family doctor."

"Do that, with my blessing." He knew he sounded sarcastic.

"Any idea how she got hold of it?"

"No."

"Everything's okay in your marriage, I assume."

Dr. Peterman spoke gently, but Steve found her tone condescending and intrusive. "What's our marriage have to do with methadone?"

"Sometimes people do drastic things for attention from a spouse. You told me earlier that you hadn't seen her all evening and only found her by accident, though you were both home."

"We have the normal stresses," he said. "Because we have our own professional lives . . . we don't spend every hour together, and the house is so big it's easy to get lost in it. But our marriage is solid. And she wanted this baby as much as she ever wanted anything, believe me. She'd never do anything to endanger the baby. She hasn't had a drop of alcohol or an aspirin tablet since getting pregnant. She's read every book on healthy pregnancies ever published." He gave her a hard smile. "In fact, didn't you tell her she didn't need to see you as often as she thought she did?"

Dr. Peterman ignored that. "Once you get home, you might want to look around, be sure your wife hasn't hidden anything. We don't want to see her back here."

Steve was nonplussed at the implications of that.

"I know this is hard, but bear with me, Mr. Wright. Let's just say for the sake of argument she took a drug she shouldn't have. Do you have any idea how she might have gotten hold of it? Does she have any contacts in the drug world? Or do you?"

Now Steve was angry. He spit out the words. "My wife didn't get hold of anything. She didn't take methadone or any other drug voluntarily. And she has no connection whatsoever with the drug world. We're respectable people."

And then he thought of Drago. Once upon a time, he'd been the enforcer for Lexie's brother, Rolland, who'd spent years dealing pot before he died. There was even a rumor that Drago had killed a rival drug dealer. But with Lexie's help, including a good job at the Royce family Scrapyard, Drago had gotten out of that world over a year ago -- or had he?

"What?" Dr. Peterman asked. "What's that expression?"

"Nothing. . . . What's scaring me is I have no idea how any drug got into my wife's system. No idea at all. . . . So what the hell do I do now? How do I protect my family?" Sterling Steven Wright never cried, especially in front of a strange woman. But his eyes burned and he couldn't stop the tears.

A week ago he'd been suspected of child abuse. Now he was suspected of driving his wife to drugs -- or worse, procuring them and then lying about it. How had his life taken such a terrible turn?

No new year had ever started out so ominously.

47

The Breakers
Wednesday, January 5, 2011

"Oh, I love a good spa. That massage hit the spot," Lexie said, adjusting her sunglasses. She and Jessica were sitting on lounge chairs at The Breakers in Palm Beach, mesmerized by the sound of the waves lapping the beach. "And the sun! I haven't seen it in weeks. No wonder the ancient civilizations that were so good at astronomy were located in the southern latitudes. If they'd been living in Indiana, they'd have thought the heavens were slate gray and about a mile high."

Jessica laughed. "Why didn't we come to The Breakers two years ago instead of Rancho Salud? Do you remember how bad that was? No food, no wine, ten-mile hikes everyday until we threw up. Lectures on healthy eating, given by a woman with gray hair, no makeup, and a church-lady smirk. Up at 5:30, in bed by 8:30. No phones, no television. Downward Facing Dog and the lotus position to the sounds of a very tiresome sitar. And we paid dearly for the torture. Ed thought we were nuts."

"We weren't nuts until we'd been there for three days, being forcibly detoxified. I like this part of the country much better. Sun, sand, palm trees, crab salad, and cocktails."

"Just think, Lexie, how much has changed in your life since Rancho Salud. You're married, you have a new house, and you're a step-mother."

"But not a mother the way I wanted."

Jessica clapped her hand over her mouth. "Oh, sorry. Didn't mean to bring that up. Gosh, did I make you cry? Here." Jessica scrambled in her tote for a tissue. "What was I thinking?"

Lexie blew her nose. "If you can stand a little crying on my part, I'd just as soon talk about it as avoid the subject. I'm not only grieving that I lost the baby, but I feel like a murderer, the way everybody's looking at me. As if I deliberately took something that caused it and now am lying about it."

"Steve told me the doctors think you took methadone."

"Oh, for heaven's sake. I didn't. Why would I? Wouldn't there be a record somewhere if I got a prescription for methadone? Wouldn't you or Steve or somebody have noticed if I was once a drug addict?"

"They have to be thinking you got it some other way. And the doctors don't know you the way Steve and I do."

"Frankly, I can't believe there was anything in my system. It's a nightmare."

"You realize then, don't you, that somebody slipped it to you in your food or your drink?"

"It wasn't in my food or drink. I didn't eat or drink anything different from what Steve and JayCee had that night."

"Were you taking any pills at all?"

"Just prenatal complex vitamins and a calcium tablet."

"All tablets or gels?"

"No. The vitamins are capsules. I took two of them and a calcium tablet before I headed to the atrium."

"Why weren't you headed for bed?"

"It was one of my bad nights when I knew I wasn't going to be able to sleep."

"Were the vitamins in the original bottle?"

"No. They were laid out on the counter with the calcium tablet."

"Who did that? Phyllis?"

"No." Long pause. "I assumed Steve did so I wouldn't forget them. They were right beside the kitchen sink."

"Did you notice whether the capsules had been tampered with?"

"Never thought about it. I just popped them in my mouth."

"What did you take with the capsules?"

"Water from the tap." Lexie pushed her sunglasses down and looked at Jessica. "What are you thinking?"

"I'm thinking somebody slipped methadone into your vitamin capsules."

"That's so nefarious."

"True. But if you didn't deliberately take methadone -- and of course I believe you didn't -- then somebody slipped it to you."

"But who would do that? Not in a million years would Steve do that. Or Phyllis."

"How about your step-daughter? You said she told you to call the baby 'no-name.' That's kind of a big clue, don't you think?"

"No. My reaction when I heard Rolland was coming was ten times worse." Lexie stared at the waves. "Anyway, where would she get methadone?"

"That I can't tell you, but kids find a way to score drugs all the time. You know that." Jessica snapped her fingers. "What about Drago? He used to be in the drug business with your half-brother, didn't he?"

Lexie nodded. "Yes, but they only dealt pot. And he's never been anything but good to me."

"Come on, Lexie. Are you forgetting he set your car on fire after pouring acid on it?"

"That was Rolie's idea, not Drago's. Besides, Drago also saved my life. He has a good job and a house because of me. What motive would he have?"

"When you talk to Steve tonight, why don't you suggest he have a sit-down with Drago? Maybe Steve should also have the other vitamin capsules sent to a lab for testing." Jessica began reapplying suntan lotion. "I could be talking out of my arse, of course, but I'm telling you, Lexie, you've got a rat in your midst. That dose of methadone could have killed you, or so the doctor told Steve, and it did kill the baby. . . . Sorry to be so blunt, but that's the truth."

"A rat in my midst," Lexie repeated, trying out the words.

"To my mind, the difference between attempted murder and actual murder is nothing but luck -- bad luck for the rat, good luck for you. I don't know who the rat is, but if I were you, I'd start looking under every floorboard, behind every door, and in every closet."

"For what?"

"Rat droppings. Whoever did this to you is a sneaky, dirty rat who needs to be exterminated. The rat's left a trail. Rats always do."

"Specifically, what kind of trail am I looking for?"

"I'll have to get back to you on that." Jessica looked behind her and raised her arm. "Hold on a minute. A waiter's coming over. Do you want another Prosecco?"

"Why not?"

When the waiter left, Lexie said, "How depressing! . . . . Where do I go from here?"

"Well, let's be practical. Get those vitamin capsules tested. Buy all new ones and lock them away. Tear the house apart, if you have to, but make sure there aren't any other bad drugs around."

"And the trail left by the rat?"

"Rats that don't get caught become very bold."

"Too vague."

"I know. Let me think about it."

"You mentioned exterminating the rat. If the rat is somebody I know, I can't do that. That's so . . . so . . . ."

"So final? So vengeful?" Jessica fluffed up her long blond hair and adjusted her straw hat. "So illegal, not to mention sinful? I know, I know. Forget I said it. What you do about the rat once you're sure you've found it -- that's up to you. Just be aware that rats don't change their ways."

48

Trust

Wednesday, January 5, 2011

Wednesday night, after a phone conversation with Lexie, Steve called Drago and asked to meet him anywhere he chose. Drago chose a sports bar at Leo Crossing where they could smoke.

Steve, the first to arrive, took a seat at the bar. He was gazing at a college basketball game and ordering a beer when he felt a tap on his shoulder. "How's it going, Mr. Wright? Haven't seen you for awhile."

"You're right, Drago." He held out his hand. "You want a beer?"

"Sure. And a cheeseburger if you're eating too. . . . So what's up?"

"You heard about my wife."

"Mom told me. I was sorry to hear about it. Especially the baby."

"Me too."

"Women are nuts about babies, Mr. Wright. Know that."

"Did Phyllis tell you what caused the miscarriage?"

"No," he lied.

"Methadone."

"I've heard of it."

Steve gave him a long look. "Addicts take it to get off drugs."

Drago nodded.

"Did Rolie ever take it? Or sell it?"

Drago took a swallow of beer, then shook his head. "Weed was his game. He stuck to weed." He held out a package of Kools. "Smoke?"

Steve shook his head. "Lexie didn't take methadone. She's never been addicted to anything. She doesn't have a prescription for it. So the question is, where'd she get it?"

"Why you asking me?"

"You were Rolie's . . . ."

"I was Rolie's what?"

"Partner."

"That was a long time ago, Mr. Wright."

"Not that long ago. You have contacts."

"No, I don't. Things change, know that. I left that world for good when Mizz Royce made me an offer I couldn't refuse about the Scrapyard."

"An offer you couldn't refuse? You make it sound like she's Tony Soprano."

"Don't mean it that way. I just mean, there's no going back."

"Anybody you know ever addicted to cocaine, heroin, anything like that?"

Drago looked off into space, remembering faces and street names. "I didn't *know* anybody who did that, not by a real name, not as a friend. You got somebody in mind?"

"How about a relative? Your mother, for instance -- ."

Drago cut him off. "Don't even go there. She's clean as a whistle. So's Lucy. Even the Scrapyard guys don't do drugs. We test everybody; I'm sure you know that. 'Surprise, José, it's your lucky day -- pee in this cup.' The Yard guys did anything stronger than tobacco, Mizz Royce would boot 'em out so fast it'd take a week for their ass to reinflate from the boot marks. Mizz Royce don't put up with any nonsense."

"Forget I mentioned your mother. I'm clutching at straws."

"Okay then," Drago said doubtfully.

They sat in silence. "I didn't mean to insult you. I'm just desperate, Drago, that's all. Where the hell did the methadone come from?"

"You sure it was methadone?"

"No, I'm not personally sure because I didn't run any tests myself, I know nothing about methadone, but I have to believe the doctors."

"Sort of like believing the earth is round or gravity works. Right? You have to trust somebody smarter than you."

"You want to know the truth -- I don't trust anybody."

"Don't blame you, but it won't get you anywhere, thinking like that. You gotta trust somebody. You can trust me. I'd die before I'd hurt Mizz Royce, know that."

"I know you would. But I'm going to need some help."

Just then, Drago's phone buzzed. He furtively glanced at the screen, then thrust it back in his jacket pocket. JayCee again.

49

Daddy-Mine
Wednesday, January 5, 2011

JayCee was pleased. Libby was dead and Joey might as well be. Jean had been fired and Gilbert DeWitt shot himself. The stupid little no-name worm was gone forever. Her pious witch of a step-mother was licking her wounds somewhere in Florida. Phyllis, Sadie, and Todd tip-toed around, deferring to her every whim -- like the good servants they ought to be. And in the evenings she had her generous -- and clueless -- father to herself. Sometimes their little *tête-à-têtes* lasted no more than an hour, but at least all his attention was focused on her.

During the Christmas break, she had begun pursuing a new interest -- writing lyrics for the likes of Duffy, Adele, and Katy Perry. JayCee knew she was as talented as they were and deserved to be just as famous. She was already rich, but making her own separate fortune would be such a triumph.

She had lots to offer the world. The deep wellspring of her life was filled to the brim with dark emotions powerful enough to bring chills and goosebumps to ordinary people if only the right voice belted out her words.

On her computer JayCee made a clean copy of lyrics she would send to Adele, the British songbird whose distinctive voice, dissonant chords, and falling notes were just right for *Daddy-Mine*. She hand-wrote a personal note congratulating Adele on her popularity. She added that she was in the process of composing the music on her Casio keyboard and then would record a demo in a professional studio. She'd send the disc along in a few days, but Adele could be assured the song would have the beat of *Rolling in the Deep* and a soulful melody. The "ohs" in the chorus -- to be performed with background singers -- should strike a falling, heartbroken note. Though she wasn't yet a music mogul, she listened to a lot of popular music and sang in high-school musicals, so she could practically guarantee a platinum hit for Adele and a songwriting Grammy for herself.

Like Adele, by the way, she was known simply by one name, JayCee. Wasn't that a neat coincidence? Perhaps they should start thinking about a formal musical collaboration.

Daddy-Mine

Verse 1

I searched for you everywhere,
Finally found you in a scrapbook,
Dear old daddy-mine.
Why'd you leave me where
I'd rot till I took a closer look?
I love you, daddy-fine.

Chorus

Had to make my own way, daddy-mine.
Had to clear a path, so many down.
Oh, oh, how many more, my daddy-fine,
Until I wear the daughter's crown? Oh.

Verse 2

Don't leave me here to rot again
Unless you want to disappear,
Dear old daddy-mine.
Once they're gone, and only then

Will my happiness appear.
I love you, daddy-fine.

Instrumental Bridge (upbeat but sad)

Verse 3

You know I am the princess bride
Who the witch did try to kill,
Dear old daddy-mine.
But I have too much pride
and she has not my skill.
I love you, daddy-fine.

Repeat Chorus

Verse 4

They say there is a bridge too far
But not for me at all,
Dear old daddy-mine.
I walk out to the foggy dark
And dance to see her fall.
I love you, daddy-fine.

Verse 5

Please don't leave me all alone
A prisoner in the dark,
Dear old daddy-mine.
Unless you have a heart of stone,
You'll give me back my spark.
I love you, daddy-fine.

Repeat Chorus

She knew from a poetry class the lines didn't scan well, but in re-reading the lyrics to Adele's hit, *Someone Like You*, she thought her lines were no worse. Adele would know how to tweak them.

In a flash of inspiration she added at the bottom of the page:

As she read and re-read her lyrics, sometimes humming them to herself to various familiar tunes, a few tears fell -- not so many as to ruin her mascara but enough to prove she had a soft heart. "Foggy dark" and "dance to see her fall" were truly inspired lines! Anyone could see that her emotions were dark and deep -- profound for a young girl. When they heard the song, Adele's fans would know how much life had wounded her, the lyricist, yet how brave she was.

She walked over to a mirror and gazed deeply, soulfully into her own eyes. So young to have talent brighter than the heavens! How could anyone not be moved by her lyrics? The world would swoon when it learned these lyrics were not only great but the first ones she ever wrote! She was Mozart in Juicy Couture.

JayCee returned to her desk, where she folded a copy of the lyrics and her personal handwritten note in threes, then as an afterthought tucked in a picture of herself as Adelaide in *Guys and Dolls*. After pasting a stamp on an envelope made out to Columbia Records, she laid the envelope aside and called Drago.

50

BFFs

Wednesday, January 5, 2011

Drago left the bar at Leo Crossing more disturbed than he pretended to be. Steve Wright, a man he looked up to and whose good will was vital, suspected him of dealing drugs or harboring a recovering addict. Lucy -- his once giggly, cuddly wife who now accused him of having an affair with JayCee -- was so cold he felt like an Eskimo banished to an iceberg floating out to sea. When his loving mother wasn't busy with Todd, she nagged him to come talk to her, the way they did in the old days, but he couldn't face her. The twins and the puppies obeyed him but more out of fear, he suspected, than respect. And he'd begun drinking a little too much.

And then there was JayCee. He felt very sorry for her. She'd been beaten and raped. The girl bravely tried to protect her boyfriend but finally was pressured to confess. Now she was ashamed of what had happened to her and sought Drago's friendship.

Her friendship was disturbing. All his life he'd sought adventure in his work life. Before accepting a job at the Royce Scrapyard, he worked with Rolie Royce in the drug trade, where he took daily chances with death because the payoff, both in power and money, was so big. But in his love life he'd never been like that. He wanted to know which girl loved him and where she'd be, preferably waiting for him. Early on, he found that emotional security with Lucy. But now -- married, with kids, a suburban house, and a steady job -- every part of his life was boring, a quietly flowing river of kids and bills and scrap with no tides or whirlpools or sudden floods to break the monotony.

JayCee rolled into his life like a tsunami, a hundred-foot wave of unfamiliar emotion and danger. He knew he should run to the highest hill, but his feet wouldn't move.

Besides, their friendship was only natural, for they had a lot in common. She didn't have a father until the Wrights adopted her. He'd really never had a father either. She said her mother's boyfriend, Tug, called her ugly names and tried to touch her once. He countered that his father beat him up and put him in the hospital when he was only six. She was bullied at school. Not to be outdone, Drago said he'd been bullied too, for being black, though in fact that never happened; when he got in trouble, it was because he started it trying to prove how tough he was. Her burning goal in life was to get rich and famous. His goal was the same, though he'd given it up a year ago. He'd let go of the brass ring and couldn't get it back.

Drago felt like a man standing in an ice-cold room with one shoulder turned to a blazing fire: freezing to death in one direction, burning up in another.

After starting his engine, he idled in the bar's parking lot until he saw Mr. Wright pull out onto Tonkel Road, then returned JayCee's call.

"What's up, girl?"

"I've written the most glorious song you've ever heard. *Daddy-Mine*. It'll go platinum if I can get Adele to sing it."

"Who's Adele?"

"Oh, for Christ's sake, Drago, just the best singer in the world."

"Didn't know you wrote songs."

"Mom says you're a great singer. Got a good voice, she said."

"That's nice of her."

"Well, do you?"

"Do I what?"

"Have a good voice?"

He struggled with his pride. "Some people think so."

"Do you play guitar or anything, Drago?"

"No."

"Would you sing a duet with me?"

"Why?"

"I'm writing music now to go with the lyrics I'm going to send to Adele. I'll have everything done by the weekend, so Saturday I'm going to go to Digitracks Recording Studios on Speedway for a professional recording session. Then I'm sending the disc to Adele."

"You have a band set up?"

"Don't need one. I'll accompany myself."

"You're ready for that? Singing professionally? At your age?"

"Of course. But I'm not telling Adele I should sing the song. I'm just going to show her how it could sound. If you don't want to sing with me, at least you can listen and give me pointers. You can be my coach. I'll give you credit when I'm famous. Maybe then you can leave that stupid job at the Scrapyard, go on tour with me."

"What'd you say about my job?"

"Stupid. You're too good for the Scrapyard. So how about Saturday?"

"What do your parents think?"

"Dad does anything I want. He'll pay for it."

"I mean, do they want me to go with you?"

"They don't care who I hang out with."

I doubt that's true. "Is your mom home yet?"

"No. The witch isn't coming back from Florida until Sunday."

"What's this witch stuff about?"

"Just a joke. You know the fairy tale -- the queen who gives her step-daughter a poisoned apple. . . . I know you like Mom, Drago, but she's not the mother you think she is. She never wanted me. Anyway, all step-mothers are wicked, you know that." She laughed as if it were a joke. "So let's not argue about Mom."

He felt like arguing about that but held his tongue. He didn't know what fairy tale the girl was referring to, but if in her mind the queen was Mizz Royce, it looked like the queen had been on the wrong end of the poisoned apple.

When Drago said nothing, JayCee whimpered. "Don't get mad at me, Drago. You're the only friend I've got. We're BFFs for sure. I'm just as bummed out about what happened to Mom as anyone else, but here I am, all alone. I need you."

"What time should I pick you up Saturday?"

"Nine."

"Okay, then."

The moment he hung up with JayCee, his phone buzzed again and S. Wright's name appeared on the screen. "What's up, Mr. Wright?"

"I wonder if you'd do me a favor."

"Shoot."

"My daughter's been moping around, in need of some company. Would you be able to take her to Keystone Mall in Indianapolis sometime soon, spend the day with her? Maybe shopping will change her mood."

Drago hesitated. What the hell was going on? "She wants me to take her to a recording studio Saturday."

"She does?"

"I thought you knew about it. She's recording a song she's written."

"How long will she be at the studio?"

"Don't know. Just the morning, I assume." Drago hesitated. "I haven't checked with Mizz Royce yet about taking Saturday morning off."

"I'll take care of that. I want you to make a day of it, keep her busy. Take JayCee shopping afterwards. Then some place like Five Guys. She loves their hamburgers."

"Does she have a curfew?"

"Let's say, get her home by nine o'clock."

"If you say so."

51

"M"

Saturday, January 8, 2011

From their telephone conversation Friday night, Steve knew Lexie was right. Turn the house upside down. Get the vitamin capsules tested, then buy all new ones and lock them up. Find the damned methadone.

Saturday morning, the moment JayCee left the house, he strode to the butler's pantry, where Phyllis and Todd were waiting. "Pull every cookbook off the shelf, unpack every drawer and cupboard. Make sure the spice bottles only hold what the label says. Dig through the pantry. Throw out anything that looks suspicious -- all the aspirin, all the Tums, flour, sugar, anything in pill or powder form that's already been opened. If in doubt, show it to me first."

"I have a printout showing the various forms methadone comes in," Todd said. "You want to look at it?"

Steve smiled at Todd. "Sure."

"You have any idea whether we're looking for pills or powder, Mr. Wright?"

"No."

"I'm no pharmacist, of course, but you're right -- if in doubt, throw it out. I'm just sayin'."

"You're sayin' right, Todd. When you're done here, do the same thing in the media and game rooms. I'm going upstairs."

After spending an hour in the master bathroom, Steve walked

down the corridor to JayCee's suite. Because it was Sadie's day off, the place was a mess. He had no idea his daughter lived like this. Why hadn't anybody told him? He'd have straightened her out.

He started in the bathroom, where he found talcum powder and bath salts but nothing else. Then he moved to the study; he found a stamped envelope made out to Columbia Records. He stuffed it into his pants pocket to be mailed later.

Returning to the bedroom, he stood there a few minutes, trying to think like a young girl with a secret. He hated thinking like that but until he got to the bottom of the mystery, he had no choice.

When he found the stained and battered messenger bag under the four-poster bed, he was stunned at the array of bottles inside. Excedrin, Advil, Midol, Tylenol, Aleve, aspirin. Why weren't they kept in the girl's bathroom? He shook out a few pills from each bottle; so far as he could tell, they looked right and were appropriately marked. Still, he'd send them out for testing.

He was about to leave the room when his eye was drawn to the window seat. Was it solid or did it open for storage? When he removed the long cushion, he saw the hinges. He lifted the seat and peered in. A dusty, bleach-stained sweatshirt was wadded up in a corner. Lifting it, he discovered a plastic baggy underneath. Inside was a brown prescription vial. He removed the vial. It had a child-proof cap and a label reading "Methadone 5 mg," issued to "Antoinette Delamarter" in April of last year.

Taking a deep breath, he shook out a tablet. It was white, rectangular, imprinted with an "M". The computer printout Todd showed him didn't include an image of this particular pill, but he had no reason to think it was anything other than what the label said it was.

He started to return the tablet to the vial when he noticed something metallic inside. Walking over to a dresser, he shook out all the contents of the vial. A ring clinked as it hit the dresser, then rolled onto the floor and under the dresser. He had to stretch flat on the floor to retrieve it: A thin gold band with two stones, one dark green, the other pinkish-red. He'd heard the stones described as an emerald and a ruby. He stared at it, weighed it in his hand. He looked for an engraved inscription, but there was none.

This couldn't be the ring he'd heard so much about, the ring that Libby's mother was looking for, could it? He looked around his daughter's room in disbelief. How had she gotten Libby's ring and why had she hidden it? For that matter, why had she kept her mother's methadone prescription? Had she used it to poison Lexie?

When he fell into an armchair to think, the envelope in his pocket crackled. Absent-mindedly, he leaned aside and pulled it out. Addressed to Columbia Records. What in hell was that about? Should he open it or not? He'd already invaded his daughter's privacy by searching her room, so what was the harm in a little more spying? He opened the envelope.

The chutzpah of the note to Adele -- apparently a famous singer he'd never heard of -- made him smile. Adele and JayCee should form a musical collaboration! Leave it to a starstruck teenager to think she was so formidably talented as to link up with a popular singer.

Then he read the lyrics. Complete drivel! The theme was so juvenile, the rhymes so painfully awkward, the phrases so cliché, he would have laughed in other circumstances, but one stanza almost stopped his heart:

They say there is a bridge too far
But not for me at all,
Dear old daddy-mine.
I walk out to the foggy dark
And dance to see her fall.
I love you, daddy-fine.

Bridge -- foggy dark -- fall. Halloween night. Was that a confession about what happened to Libby? If so, it explained how the ring ended up in this room.

"Unless you want to disappear." Was that a threat to him? If he was daddy-mine, daddy-fine, what sense did that make?

"Had to clear a path, so many down." He shuddered.

He was still sitting in his daughter's armchair when Phyllis appeared at the door. "We're done in the kitchen, Mr. Wright, ready to start on the media room. Did you notice, it's starting to snow? . . . Oh, my gosh, are you all right?"

He took so long to respond, Phyllis wondered if he had heard her. Finally, he said, "You and Todd can go now."

"You found something? The meth -- the thing we were looking for?"

"I don't know. But we're done for now. I'm paying you both for the full day, of course. I'll see you Monday."

"You sure there's nothing more we can do before Mizz Royce gets back tomorrow?"

"I'm sure."

"There's some leftover roast turkey in the refrigerator if you want to make a sandwich later."

After a few seconds' of silence, she said, "If you want it now, I'll make it for you, bring it up here."

No response. He didn't even look at her.

"Mr. Wright?"

Phyllis thought she heard him whisper, "What?"

She tiptoed down the corridor. If he'd found the methadone -- if that was the reason she and Todd were being dismissed early -- why didn't he just say so?

52

Getting Clean
Saturday, January 8, 2011

Steve idled behind Scuttlebutt's, wondering if he should turn around and leave without seeing the owner. Did he really need to confirm the methadone he found in his daughter's room belonged to Antoinette Delamarter?

For a few minutes, he absently watched a beer truck maneuver down a ramp to a loading dock, then stared at the Lexus he'd parked next to. If it was the owner's, then gentlemen's clubs must be a damn good investment, even in a bad economy. He looked at his watch. He either had to get out of the car or cancel the meeting.

He got out of the car, walked to a gray metal door, and pushed a button. He heard the faint ring of a bell inside the building. Then he was buzzed in. The cinderblock corridor was dimly lit. Straight ahead, then a right, he'd been told. When he saw a cheap metal wall sign reading "Office," he knocked on the door.

He did not expect the man on the other side to look so . . . well, so young, so respectable.

"Mr. Scutter?"

"Scut. And you're Steve Wright, I suppose."

"I am. Thank you for seeing me."

"Have a seat. Cigar?"

Steve hesitated. This wasn't a social call, but why not? Establish a little rapport. "Great."

"I've seen your picture in the papers from time to time, but never in here," Scut said.

"Not my thing. No disrespect."

"Not really my thing either, but it's a living, so no offense taken."

"Judging from the Lexus outside, it's a good living."

"That it is. The worse things get out there," Scut said pointing to a wall, "the better in here. Pop always told me that. Some men even try to use food stamps to pay for their beer, if you can believe that."

"You allow that?"

"No. But we cash welfare checks."

"What a world!"

"So, what I can do for you?" Scut checked his watch. "Don't mean to be rude, but Saturdays are hectic."

"One of my employees, Dover Pitt, came to see you last year about Antoinette Delamarter's daughter."

"I remember. He said he was a school counselor."

"He was then. After that, I hired him to be my golf pro."

"Nice guy. He thought Pop or me might be her father. He was so nervous, I offered him a beer before he left, but he shot out of here like the Road Runner being chased by the Coyote. So, did he ever find what he was looking for?"

"I'm afraid so. It turns out her daughter was -- is -- my daughter too."

Scut suppressed a smile. "You?"

"Me. A teenaged mistake. But my wife and I adopted the girl last year."

Scut rolled the ash off his cigar. "If I went home with that news, my wife would kill me. Or I'd be missing a few important parts."

Steve winced. "I think that was on my wife's mind for awhile."

"So, has anybody ever figured out what happened to Tawny?"

"The cops are still working on it. Tawny is why I'm here. I never knew her except -- except for a few minutes at a party when

I was eighteen."

"A few minutes too many."

Steve nodded.

"Sorry, that was uncalled for."

"I deserve it. My question is, was Tawny ever addicted to anything? Cocaine, maybe. Or some other street drug."

"What do you think?"

"I don't know. That's why I'm asking."

"Most of the girls have a habit. For some, it's just alcohol or pot. But others . . . ."

"Like Tawny?"

Scut nodded. "Alcohol *and* drugs. A lethal combination, not just for their health, but their pocketbooks, their family life, their work habits. Drugs tear up their looks so bad, most are out of here before they hit thirty. Tawny did better than most in the looks department, but still it got bad for her. She missed a lot of work, tried to borrow money from everybody. No customers ever invited her to the champagne room for a lap dance."

"Champagne room?"

"Private room where the girls make their real money. Lots of red velvet and mirrors."

"Real money, real champagne?"

Scut laughed heartily. "Let's just say, the money's green and the box wine's got some fizz. Anyway, in that room, there's no touching of body parts but plenty of everything else. It's where the girls make the big tips and I make the big profits on the liquor. I told Tawny she was either going to get off the coke and get clean, or be fired."

"She got clean, I take it."

"Clean! I suppose you could say that. If you ask me, though, switching from coke to methadone isn't going clean except in some alternative universe."

"Do you know for a fact that she was taking methadone when she died?"

"After I issued the ultimatum, I made her show me the prescription to prove she was off drugs, but I didn't demand she swallow a pill in front of me." He smiled wryly. "Who knows whether she took it as prescribed? I do know, she continued drinking after that, so if she was mixing methadone with vodka, she was playing with fire."

From his jacket pocket, Steve extracted the prescription vial he'd found in JayCee's bedroom and offered it to Scut. "Does this look familiar?"

Scut glanced at the label but made no move to take the vial. "I'm not touching that."

Steve was momentarily puzzled.

"Fingerprints."

"Oh. . . . I'm not trying to set you up, Scut. I'm just trying to decide whether I'm seeing what I think I'm seeing."

"Where'd you find it?"

Steve shook his head.

"Ah, got you." Scut looked off into space. "You searched her house before the cops got there."

"No. But no need to go into that now. I'll hold it so you can read the label."

Scut leaned in. "Looks pretty much the same as the one I saw. She started on methadone more than a year ago -- in 2009, I think -- so the date of 2010 isn't the same as I saw. But I recognize the doctor's name, the pharmacy chain. And, of course, that's Tawny's name." Scut stood up. "Are we done with Tawny and her drugs?"

We're just beginning. Steve stood up too. "I think so."

"You're a businessman, might be interested to see how we operate. You want a tour?"

Steve hesitated.

"I'm not expecting you to become a customer, Steve. But Pop and I are thinking of franchising the business, so if you're interested in getting in on the ground floor, here's your opportunity."

Steve wasn't thinking of getting in on the ground floor of anything, especially a gentlemen's club, but what could it hurt to see where his daughter's mother had worked? Maybe he'd learn something. He couldn't admit, even to himself, the real reason for accepting Scut's strange invitation: it would let him put off a painful telephone call to his wife.

53

Fat Eddie's

Saturday, January 8, 2011

JayCee had no interest in eating a hamburger at Five Guys. She wanted a steak and she was paying. Drago thought that sounded okay. If steak was on the menu seven days a week, he'd be happy, and somebody else paying was always a good thing.

"So, where to?" he asked when they were back in his Jeep. The back seat was stuffed with JayCee's purchases at Glenbrook.

"Fat Eddie's Roadhouse. You ever heard of it?"

"No."

"Mom -- my real mom -- took me there once. It's out on Illinois Road toward Roanoke. It's very old-fashioned, dark and smoky, but the booths are romantic. Just start driving, I'll tell you where it is."

Fat Eddie's was a low-slung, brown-clapboard assemblage of tacked-on rooms, breezeways, and porches, stretching out along the highway like a derailed train. Though the parking lot was almost full and the bar bustled with noisy patrons, they were immediately escorted to a booth, where a little tea light provided the only illumination. First, a busboy covered the table in butcher paper and laid out the cutlery. Then, a fortyish waitress named Madge, wearing a black dress, a white apron, and a little paper crown, appeared. She set a bread basket on the table and asked if they needed an ashtray. JayCee said yes and she also wanted a gin and tonic. Drago ordered a beer.

When the waitress left, Drago looked at his companion. "She never even asked how old you are."

"It's dark. Besides, I look twenty-one, don't I?"

He studied her face. Lucy didn't own as much makeup as JayCee was wearing. "I guess. Is that your rocker look?"

"I'm tired of looking like those stupid girls at school. You know what this is?" she asked, pointing at her chest.

Drago was afraid to answer.

"A bustier. Madonna wore stuff like this. It's my Madonna-Amy Winehouse look. If I'm going to sing, I need to look like a rock star. Don't I look like her?"

"Like which?"

"God, Drago, guess. Like Amy Winehouse. She's thin with big eyes and hair, looks like she just got out of bed."

"Don't know who that is."

"She's famous, that's all. A great contralto voice, always sounds a little drugged up. Maybe I should send *Daddy-Mine* to her. She's more like me than Adele." JayCee lit a cigarette. "So, what'd you think of my song?"

"I didn't understand it."

"What do you mean?"

"What's that stuff about a princess bride?"

"That's what I am. I'm the princess now. And you're my prince. We go everywhere together. You like me, I know you do."

Drago was at a loss for words.

"You're a good driver, you know that?"

"That's what people tell me."

"Are you a good kisser too, Drago?"

"You'd have to ask Lucy that."

"You don't kiss other girls?"

"Course not."

Suddenly she slid out of the booth and moved to his side, nudging him over, and putting her arms around his neck. "Forget Lucy. I'm asking you. Show me." She kissed him on the mouth so quickly he couldn't pull away. He found himself kissing her back.

When the waitress appeared with their drinks, JayCee looked up at her. "My boyfriend's shy." She slid away and returned to her side of the booth. "See what I mean? You like kissing me, tell the truth."

Drago had no time to consider what was happening to his heart -- or at least his nether regions. Out of the corner of his eye he caught someone running his way.

He couldn't believe his eyes.

Lucy! Where had she come from? How did she get here? Where were the boys?

Standing a foot away, dressed in rumpled red sweats on which she appeared to have spilled a gallon of coffee, her hair wild, her plump cheeks on fire, Lucy glared at Drago. "What's this? What's going on here?" she yelled. "I've followed you all day. The boys are in the car, screaming their lungs out, I haven't had a minute to myself, and you -- you piece of crap -- are sneaking around with this little tart."

Incongruous thoughts crossed Drago's mind. If he and JayCee had really been sneaking around, then Lucy wouldn't have found them. Somebody must have told her he'd be with JayCee all day -- but without explaining that Mr. Wright had planned the whole thing for reasons he couldn't explain.

His wife leaned in, her face inches from his, yelling and gesturing. He tried to wipe the spray of saliva off his face. When he started to slide out of the booth, Lucy punched him in the shoulder, then swept JayCee's cocktail into her lap. "What are you doing with my man? Trailer trash -- that's what you are! Nothing but garbage. A scarecrow with mean eyes. Keep your hands off him or you'll be eating with stumps."

JayCee giggled. "He's mine, fat girl, not yours. And if you touch me again, I'll call the cops."

"I didn't touch you yet, you skinny little whore. When I do, you'll know it." She turned back to Drago and in a suddenly calm voice said, "Don't even think of coming home again. I'll see you in hell." And then she was gone.

After Drago had returned JayCee to her house, he realized he was either going to have to sleep in the car or face his mother.

54

Liar, Liar
Sunday, January 9, 2011

Steve and Lexie's confrontation of their daughter didn't go the way they expected.

In fact, in their heart of hearts, they hoped there would be no confrontation at all. Lexie warned Steve to go easy on the girl. There might be an innocent explanation for everything.

"You didn't think there was for Jean. You assumed from a few bottles Sadie found under her desk that she was secretly boozing it up on the job."

"And you thought I should have assumed her denial was true, so all I'm asking is, do the same with your daughter. Just see what she says without making her defensive."

Late Sunday morning, they walked to JayCee's room and told her they needed to talk. She was sitting at her Casio keyboard, practicing her music. The black curtains were closed; the only light in the room came from a floor lamp behind her right shoulder.

JayCee looked up and smiled when she saw them in the doorway. Her eyes sparkled. "You want to hear what I've composed? First, I'll play it, then I'll sing the song."

"Okay."

"Sit on the window bench, why don't you?"

The four minutes it took for her to sing the song from beginning to end felt like an eternity.

"Is that what you recorded yesterday?"

"It is. So, how do I sound?"

"Very good," Steve said. "That sounds like the song I found in here yesterday -- *Daddy-Mine*. The one you're sending to Adele in care of Columbia Records."

JayCee's face darkened. "How do you know about that? I didn't show anything to you."

"As I said, I came in here yesterday, just to look around."

"For what?"

"I'd never really been in your room before."

JayCee glared at her father. "You've no right to be in here unless I say so. This is my room. I'm entitled to my privacy. You can't come in here just because you live here too."

He kept his voice very quiet. "We don't just live here; we own the place. And parents have every right to know what's going on with their children, so we don't need anybody's say-so to enter any room in the house, including yours. You're a smart girl. I'm sure you understand that."

JayCee seemed to consider the situation. Her frown disappeared, replaced by a tight smile. "Did you mail the envelope?"

"No."

"Give it to me then."

"I have it here," Lexie said. "We've been trying to understand your song. Let me read the chorus: 'Had to make my own way . . . had to clear a path, so many down . . . how many more . . . until I wear the daughter's crown.'" She looked up. "What path are you clearing? What do you mean, so many down?"

"Oh, for Christ' sake, Mom. It's art. I had to rhyme something with crown."

"'I walk out to the foggy dark and dance to see her fall.' Is that just art too? Or are you telling us something about Halloween night at the bridge?"

JayCee giggled. "You are so lame. Really. I did see Libby fall."

"You did?"

She sneered. "Like, in my imagination."

Steve got up, pulled the ring out of his trouser pocket, and walked over to his daughter. "I found this too. Recognize it?"

JayCee hesitated, involuntarily flicking her eyes at the window seat, where Lexie was still sitting, then asked in an accusatory tone, "Where did you find that?"

"I think you know where. Tell me what this is."

She tossed her head defiantly. "You know what it is. Libby's ring. The one Joey gave her."

"How did it get in this room?"

She gave her father her most innocent look. "She gave it to me."

"Why? How did that happen?"

"She was mad at Joey. She wanted me to keep it where nobody would see it but made me promise I'd give it back if they got back together. After she died, Joey told me to keep it. My birthstone's an emerald, same as Libby's, so it works."

Then Steve took the prescription vial out of his other trouser pocket and held it toward her. "How about this? Look familiar?"

She merely glanced at it. "No."

"It's your mother's methadone pills."

"How do you know they're hers?"

"The label."

Silence.

"How did you come to have this in your possession, JayCee? Why was it in this room?"

"You know where I found it. In the stupid trailer I grew up in, poor as dirt, while you were living here, rich as a king."

Steve ignored the taunt. "You took it from your mother's things?"

She scrunched up her face as if she was about to cry but didn't answer.

"You took it after your mother died, I assume. But why?"

"I didn't want the cops to know my mother was, like, an addict. I was protecting her."

"If you didn't want the cops to see this, why didn't you just throw it away when you were tossing other stuff into the dumpster the night you were told she was on the way to the hospital?"

"What stuff?" Lexie asked. "What are you talking about?"

"A conversation I had months ago with Duke. I'll tell you about it later." He returned his attention to his daughter. "Why did you keep this medicine?"

"I don't know. I wasn't thinking, I guess."

He shook the vial. "Some pills seem to be missing."

"How do you know that?"

"I can count. The date on the label, the number of pills originally in there minus the maximum she'd have taken before she died. Six are missing."

JayCee shrugged. "Maybe she took more than she should have."

"Maybe. Why was this vial and the ring hidden together in the window seat?"

"I didn't *hide* them. I just didn't know where else to put them. But you can throw them away now. I shouldn't have kept the pills." She reached for the vial but Steve held on to it. He stepped away and sat down in an armchair.

"Do you miss Libby?"

JayCee was confused. "Why -- why are you asking that? What's she got to do with Tawny's prescription?"

"Nothing. I'm just concerned about you -- we both are," he said, glancing at his wife. "There's been a lot of tragedy among your friends in a very short period of time. It has to affect you."

"It does," she said, scrunching up her face. "It's, like, lonely. Libby and Joey were my best friends."

"Were you and Joey sleeping together?"

"Dad!"

"Were you? Before the night you said he raped you, I mean."

"He did rape me! I'm not just saying it. He forced me. And, yes, that was the first time."

Steve held out his hands, one holding the ring, the other the prescription vial. "I'm going to have to take these to Duke, ask him what to do about them." He glanced at Lexie, still holding the lyrics page. "And the stuff you were sending to Adele. Finding the ring clears up the mystery about what happened to it and eventually Mrs. Stuart should get it back. And methadone is what made Lexie so sick, so that mystery is cleared up too. Except, of course, how it got into her system. I don't know if that song you wrote means anything, but maybe it does. We also have to tell Duke what you told Lexie about letting Libby out of the house that night, hearing her voice and Joey's at the bridge, even hearing her scream." He paused. "That story's true, isn't it?"

"It's not a story." She wiped her eyes with the back of her hand. "You don't believe anything I say."

"Well, what you're saying now is different from what you told all of us after Libby was first found. Then you said you didn't know how she got out of the house without setting off the alarm. Now you tell us you let her out and heard their voices." Steve paused. "By the way, how could you hear Joey and Libby arguing on the bridge if you were still in the house?"

"I wasn't in the house. I never said that."

"I think you did."

"You don't listen to me at all. I was standing on the patio off the media room."

Steve ignored the taunt about not listening to her. "That's what? at least two hundred yards away and around a corner."

"They were yelling. Libby screamed. You know how sound travels through fog."

"I didn't know it did."

"I googled it."

"You googled what exactly?"

"How sound travels through fog. Most of the articles are about Seattle -- ."

He cut her off. "Why?"

"Because I knew you wouldn't, like, believe me otherwise."

Steve cleared his throat. "But you didn't call anybody when you heard Libby scream. Why?"

"It wasn't any of my business. Besides, I didn't think it meant anything. How was I supposed to know Joey would do something horrible to her?" She sniffed as if fighting back tears. "But then I found out he is horrible. You know that too."

"I see. So can you tell us how you got that strange bruise on your temple?"

She turned and pointed at the panther statue. "That's what he hit me with."

Steve got up, took a handkerchief from his pocket, and walked over to the dresser.

"What are you doing?" JayCee asked.

He draped his handkerchief over the statue and picked it up. "It might still have his fingerprints on it. Why didn't you tell us earlier about this?"

JayCee stared at her father. Finally she asked, "Why can't we just throw that stuff away. Why does that stupid man have to know anything?"

"The more he knows, the better we can protect you."

"If you're really going to do that, then there's something else to show him."

"There's more?"

JayCee shot her father a triumphant smile. "Joey wrote a confession."

"You're joking."

"No."

"You have it?"

"Don't look like you don't believe me."

"How did you get hold of it?"

"It's a love note he wrote to me."

"Where is it?"

She got up and went into the study, returning a few seconds later. "Here."

He unfolded a small piece of notebook paper and read aloud: "'My darling JayCee. She's out of the way now. Your loving BFF, Joey.'" Steve looked up. "Is this Joey's handwriting?"

She shook her head in disbelief at the foolishness of the question. "Of course."

"How do you know?"

"I've seen it plenty of times. And it's the same notepaper he used to get Libby to the bridge that night. BFF, in case you're wondering, means boyfriend forever. That's what he told me anyway."

Lexie spoke up. "What does that line mean, 'She's out of the way now?'"

"Duh! She's dead."

"By whose hand?" Steve asked. "Joey's, I suppose?"

"Or yours." She stared at him with glittering eyes.

"What?" Lexie and Steve asked in chorus.

"Maybe I heard your voice out by the bridge, Dad."

"JayCee!" Lexie cried. "How can you say such a thing? We were at the Club that night. Your father would never do such a thing."

"You weren't there."

"I was with your father until we got home from the Club. By that time, I assume Libby was in the water, if not dead."

"Whatever. Just testing you."

"That's not a test," Lexie said. "That's the most horrible lie you could concoct."

JayCee was defiant. "It wasn't a lie. I said *maybe* I heard Dad at the bridge."

"You shouldn't say it at all."

"Probably it was Joey. . . . Yah, I'm pretty sure it was Joey."

"And, believing that he murdered his girlfriend, you protected him anyway! You spent time alone with him! . . . Weren't you afraid he'd do the same thing to you?" Lexie asked.

"No. What he did at the bridge proved he loved me."

"In what universe . . . ?"

Steve got up and took his wife's arm. "It's time to go. Things aren't adding up."

"Or else they are," Lexie said under her breath.

"I want that note back," JayCee said, standing up and reaching toward her father.

"Afraid not." Steve handed the note to Lexie. "We have a lot of thinking to do."

55

Limbo
Sunday, January 9, 2011

Sunday afternoon, in an old Victorian on Forest Park Boulevard, Duke Simmons was installing shelving in his garage to hold fishing equipment when he heard a car pull into the driveway. He put down his drill, opened the garage door, and walked out. He didn't recognize the Expedition.

"What a surprise," he said, when Steve Wright put down his window. "What's up? Haven't seen you for awhile."

"It's rude of us just to come over like this, Duke, no notice, but we really need to talk to you."

Duke hesitated. He didn't normally see clients on Sunday, and then only by appointment in his office. Furthermore, in this case, the interruption meant he might not get through his honey-do list before the Packers-Eagles game. But his clients looked like somebody had died, so he said, "Sure. You want to stay to watch the Packers kick the stuffing out of the Eagles? I'm sure my wife can stretch the chili she's making."

"Some other time. We can't stay long."

"Do you have time to see my newest vintage lunch box?" Duke asked when they were settled in the family room. Without waiting for an answer, he opened a display case and removed a metal lunch box with an American flag motif. "Stars & Stripes Dome Lunch box, 1970. Even a thermos. What do you think?"

Steve smiled. "And this set you back, what? Fifty dollars?"

"Oh, man, I wish. Try ten times that."

Steve whistled. "You're serious about this stuff."

"Somebody's got to preserve the best of the past."

"Which is what?"

"A simpler way of life. When there were no food police and your mother sometimes surprised you with your favorite bologna sandwich and a Twinkie. At most you might have to eat a few carrot sticks -- unless you traded them for a great big old dill pickle. The lunch boxes remind me of that. Everything looked so good then, didn't it?" Duke returned the lunch box to the display case. His attempt to lower the tension emanating from his clients had accomplished nothing, so he tried again. "Just let me ask Dorothy to make some coffee." He studied their faces. "Or do you need something stronger?"

"Coffee's good," Steve said.

"So," Duke said, after returning with a tray of coffee cups and cookies and settling into an armchair, "what do you need to talk to me about?"

"JayCee," Steve said. "Are you ready for a little show-and-tell?"

"Try me."

Steve laid out on the coffee table the lyrics to *Daddy-Mine* with the note to Adele, Tawny's prescription vial, Libby's ring, the panther statue, and Joey's confession. He explained each one in turn. The narrative took an hour, Duke interjecting many questions.

When Steve was done, Duke gave his clients a long look. "So what's the question?"

"What do you think? Are we imagining that JayCee might have done some very bad things? And if we aren't imagining things, is there a way to stop her?"

"You mean, if you turned all this over to the authorities -- which I'd advise you not to do -- would the State's Attorney charge her with murdering Libby, falsely accusing Joey of rape and battery, and poisoning Lexie?"

"That's what we mean."

Duke leaned toward the coffee table. "Okay, let's take these one by one. The song has an ominous tone, suggesting your daughter killed her friend at the bridge. But it isn't a typical confession, is it? It's arguably no more than an expression of a teenager's overactive imagination. True, her suggestion that her first song is worthy of a Grammy is grandiose, and typical of a . . . I hate to say it, but typical of a sociopath." He looked at his clients apologetically. "I'm not saying JayCee's a sociopath, but if she did the things we're talking about, then chances are she is. Though grandiosity is a characteristic of sociopaths and can lead them to do terrible things, by itself it's not a criminal offense. Have either of you read a book called *Without Conscience* by Dr. Hare, by the way?"

Lexie and Steve shook their heads.

"Well, you might want to read it. It explains some of the elements of a sociopath's personality. Let me tell you, a lot of my clients are sociopaths. Anyway, back to your array of . . . artifacts. The methadone is alarming because there's no reason JayCee should have hung on to it or hidden it. She didn't want the baby, you say, but there's no proof that the methadone in Lexie's system came from this vial, or that the girl tampered with your vitamin capsules, Lexie -- or that she knew the methadone would cause a miscarriage.

"Then there Libby's ring," he said, picking it up. "Maybe JayCee took it from her friend before killing her. Or maybe she's telling the truth -- Libby gave it to her and then Joey told her to keep it. It's JayCee's word against that of a dead girl or a boy who's been charged with rape.

"The panther statue might match up with the photographs of her injuries, but a match doesn't tell us who was holding it when she was struck in the temple. As I understand it, the doctor himself said her injuries looked pretty superficial, but that doesn't mean she inflicted them on herself.

"And then we come to Joey's note implying he got rid of Libby. If the cops got their hands on this, they might find a handwriting expert to determine whether he wrote it. The torn left edge might match up with a notebook either JayCee or Joey had. If the boy's fingerprints aren't on the note, we have a question about the author's identity -- but not an answer. JayCee's fingerprints on it simply means she received it, not that she wrote it. If other people -- like JayCee -- had access to Joey's notebook, then she or someone else could have taken the paper and used it to frame him."

Duke sat back, his eyes still on the coffee table. "You tell me she also changed her story about Halloween night at least three times and about Joey's alleged assault more than once. I understand why that raises red flags in your mind -- it raises them in mine too -- but it doesn't support the kind of case a prosecutor will stake his career on."

"You think we're nuts, even to suspect that JayCee could . . . could kill Libby or falsely accuse Joey of rape?"

"No." Duke rubbed his chin. "Without divulging information I shouldn't, let me just say I have a hunch the cops want to talk to JayCee about her mother's death because no one else had access to her mother's thermos. They never found the antifreeze, or I think we'd have heard about it, but the garbage bag JayCee dumped the night her mother died might have contained it. We'll never know now -- unless she confesses. The motive for Antoinette's death seems insubstantial if you're normal, but it's rational if you're a sociopath."

"Hold on," Steve said. "Sociopaths are rational?"

"Yes, in the sense that they know the difference between right and wrong, they plan their crimes, and they try to cover them up. And, as I said before, I'm not saying your daughter is a sociopath -- I'm not qualified to say that, though I have my inexpert opinion after talking to her -- but let's assume she is a sociopath just for the sake of argument. You with me?"

Steve and Lexie nodded.

"Let's also assume for the moment -- just for the sake of argument -- that she killed her mother, her mother's boyfriend, and her girlfriend. That makes three murders. Experts disagree on whether two or three murders are necessary for someone to be called a serial killer, but either way, JayCee meets the criteria.

A serial killer is typically motivated by anger, revenge, or financial gain. Some seek attention, but I don't see that as operative here."

Duke leaned forward, his face tight with concentration, a few strands of hair failing over his forehead. "Here goes. As you know, the cops don't have to find a motive to construct a prosecutable case, but juries sometimes have a hard time convicting if they can't figure out a plausible motive. So let's contrast the girl's situation before and after her mother died. Before the death, JayCee wanted her mother to name you as her father and make you, Steve, pay child support so they'd live better, but Antoinette wouldn't do it. Afterward, once her mother was out of the way, JayCee was free to find you. Even if you hadn't acknowledged her as your daughter and taken her into your home, at least she stood a good chance of living a lot better on whatever money the courts forced you to cough up. As it is, however, she won the lottery."

"So the death of her mother produced financial gain."

"Looks that way. She even said as much when I interviewed her. Then there's Tug, her mother's boyfriend, who died from anaphylaxis as a result of a peanut allergy. JayCee hated the man and mentioned he never worked. Before I met with JayCee, I took a look at the Coroner's report. At the time of Tug's death, Antoinette told an investigator that Tug carried an epinephrine pen but she couldn't find it. She denied that she kept any peanuts or peanut products in the house, though I have reason to believe some might have been present without Antoinette's knowledge. Your daughter denied hiding Tug's EpiPen, but something she said calls that into question."

Steve looked stricken. "When I searched her room yesterday, I found an EpiPen attached to a key chain in a bag stuffed under her bed. I didn't give it a second thought. You don't suppose . . . ?"

Duke nodded. "So my suspicions were spot on. She got rid of a free-loader, and she kept the pen as a souvenir. You might say the same thing about her mother's methadone and Libby's ring. Murderers, especially serial murderers, often keep souvenirs to remind themselves of their triumphs."

"Getting rid of Tug got rid of a nuisance, maybe even a

financial drag," Steve said. "Getting rid of her mother meant she had a chance of finding her father. In each case, she gained something -- not enough to murder if you're normal -- but she gained something important to her. But if she rather than Joey killed Libby, what was the motive? She didn't improve her standard of living."

"Adolescent jealousy perhaps. Maybe anger at Libby, or revenge for something JayCee thought she did. Your daughter couldn't make Joey her boyfriend until Libby was out of the way, so Libby's death meant there was a change for the better. Then something happened with Joey -- maybe he broke up with her -- and she got revenge by accusing him of rape. Then she got rid of the baby because she didn't want to share the spotlight with another kid."

Lexie shuddered. "This is all just speculation."

Duke tipped his head. "Yes."

"If I understand you right, there are lots of reasons to suspect JayCee of some very bad stuff. But is there enough evidence that the police would charge her with these crimes and the prosecutor would take take her to trial? And if she went to trial, would a jury convict?"

"Even if the cops knew what we know -- or suspect -- I doubt it. The forensic evidence directly linking her to the crimes is practically non-existent. These days, juries expect a trial to be like a CSI episode. And painting a credible picture of a sixteen-year-old serial killer to a jury would be formidable."

"Can we get her institutionalized?"

"On what grounds?"

Steve groaned. "So where do we go from here?"

"We sit tight."

"We can't do that," Steve said. "More than likely, JayCee's the one who put methadone in Lexie's vitamin capsules. For awhile, when she was in the hospital after the rape, she wouldn't say what happened, leaving us hanging as suspected child abusers. This morning, in a moment of anger, she accused me of Libby's murder -- then took it back as the absurdity it is, but what if she starts spreading rumors? What if she decides to get rid of somebody else? How do we sleep at night?"

"She's a smart girl," Lexie said. "She's counting on our kindness as her parents, our unwillingness to admit we made a mistake by adopting her. We have to find the ethical way to stop her."

"You have suspicions -- reasonable ones, in my view -- but no proof of anything. I suppose you could think of this as an ethical problem, but really you need to be practical. If you want to be sure your suspicions are spot on, then try to get a confession from her. Given what I know about her, I don't hold out much hope that she'll cop to anything. She's manipulative and has an answer for everything, even when she's caught in a lie. But if you don't try to get a confession, you'll live in limbo."

"A private confession to me won't mean much, will it?" Lexie asked.

"By itself, no, unless you want to wear a wire."

"I don't know if I could bring myself to do that. Meanwhile, you're right -- we live in limbo!" Lexie said. "If we live at all."

Duke stood up. "There's nothing stopping you from going to the police with the same information you've given me, but in that case, you realize, you might be subjecting your own daughter -- and yourselves -- to a hellish investigation that in the end resolves nothing and even makes things worse."

Lexie looked at the coffee table. "For the moment, what do we do with these -- artifacts, I think you called them?"

"Leave them here."

Just as Steve stood up too, his phone bleeped with a text. "Excuse me. It's Dave Powers." He studied the screen. "I can't believe this."

"What?" Lexie said, standing up and trying to read the text.

"Dave says JayCee called him. Tomorrow she's filing a complaint against me, claiming I hit her when I found her with Joey. She's hinted that she knows something about Libby's death the cops don't know." He stared at Duke and Lexie. "What in hell is that about? What does she know she hasn't already said?"

"A child endangerment charge against you! You said she

accused you of murder this morning, so maybe that's the new charge. That complicates things," Duke said wryly. "You're going to need a good lawyer, but in the circumstances I can't represent you in a matter between you and your daughter since I already represent her. However, I can recommend someone." He put his arm on Steve's. "Let me give you a piece of friendly advice anyway. Don't go home tonight. Stay away from your daughter until this is resolved."

It took a second for Steve and Lexie to process that counsel. "But then I'll be alone with her," Lexie said. "It isn't safe."

"Ask a friend to stay with you."

"Who?"

"Jean," Steve said. "Ask Jean."

"Why would she do me a favor after what I did to her?"

"Phyllis then."

"Poor Phyllis."

Suddenly, Steve felt sick. He slumped into a chair, his head in his hands. "What in hell have I done?"

Part Three

And when she was bad she was horrid.

Final line of an old nursery rhyme

"I will have mercy on whom I will have mercy . . . ."

The Lord speaking, Exodus 33: 19

56

A Terrible Jam
Sunday, January 9, 2011

On the drive back home, Steve and I made a decision. He would bolt upstairs, throw a few things into a duffle, then drive to Woodburn to stay with his brother Frank until it was safe to come home. He'd hire the lawyer Duke Simmons recommended and then, if the cops asked him to appear for an interview, he would do so.

While Steve was packing, I called Jean and told her I was in a terrible jam. I needed her. She was a little stiff on the phone, but I told her I was wrong about suspending her, she had her job back if she wanted it, and I would explain the whole situation if she'd just come over. I pleaded with her to give me a chance to make things right. Without trying, I'm sure I sounded as hysterical as I felt. "Plan to stay a few days if you can manage that. Do you have a gun?"

"Of course."

"Bring it."

"You're kidding!"

"No."

"Do you want Dover to come with me?"

"No. Just you. Please." Over the phone I wasn't about to tell her that no man would be safe in our house. He could be accused of rape, even murder.

When Jean arrived, JayCee was upstairs in her suite. I took Jean to the atrium, where I hugged her.

"Why are you crying, Lexie? What's going on?"

It took a few minutes to compose myself. "I'm ashamed and I'm scared." I told her about our afternoon with Duke Simmons, leaving out nothing.

"Where do I come into this?"

"If JayCee can do the things we think she has, she could have set you up. I realize that now. Those liquor bottles under your desk were probably taken out of our trash."

"By your daughter?"

I nodded. "I don't know that for sure. I can't think why she would, but who else in this household would do such a thing?"

"*I* can think why she would," Jean said. "I'm the one who told you she stole some clothes."

"I don't even know if she read your note. I don't think she did."

"She and I had a very odd conversation one afternoon. She wanted to trade secrets. I told her I was an alcoholic -- not really a secret -- and then she told me about stealing a garment from Forever 21. She also asked me who you loved more -- her or me and said something about how you could fire me but not her. She warned me not to tell you what she'd done. When I left the office that evening, she saw me carrying an envelope to your cubby, so she knew, if I was going to tell you about the theft, where she'd find the note. She couldn't have known for sure I'd rat on her, but she might have suspected I would, especially because I told her how wrong it was to steal. If she did read the note, then the revenge she got was just what you'd expect. She knew exactly how to make it look like I was doing something you'd fire me for."

"That's awfully devious for a teenager. But given our conversation with Duke, I can believe it."

"So . . . ."

"So, Jean, I'm sorry for what I did to you. It was unfair. Steve told me that in no uncertain terms, and we were at odds for weeks over it."

"And?"

"And you have your job back if you'll forgive me."

It took awhile before Jean was mollified. She felt the need to defend herself and chide me for going off half-cocked. I felt the need to let my defenses down and listen for once. Really listen.

Finally she said something to the effect that I was forgiven. Just then there was the rumble of thunder. We both looked up at the glass ceiling of the atrium. "Good heavens, can you believe this?" Jean said. "It's snowing and thundering at the same time. Only in Fort Wayne!" She looked around the room. "Whatever made you build an atrium like this?"

"Over a year ago, before Steve and I were married, I stayed in a New York hotel with an atrium like this. I loved the feeling of indoors-outdoors. And that night I made a call to Steve that changed our relationship for the better, so I associate this kind of space with a promising future."

"You never expected then that you'd be facing what you're facing now, I'll bet."

"Never."

"You know what scares me?" Jean suddenly stood up and looked around. "Where do you keep the ashtrays? I need a cigarette."

I pointed to a cabinet. "I'll have one too. Anyway, what scares you?"

"Steve made a mistake years ago . . . a common one for boys that age. In the eyes of a lot of people who made the same mistake, it probably seemed pretty minor, with no consequences."

"Are we talking about his encounter with Antoinette Delamarter?"

"That's what we're talking about. A few minutes of teenage indiscretion ended up poisoning his life."

"And mine too. I didn't think it would. Once I accepted the situation, I wanted to be the best step-mother ever."

"You always want to be the best at whatever you're doing."

"You make that sound like a fault, Jean."

"Sorry."

I knew from her face she wanted to remind me that being a perfectionist wasn't a virtue, but she restrained herself.

"So now what happens, Lexie?"

"Tomorrow Steve's going to talk to the police, if necessary. He's hiring a lawyer."

"How about tonight? How can we go to bed knowing we're in the same house with a girl who might have killed her mother, her mother's boyfriend, and her best friend? I don't plan to sleep a wink."

"This may be one of those nights I can't sleep anyway."

"Then, if I'm going to stay awake with you, I'm going to need some coffee. How about you?"

"Big pot, full caff."

"You have anything to eat in that vast pantry of yours?"

I laughed. "Phyllis stocks every snack you can think of, so I'm sure we'll find something."

She was making coffee while I laid out smoked oysters, a good brie, and rice crackers when my cell phone played *Nine to Five*. I looked at the screen, then at Jean. "It's Phyllis."

"This time of night? On a Sunday?"

Phyllis, in an agitated voice, said she had to see me immediately. I told her this wasn't a good time, but she wasn't about to be put off.

"If you don't see me right now, you won't see me tomorrow morning or any morning after that."

I looked at the phone in shock. After more than twenty years, she was prepared to quit, just like that? "I don't understand."

"You will."

I told her to come through the garage to the kitchen without ringing the bell. The last thing I needed was to arouse JayCee, assuming she was asleep, or lose Phyllis.

57

Things Left Unsaid
Sunday, January 9, 2011

As Phyllis opened the door, we could hear it thundering. When she turned toward me, I saw that her pinched face was more pinched than ever, a study in repressed fury. Before I could invite her to take a stool at the island, she said, "I can't believe what you've done to my son and his family."

"What *I've* done?"

Jean did her best to calm the troubled waters, urging Phyllis to sit down, take a deep breath, and have some coffee or a glass of wine if she wanted. Suddenly, Phyllis registered Jean's presence as if she hadn't realized who was speaking to her. "What are you doing here? I thought you'd been fired."

I explained that we had an emergency, Steve had left to stay with his brother and Jean had come over to keep me company. When I started to explain why I had reinstated Jean, Phyllis interrupted, as if she had no time for anyone else's story.

"Your daughter's the problem."

"She is that," I conceded, though I had yet to hear why Phyllis was so angry.

"She spent yesterday with my son -- at Mr. Wright's request, I might add. Did you know that? Lucy, poor girl, followed them all day, driving all over hell with the twins in the back seat. She finally found them having a cozy dinner at Fat Eddie's out on 14. Now she won't let Drago go home. She calls either him or me every hour, crying, screaming and threatening divorce. My son is staying with me, hiding up in his old bedroom like a whipped boy. He claims he's not having an affair with JayCee but he won't explain anything. Our life has been ripped apart by that girl."

"All this because Lucy found them having dinner together?"

"Oh, wake up." Phyllis had never spoken to me in that tone before, and I was taken aback. "She's been at the Scrapyard with Drago pretending to be a reporter. They've gone to lunch at least twice that I know about. She's gone puppy training with him. He drives her to the theater on Lucy's birthday. Then Mr. Wright tells him to spend the day with her at a recording studio and then take her shopping and out to dinner." She paused and in a quieter voice said, "It's awful what you've done. You keep throwing your daughter and my son together, as if you want to drive a wedge between him and Lucy. What in the world are you thinking?"

There was more. Lots more. I didn't want to sound defensive, but I did try to explain that we had no intention of causing problems between Drago and Lucy.

And then, instead of continuing the verbal exchange, Phyllis pulled a rabbit out of a hat, so to speak. Well, out of her purse. On the counter she laid out the silver Juicy Couture necklace I'd given JayCee when she first moved in. The heart pendant was partially crushed.

I stared at the thing. It had been lost so long I'd almost forgotten about it. I'd instructed Sadie to look for it more than once, but nothing had come of those searches. Now, here it was, as if by magic. The necklace had the same effect on me as if Phyllis had suddenly laid a dead rabbit on the counter. I couldn't bring myself to touch it. "Where did this come from? Why do you have it?"

"Todd found it near the bridge."

"When?"

"A few days before Thanksgiving. It was smooshed in the mud made by the tires of a fire truck."

The hair rose on the back of my neck and I had a hard time

catching my breath. "How long had it been there?"

Phyllis looked at me as if I were brain dead. "The last time a fire truck was parked near the stone bridge."

"I see. . . . Why didn't Todd give it to me when he found it?"

"We planned to give it to you when the time was ripe."

"And it's ripe now, is it?"

She took her time explaining. "Think of it as a trade. The police don't have to know about it if you keep JayCee away from Drago."

I looked at Jean, then back at Phyllis. "Why do you think the police might want to know about it?"

"You really want me to spell it out?"

I nodded.

"Your daughter was at the bridge the night Libby died. Did this necklace just drop off her neck? I don't think so. I think she lost it in a struggle with Libby. Todd knows he set the alarm, so if it didn't go off, JayCee shut it off. Why lie about a little thing like the alarm unless it was to cover up a big thing -- like what actually happened out there?"

I knew that part about the alarm was true. And I knew JayCee lied about what she did that night because she told me she did. First she was asleep and didn't know why the alarm didn't sound, then she turned off the alarm and let Libby out, finally she not only let Libby out but stood on the patio listening to some kind of scuffle on the bridge. It wasn't illogical to believe that the next iteration of her story would be an admission she was actually at the bridge.

I wanted to tell Phyllis about the conversation Steve and I had had with Duke Simmons earlier that day, but I knew that was pouring gasoline on a fire, so I simply mused, "Nothing has been right since she arrived here."

"I thought I'd never hear you admit that," Phyllis said.

"She's at the center of a whirlwind that's destroyed a lot of lives. Her mother and her mother's boyfriend are dead. Libby Stuart's dead too. Joey DeWitt's been charged with rape, and his father killed himself. Drago and Lucy are at loggerheads, on the verge of divorce from what you tell me. Jean's been falsely suspected of drinking on the job. I was poisoned with methadone and lost the baby. She's connected with every single event."

"She personifies chaos," Jean said. "I hate chaos."

"Those are death penalty cases -- some of them anyway." Phyllis made her pronouncement as dispassionately as if describing *bouillabaisse* as a Provençal fish stew.

I shuddered. "I hope it doesn't come to that. In fact, it won't. She's been too clever for the law."

"What do you mean?"

"She's covered her tracks so well it's unlikely she can be successfully prosecuted for the crimes we think she's committed."

"Where is she?" Phyllis asked.

"Upstairs in her bedroom. Why?"

"It makes me nervous to be in the same house as her. That's why I have to quit."

A long silence ensued. I didn't know what to say.

Jean was the one to break the silence. "Before there was such a thing as the Law -- with a capital L -- before there were sheriffs and detectives and prosecutors, how did people deal with a murderer in their midst? Does anybody know?"

Neither Phyllis nor I answered her.

"You know what I'm talking about, right?" Jean continued, oblivious of my pain. "Everybody in the village knows who robbed and killed the old widow living alone in the forest. The villain blithely continues on about his business -- cutting wood all day and getting drunk at night, sneering at his neighbors, maybe even wearing some token he stole from the widow. Everybody knows the bastard will do it again unless he's stopped, but the sheriff won't help or is off in another county or something. So what do the villagers do?"

Phyllis gave each of us a long look. "Surely you know the answer."

Jean shook her head. "No, I don't."

"A family member of the victim finds the culprit and kills him."

"That's vigilante justice."

"At least it's justice. Or the criminal's family pays blood money to the victim's family. But, either way, the villagers stop the killing."

Jean shuddered. "Well, that's not possible in this day and age, is it?"

As if we'd heard the same prompt, both Phyllis and I returned our gaze to the Juicy Couture necklace.

On impulse I went to my cubby and opened a little wall safe. I returned with the silver ID bracelet Todd found out by the creek and laid it beside the silver necklace. I didn't look at Phyllis. She and I both knew who the initials belonged to. We also both knew whose bones were found at the creek over a year earlier.

"What's that?" Jean asked, picking up the bracelet and spelling out the initials. "GWCB. Who does this thing belong to? What's it have to do with what we're talking about?"

Neither Phyllis nor I answered. Each of us possessed something the other wished had never been lost in the first place. Each of us knew about a deed that couldn't be undone. Those two silver mementoes balanced the scales.

So I let the silence grow and grow like an underground fungus. Suddenly, Phyllis jerked her head up.

"What?" I asked.

"Nothing." With an enigmatic little nod, Phyllis reached for the ID bracelet and put it in her purse. "Tell JayCee not to try to see Drago."

"I'll do that."

"He's at my house, you know."

"That's what you said."

"I'm not staying there tonight. I'm going to Todd's, so Drago will be alone."

Jean looked puzzled, as if listening to code. I wasn't sure I understood it myself until later. After a few minutes that felt like an hour, Phyllis put on her coat and let herself out through the garage.

"Now, what was that about?" Jean asked, picking up the necklace to examine it more closely. "Why did you let her take the bracelet?"

I looked at the cold cup of coffee I'd barely touched. "I think I need a glass of wine after all."

"No problem, Lexie." She moved to the wine refrigerator, took out a bottle, found the corkscrew and poured a glass of wine for me before saying, "But you didn't answer me."

As Phyllis opened the door to the garage, I had caught JayCee's ghostly reflection in the French doors to the kitchen terrace. For a second, I wasn't sure whether she was outside the kitchen or somewhere in the house. Now I slowly turned to see her standing in the doorway of the family room. Her glittering eyes were in shadow, her face pale except for the feverish glow of her cheeks. She was clad in a long white nightgown I didn't even know she owned.

Had Phyllis seen the same apparition?

"Some things are best left unsaid," I whispered.

58

The Apple of Dad's Eye
Sunday, January 9, 2011

"How long have you been standing there?" I asked JayCee.

"Oh, my God," Jean exclaimed, suddenly noticing her.

"Long enough. Long enough to know you think I killed my real mother and Tug and Libby. That I accused Joey of rape and put methadone in your vitamin capsules."

"You didn't hear me say any such thing. "

"I did."

What in the world did she think she had heard? "I only said you're connected with all those events, at the center of the whirlwind. But you could put our minds at rest. Tell us you didn't do those things," I whispered.

"Why? You wouldn't believe me anyway."

"With the right explanation, I would."

"Whatever." She walked over to the counter and grabbed the wine glass. Without thinking, I tried to grab it back. In my haste, the glass hit her lip before crashing to the counter. "Ow!" she cried, holding her bloody lip and backing away from me in an exaggerated pose of fear. "Now see what you've done."

I babbled assurances that I hadn't meant to hurt her and tried to use a towel to dab at the blood on her mouth. She wouldn't let me near her.

"I'm going to call your cop friend and show him what you did to me. Dad beats me, so do you." She twisted her mouth into a smile as she watched Jean gathering up broken glass and mopping up wine. "What's she doing here anyway?"

"She'll be staying with us a few days to keep us company."

"Why?"

"Dad had to leave for awhile."

"Why?"

"You know why. You told Dave Powers he beat you up. He can't risk being around you."

"I want him. I want him now. I want to show him what you just did to me."

"Why would you want him if he beats you up, as you claim?"

"I just made that up. He didn't kill Libby or beat me up. Joey did."

"Then why did you accuse Dad of those things?"

"Just to see what he'd say. God, Lexie -- ."

I cut her off. "I'm Lexie now, not Mom?"

"You were never Mom. Jean told me to call you that so you'd think I liked you. But I never did. I hate you. I, like, hate you so much that I could . . . ."

"You could what?" Jean asked.

"Kill both of you."

I did my best to conceal my horror. "Then what? If we were dead, then what?"

"I'd have Dad to myself. I'd be the queen." Suddenly she drew closer to the counter and scoured it with her eyes. "Where'd my necklace go?"

Neither Jean nor I answered. I didn't know where it had gone either, so Jean must have hidden it during the scuffle over the wine glass.

"Where is it?" she screamed. Without warning, she lunged and struck me in the shoulder. If Jean hadn't thrown herself between us, I don't know what would have happened.

"Stop that!" Jean shouted, taking the blows I would have received. Gripping the girl's shoulders, doing her best to dodge the blows, she shoved JayCee backward. "Go sit down in the family room, get hold of yourself. You're not hitting anyone. Stop that or we'll call the police."

JayCee backed up a few steps. "The police!" she sneered. "I heard you admit they can't do anything to me, no matter what I did."

"Tell us, what did you do?"

"Everything I had to do to get where I am."

"And where is that?"

"The apple of Dad's eye. The most talented songwriter in the world, soon to be famous. And Drago's girlfriend."

"If you heard everything, then you know Phyllis doesn't want you anywhere near Drago."

She laughed. "Watch me," she yelled over her shoulder as she ran upstairs.

59

Like Sin Itself
Monday, January 10, 2011

Phyllis is dressed in her nightgown and terry robe, sitting in the dark, facing the front door. A cup of coffee and her semi-automatic Luger lie on the table beside her. She has sent Drago home with Todd, pleading a migraine and saying she needs some time to herself, just for one night. The only tricky part has been purloining Drago's cell phone. After the men leave, she listens to it bleep over and over and reads "JayCee" on the screen with grim satisfaction. This night, the girl won't get no satisfaction.

The front door is locked, but that will be no barrier to the girl, for she learned where the front door key is hidden Christmas week when she and Lexie brought over gifts to welcome her and Todd home from Dollywood. The girl might fumble a little in the dark, locating exactly where the magnetic box is affixed to a leg of the iron chair on her porch, but she'll find it.

Phyllis doesn't know why, but after Drago and Todd leave, she fastens Carver's silver ID bracelet on her left wrist. It feels foreign and heavy, like sin itself. She is resentful that once more the burden of avenging her son falls upon her shoulders.

She wishes none of this had to be done, but as Todd told her in Las Vegas, the kinsman avenger plays an important role in a world without justice. A few hours ago, when she glimpsed the girl's reflection in the French doors of Lexie's kitchen, for an instant she considered screaming at her for sneaking around or throttling her, right then and there. But then, from nowhere, some instinct took over. Keep quiet. Pretend she's not there. The words that would set everything into motion tumbled out of her mouth as if scripted by an unseen presence.

Tell JayCee she couldn't do something and she would be sure to do it. Order JayCee never to see Drago again and she'd die trying, just to prove she could.

60

Listen and Learn
Monday, January 10, 2011

Todd drove to his villa in Pine Valley, Drago following in his Jeep. Todd's house was old-fashioned and ugly -- dark woodwork, shag carpet, faded wallpaper, heavy oak furniture -- but he bought it cheap at auction, completely furnished, after the former owner died. He added a big flat-screen television, two Barcaloungers, a good floor lamp, and a computer that worked most of the time. The dining table was loaded with stone grinding and polishing equipment. The refrigerator was well stocked with snacks and beer. It wasn't a beautiful home, but -- except for the absence of a good wife -- it suited Todd perfectly.

When Drago had thrown his duffel into the guest bedroom and the two men had kicked back in the gold frise Barcaloungers, drinking beer out of the can, Drago finally said, "I didn't know Mom got migraines."

"I didn't know it either. This is the first I ever heard about headaches. She never gets sick. Strong as an ox, that woman. I call her my steel hydrangea, she's so solid."

Drago snorted. "Smooth tongue you got there, Todd. Never heard more romantic words. You must be quite a hit with the ladies."

Todd let the sarcasm pass. "Never tried to be a hit with the ladies. Never wanted more than one. The right one."

271

"And my mom's the right one?"

"She is for me."

"And you're the right one for her?"

"That I don't know yet. I think the experience she had with your father wounded her." He caught himself. "Not trying to disparage your father. Don't mean that at all. It's just that Phyl's pretty reserved -- has a hard time letting herself be loved -- and I don't know how to account for it except what happened long ago."

"You know about my father?"

"Some."

"What do you know?"

Todd hesitated. "I know what he did to you. I know how he died."

"Is that right?"

"And I know he was dug up."

"No shit. Who told you?"

"Phyl, of course. I found your dad's silver bracelet out by the creek. I didn't know what it was for quite a while, but finally Phyl enlightened me."

"What silver bracelet?"

"An ID bracelet your mother gave your father a few months after they met. It has his initials on it."

"Oh, yeah? Tell me what they are."

Todd smiled. "Is this a test?"

"You could say that."

"GWCB."

"So what happened to the bracelet?"

"I gave it to Miss Royce. I found it on her property, so I thought it belonged to her. I tried to get it back a few months ago, but she said she doesn't know what she did with it."

Drago suddenly stood up. "I'm going to call Mom, see if she needs anything. We shouldn't have left her alone." He reached into one jeans pocket, then the other. "Where the hell's my phone?"

"Is it in your jacket? I think you threw that in the bedroom."

Drago returned a few minutes later. "Not in my jacket, not in my duffel. What the hell happened to it?"

"Calm down, Drago. You'll find it. If you really want to call her, use that phone over there. But I wouldn't call her."

"Why?"

I heard something in her voice I never heard before. She wants to be left alone. "She might finally have fallen asleep. The last thing you want to do is wake her. A migraine's not a picnic, you know. It's hell. I've never had a migraine; I'm just sayin'. So if you're going to call anyone, it ought to be Lucy. Use my phone, talk as long as you want."

"And say what?"

"Apologize. You've made a mess, my boy, and you're the only one can clean it up."

Drago bristled. "Who are you to tell me what to do?"

Todd lowered his eyes. "I'm nobody. I'm not your father and never will be. But I love your mother. It follows that I care about what happens to you because she'll be crushed if you leave your wife and kids, the way your father left you."

"He didn't leave me."

"I know that, Drago. He didn't walk out the way everybody thought. I know far more than you think. But in a way he gave your mother no way out, and if I dare say so, it wasn't manly of him to do what he did to you and Phyl. Not manly at all. I'm no expert on what it takes to be a good husband and father, having never been either one. I'm just sayin'."

"I think I should drive back to Mom's."

Todd stood up, deliberately blocking Drago's path to the front door. "Why don't you get comfortable, have another beer? Let's watch something -- a reality show maybe. Reality shows are my favorite."

Something in Todd's voice startled Drago.

"You know what your problem is?" Todd continued.

"I don't have a problem. Know that."

"You don't listen very well, Drago. Listen and learn, that's what I always say. You're a good guy at heart, but you've got a lot to learn about women. Life's no good at all without a good woman."

Drago snorted his contempt but his face betrayed his

shame.

61

Proverbs
Monday, January 10, 2011

After Phyllis left and JayCee ran back to her bedroom, Lexie and Jean returned to the atrium. They sat in comfortable arm chairs, feet up on ottomans, side by side, a table lamp softly lit, Henry at their feet. They drank coffee and watched the snow, grateful not to be alone.

Jean was more agitated than Lexie. "You think you should set the alarm so if JayCee tries to leave, we'll know?"

"We'll hear her without that, but I'm sure she's asleep. I don't think she's going anywhere tonight anyway. It's practically a blizzard out there."

"Do you need to call Steve, make sure he got to Woodburn all right?"

"I already got a text from him. He's fine."

They talked about this and that for another hour when Henry suddenly cocked his head. Jean stiffened and looked around. "Did I just hear a door open and close?"

Lexie took her time answering. "I didn't hear anything."

"You must have."

"No."

"You want me to see if JayCee's still here?"

"No. I'm sure you just heard the wind rattle something."

"How can you be so calm?"

"'Have no fear of sudden disaster or of the ruin that overtakes the wicked . . . .'"

"What's that from?"

"Proverbs, I think. Can't remember the rest of the verse."

62

Find a Position
Monday, January 10, 2011

Around two in the morning, despite the tension, Phyllis begins to feel drowsy. She slaps herself awake. As she stares into the dark, doubts worm their way into her mind. Perhaps she misjudged and the girl won't do the expected.

Just as she rises from her chair to refresh her coffee, the doorbell rings, over and over. Then she hears a faint sound, the experimental turning of the doorknob and a thump of hip against door. Holding her coffee cup in suspended animation, she waits, her heart knocking against her rib cage. Then comes a quiet knock, followed by the scrape of the metal chair as it is moved on the porch.

She hears the key thrust into the lock, turn the wrong way, then slowly turn the right way. As if in slow motion, she watches the door open a few inches, then a head appear around it. She recognizes the bouncy hairdo, haloed with sparks of copper by the light streaming from a streetlamp across the street.

"Drago."

The voice sounds so young, so innocent.

The girl steps into the living room. Such a frail silhouette for a demon!

Shivering, Phyllis puts down her cup and picks up the gun. She slowly backs up a few steps toward the door to her bedroom.

Get your story straight. Find a position that will seem reasonable to an inquisitive cop.

63

The Bug
Monday, January 10, 2011

Drago rose from his bed, still wearing his street clothes, and walked down the hall to Todd's bedroom door. He hovered there a few seconds, listening to the man snoring like a giant bulldog.

He tiptoed to the front door, quietly let himself out and walked, head down and eyes half-closed, through the blowing snow to his Jeep. Driving to Huntertown took longer than expected, for it was practically a white out. He had time to ponder. His mother never had a migraine before, so was she just pretending to have a headache so she could get him out of the house? Why? And if she was really sick, why didn't she want somebody with her?

And what the hell had happened to his phone? He couldn't live without it. He tried to picture where he must have left it at his mother's house.

He was shocked to see a car in his mother's driveway. He pulled in behind. JayCee's VW bug! He doused his lights and shut off the motor.

What was JayCee doing here? At two in the morning? Then he noticed footprints leading from the VW to the front door.

64

No Dispute
Monday, January 10, 2011

The front door closes. "Drago? Are you here?"

Phyllis catches her breath. She gets into position, feet planted, arms outstretched, both hands on the gun, one folded over the other, to steady it, finger on the trigger. She watches the girl stomp on the rug and try to turn on a table lamp, but all the bulbs were unscrewed hours earlier.

The girl stands still for a moment, letting her eyes adjust to the darkness, then heads haltingly toward the dining room and then the kitchen, perhaps drawn by the light of a digital readout on the oven. Bumping into a chair before reaching the kitchen, she stops and turns around. "Where are you, Drago?" The girl giggles. "Stop, like, hiding from me."

Phyllis waits until JayCee, arms outstretched like a blind woman, begins inching in her direction. If possible, let the intruder face you. When the girl is a couple yards away, Phyllis fires. As she's been taught to do, without uttering any warning at all, she fires until the 8-round magazine is empty. Always let the intruder get all the way into the house, then make sure she can't dispute your version of events.

Fortunately, the magazine is empty when Drago bursts through the door, for she isn't expecting a second intruder and has no idea who it is at first. In her agitation, she might have shot her son by mistake.

Phyllis collapses into a chair. Now she has a headache for real.

"Get out of here, son. You weren't supposed to be here."

"I can't. They'll see my tire tracks in the driveway."

Resigned, Phyllis gives Drago a few instructions.

Not until he has screwed all the light bulbs back into the lamps, scrubbed JayCee's texts from his phone, hidden Carver's bracelet and the metallic box that once held the front door key, rumpled up his mother's bed, and put her coffee cup in the dishwasher does Phyllis call 911.

65

Tragedy
Tuesday, January 11, 2011

The death of Jacintha Wright was a tragedy according to an article in *The Journal Gazette*:

Tragedy in Huntertown

Early Monday morning, a long-time Huntertown resident was suddenly awakened from a deep sleep by an intruder breaking into her house. Fearing for her life, Mrs. Phyllis Whitlow, 45 and the grandmother of twin boys, shot the intruder dead.

The tragedy is that the intruder was later identified as Jacintha Caitlin Wright, nicknamed JayCee, the adopted daughter of Mrs. Whitlow's employers, Steven and Alexandra Wright. "She never said a word," Mrs. Whitlow said, "and in the dark I couldn't tell who it was. When I came out of my bedroom, all I could see was a shadowy figure holding what I thought was a gun. I thought I was going to be shot in my own home. I had no reason to believe the girl would be anywhere near my house. I wish she'd said something so this tragedy could have been avoided."

There was no sign of forced entry. Mrs. Whitlow

explained: "The front door was locked but somehow she must have got hold of my key. Maybe she stole it while I was at work. [Mrs. Whitlow is housekeeper for the Wrights.] I'm still in shock. I'll never get over this. I am so sorry for Mr. Wright and Miss Royce."

By coincidence, Mrs. Whitlow's son, Pendragon "Drago" Bott, came upon the dreadful scene a few minutes too late. He said that despite the blizzard he'd driven to his mother's house after midnight because she'd earlier complained of a migraine headache and, not having heard from her, he was worried and wanted to be sure she was all right. "I just had an instinct something was wrong -- but I never guessed anything like what I found."

The dead girl's life was filled with tragedy. She was the daughter of Antoinette Delamarter, an exotic dancer who died last year, a victim of suspected poisoning. The girl was then adopted by Steven Wright, her biological father, and his wife, Alexandra "Lexie" Royce, the owner of Summit City Metals and Scrapyard. Last Halloween, the Wrights' estate in Gretna Green was the scene of the death of Mary Elizabeth Stuart, a close friend of Jacintha. The cause of the Stuart girl's death was drowning by unknown means; the police investigation is still active, according to Lt. David Powers of the Fort Wayne Police Department. A few months later, Joseph DeWitt, who found the dead girl and was questioned in her death, was charged with raping and beating Jacintha. While the boy was out on bail, his father, Gilbert DeWitt, killed himself.

Mrs. Whitlow has suffered tragedy before. Almost twenty years ago, her husband, Carver Bott, disappeared while awaiting trial for child endangerment. Asked if she'd ever heard from him, she said "I haven't and don't expect to." She resumed her maiden name a few years after his disappearance. She has worked for the Royce family for over twenty years.

A police spokesman indicated that no charges were

expected to be filed against Mrs. Whitlow, who has a State permit to carry firearms and was acting in self-defense. Under Indiana law, people have the right to use deadly force without first retreating to prevent serious bodily injury to themselves.

Steven and Alexandra Wright have asked that, in lieu of flowers, contributions be made in Jacintha's name to The National Association of Teen Institutes, a non-profit organization that counsels troubled teens and promotes teenage leadership.

Epilogue
Saturday, September 10, 2011

Jean Arnold was standing outside the Gretna Green Clubhouse under a pergola, admiring her handiwork. Baby sock bouquets, washcloth lollipops, and baby bottle vases adorned the long dining table, set with chartreuse and pink china bought especially for the occasion. Clothesline onesies in a rainbow of colors hung overhead, gently bobbing in the breeze. Guest favors -- DeBrand chocolate truffles in the shape of a three-layer white cake -- graced each place setting. A gift table, draped in a pink cloth with a gigantic diaper cake centerpiece, awaited the guests' gaily wrapped offerings.

The day was perfect -- sunny and warm, a faint breeze, a hint of clover and apple in the air -- and the chef had already fired up the grill on the downwind corner of the patio. Filet mignon for the hearty eaters and salmon for the dieters should make everybody happy.

Jean greeted her guests one by one -- Phyllis Whitlow and her sister Ruth Newsome, Lucy Bott and her mother Denise Flowers, Sheila Powers and her mother Lydia Johnson, Lexie's step-mother Matilda Royce and her friend Grace Venable, Steve's Aunt Maude Wright, Jessica Singer and Linda Adler, Trude Weide and Beulah Grabbendorf, Erna DeWitt and Mary Stuart, a few neighbors, and half a dozen other friends, mostly from high school and college. All the women were dressed to the nines, and there was much to be giddy about, fizzed by the Club's peach champagne "Bellini" punch.

Lexie pretended to be surprised when Steve delivered her to the patio, but Jean had dropped enough hints that she was prepared for a party. Blond and beautiful, she glowed the way a pregnant woman is supposed to glow, dressed in a floral sundress and wearing a pink straw hat. She warmly greeted each guest in turn.

When she reached her step-mother, Matilda launched an air kiss her way and said, "So it's a girl. In my day, we didn't announce that, but I suppose it's the best way to get the most useful gifts. Have you picked out a name?"

Lexie ignored the little taunt about gifts. "Lacey Pemberton Wright."

Matilda cocked her head. "Pemberton?"

"I found out from Ancestry.com that she's my great-great-great grandmother. I love the name. Don't you? Sounds like something out of Jane Austen."

"I don't like surnames for middle names, but I'll get used to it. And your due date?"

"Christmas."

"Oh, poor child. Bad timing! Just one set of presents for a whole year, a holiday overshadowing her birthday."

"Oh, I don't see it that way at all, Matilda. She'll be born on the best day of the year."

"If you say so."

No one acknowledged the dark undercurrent of death flowing just below the surface of life, meshing so perfectly with the beginning of autumn. No one spoke the name of Mary Elizabeth Stuart or Jacintha Caitlin Delamarter or Gilbert DeWitt, nor did they allude to Lexie's first baby. But from time to time the shadow of the missing passed across many faces and was quickly brushed away.

Lucy chattered like the most happily married woman in the world -- which, for the moment, she was. She gleefully cast her diet to the winds.

Erna DeWitt did not reveal that the Wrights had paid off her mortgage and set up a college fund for her son, but she did brag about the fact that Joey had been accepted at Indiana University, where he planned to major in forensic science.

Mary Stuart was wearing Libby's ring on her right hand but didn't call attention to it.

Jean accepted congratulations on her engagement to Dover Pitt and asked for ideas about a New Year's Eve wedding.

Matilda and Grace babbled about their most recent Viking river cruise down the Danube and circulated endless pictures of themselves posing in front of this Bratislava monument and that Budapest bridge.

Trude passed out her business card and urged the guests to reserve a puppy from Lord and Lady Macduff's latest litter of the cutest, smartest, healthiest Shelties anyone had every seen.

Sheila revealed that she and Lexie were establishing Summit Academy, a private college preparatory school. It would open in the new year. If all went well, they'd franchise the business nationwide.

Phyllis was quiet, weighed down by her secrets, oblivious of the fact that everyone else at the table had a secret she hadn't even told her best friend. At Lexie's urging, Phyllis finally passed around pictures of her and Todd gazing at The Great Mound, rock hunting in Nevada, drinking cocoa on Dollywood's Polar Express, and most recently riding the ferry to Mackinac Island. At least, Todd's place in her life was now out in the open.

The gaiety intensified as soon as the men rolled in from the golf course and joined the women. They were there to have a beer before carrying the mountain of gifts to Steve's car, but they too got caught up in the moment. Taken by surprise at the atmosphere but always the ready host, Steve instructed the staff to set up another dining table, start up the grill again, pipe some Sixties classics out to the patio, and add an array of top-shelf liquors to the outside bar. Part of the patio was cordoned off for dancing. The impromptu party swelled as Club members wandered out to join the fun.

The baby shower was supposed to be over by four, but no one wanted to be the first to leave. The party didn't wind down until a full moon began its nightly arc through the heavens.